FURY

OF THE

GODS

IMMORTAL RELICS BOOK TWO

STEPHANIE MIRRO

TANNHAUSER PRESS

Originally published as Her Majesty's Fury
First edition June 2019
Visit stephaniemirro.com for more information.

Cover design by Covers by Christian
Published by Tannhauser Press
tannhauserpress.com

Print ISBN: 978-1-945994-58-6

September 2020

10 9 8 7 6 5 4 3 2 1

ALSO BY STEPHANIE MIRRO

IMMORTAL RELICS
Curse of the Vampire
Revenge of the Witch

COLLECTIONS
The Outsiders: An Hourlings Anthology

Dedication

For my parents,
who always encouraged me to follow my dreams.

CHAPTER 1

Serafina

As she turned to close her bedroom door behind her, a flash of red and blue caught Sera's eye. She crossed the room, choking back a sob as she grabbed the Spiderman comic from her bedside table. The wall-crawler superhero was Hiro's favorite, and her boyfriend had saved the newest release to enjoy when he got back from Seattle. She had almost forgotten it.

Guilt gripped at Sera's raw throat, making it difficult to breathe. She held the book to her chest as tears spilled down her cheeks once again. Because of her, he would never have the chance to know what happened next to Peter Parker. A silly thought, perhaps, but after seeing his body growing cold on the floor at Danae's feet?

Not so much.

We need to kill her, Bacchus. Fast, she thought to the god as she tucked the comic inside the duffel bag she carried.

We will. The pinecone-shaped amulet pulsed as Bacchus replied. A moment later, Sera's tears ceased when his calming energy took hold. But the guilt remained.

Just over a week ago, Sera had wondered how she would ever get used to an ancient god speaking in her mind. A god who lived in an amulet around her neck. An amulet considered stolen from a national museum and hunted by vampire-like creatures called Bacchae. Minor details.

Now she couldn't imagine getting through this ordeal without his help, even if he did let Danae's Bacchae followers torture her so she would know firsthand what future was in store for humans if Danae won. It wouldn't be pretty. Sera understood his reasoning and forgave him... mostly, but she didn't have to like it.

Soon she would let the pain in; soon she would need it to drive her plan for vengeance to fruition. But she wasn't ready for that. Not yet, but soon.

A knock at her apartment door stopped Sera as she walked back toward the living room where her best friend Nora waited to drive them back to the safe house. The hairs on the back of her neck stood on end, and a chill ran up her spine.

Surely Danae's Bacchae guards hadn't come to attack her already. And besides, they wouldn't knock. Right? She took her chances, and a deep breath, confident that they couldn't come in unless she invited them inside. Or at least semi-confident.

You are correct, Bacchus said, amusement in his tone.

"I need your help," Ms. Patton said when Sera opened

the door. Her next-door neighbor's normally grim expression shaped her wrinkled face, but her eyes had an odd glossiness to them.

"Are you okay?" Sera could count the number of times Ms. Patton had spoken more than two words to her on one hand, usually after Sera had pissed her off somehow.

"Please. I need help in my apartment," the woman said and turned away. She hobbled toward her door down the narrow hall, beckoning to Sera with a hand. Blood stained the back of the woman's shirt as it dripped from a gash in the back of her head.

Sera gasped.

Serafina, wait—

Without a second thought, she dropped her duffel bag and rushed out of her apartment, hoping to catch Ms. Patton if she fell. The woman was clearly hurt and needed to go to the hospital. Sera had known it was only a matter of time before the older woman injured herself; she just hadn't realized *she* would be the one to help the woman.

Strong arms wrapped around Sera from behind, cinching her arms to her sides. Her heart leaped to her throat, and the memory of Hiro doing the same thing at the mall only a few weeks before flashed through her mind.

Only this was most definitely not Hiro.

As she turned her head to face her attacker, a stranger stood where Hiro once had. An unknown man—no, a Bacchae—with long, greasy black hair and ghostly white skin grinned at her with fangs extended. The scent of his unwashed hair, thick with cigarette smoke, wafted beneath her nose, and bile roiled in her stomach. She swallowed hard.

"Happy to see me?" the creature asked, his grip

tightening. Three other Bacchae appeared out of the shadowy stairwell next to Sera's door, their irises red and pupils dilated like cats'.

Shit, Sera thought, dismay settling around her shoulders.

Ms. Patton's door slammed shut, and the woman was nowhere to be seen. At least Sera wouldn't have to worry about the old lady getting killed. Not in front of her, anyway. She would check in on her after she took care of the Bacchae. One problem at a time.

Let me handle it, Bacchus said, and a tingling sensation coursed its way through her limbs as he took over her body's movements. The amulet lit up like a crimson spotlight, pinpointing on the arms that bound her.

The Bacchae holding her hissed and released his grasp as he stumbled backward, shaking his steaming hand.

"This will not end well for you, my children," Bacchus said, his deep voice booming out from Sera's mouth. "Go back to your mistress and tell her that death is coming."

The tallest, and meanest looking, of the four Bacchae stepped forward. His height, shaved head, and neck tattoos peeking out above his black leather jacket were intimidating enough before he raised his gun. Even with a god controlling her limbs, she found it next to impossible to stay confident as she stared down the barrel of the silencer. She gulped, her pulse drumming in her ears.

"Your time is at an end, old man. Don't make us kill the girl," he said.

"Sera, what's going—" Nora appeared at the door, her green eyes opening wide as she took in the scene in the apartment building's hallway.

Everything seemed to happen in slow motion after that.

The Bacchae with the gun moved his aim to Sera's best friend and pulled the trigger. Despite the silencer, the sound of the bullet releasing ricocheted in Sera's mind. She wasn't sure who had control of her body when she leaped from where she stood, into the path of the bullet.

Pain exploded within her arm as the bullet tore its way through muscle and bone and embedded itself in the doorframe by Nora's head. Red splattered the wall next to the hole.

Everything sped up again as Sera hit the wooden floor on her side. Nora screamed and pulled back inside the apartment, protected by one of Bacchus's safeguards when he created the Bacchae—the need to be invited in. Three sets of iron-gripped hands pulled Sera to her feet.

They hadn't learned what it meant to face a god yet.

Bacchus's roar of fury ripped from her throat like a battle cry as she pulled her arms together. The two Bacchae holding her limbs stumbled in surprise and nearly collided but didn't release their grip.

An unearthly growl echoed down the hall from the stairwell.

Sera caught just a glimpse of a dark-haired man charging up the last steps, his eyes glowing as if they housed the sun, before he raised a hand and sharp claws extended from his fingernails. He used them to rake against the Bacchae closest to him, shredding the creature's chest open to the bone. The Bacchae's scream was cut off as the new arrival's other hand punched through the exposed ribcage and clenched the beating heart until the organ, and the body surrounding it, shattered into glittering dust.

Whoa. Sera didn't have time for any other thoughts

before Bacchus took over again. The fight was over in a matter of moments with the help of the mystery man. Or whatever he was.

A golden haze settled around them as the last of the Bacchae dissipated. Sera bent over and panted, wincing as she jostled her injured arm. She had almost forgotten about the bullet. Heat spread like honey from the amulet down her arm and into the wound. She watched with fascination as the blood ceased to spill, and the hole closed.

Working with a god came in handy but had also caused this whole mess. She would consider it a silver lining.

When Sera stood straight, Theo Pratt, the detective who questioned her after the Bacchic amulet went missing, looked back at her. His dark eyes were stern as ever as he tucked the Bacchae's dropped gun into his interior jacket pocket.

"We need to talk," he said.

Shit, she thought again, her shoulders sagging.

She hadn't even stopped to think about the fact that Julia Dixon, Theo's partner, had gone missing from the detective ranks. Danae had killed her, too. Of course he would come by after Sera had been questioned by them both, more than once, and it was only going to look worse for her when they found out Hiro was gone, too.

First, an amulet she had unearthed last summer had been stolen from a national museum, and now two people she knew were dead. At the hands of an evil Bacchae witch proclaiming herself Queen, no less. Great.

But what the hell had she just witnessed? The man's eyes had glowed, and he ripped a Bacchae to shreds with his bare hands. Who was he? *What* was he?

Whatever he was, she didn't have time to stop and think and feel about any of that. No distractions. She had more Bacchae to kill, and she was beyond pissed they had shown up at her door.

"Thanks for the help, but now's not a good time." She turned her back to him and headed toward Ms. Patton's apartment door.

"Where's Julia?" Theo asked, suddenly ahead of her with an arm against the wall, blocking her path.

Are you going to help me? she asked Bacchus.

I believe in you, Bacchus replied. She could almost see him lounging on a Roman couch, sipping wine from a chalice as he dismissed her. Sometimes she wished she could throttle the god.

A low growling buzzed in her mind. Sera froze in place as she tried to decipher the odd sound and sensation, her hands half raised to push him out of her way. Did he bring a police dog with him? She didn't want to turn around to find out.

"Where's Julia?" the detective repeated.

"I don't know," Sera snapped back.

It wasn't entirely untrue—she didn't know what the Bacchae had done with the body. Either of the bodies. She braced herself for the overwhelming grief she expected to come, but Bacchus had done his job suppressing her emotions well. A hole existed where her heart should have been. She breathed a sigh of relief.

"I need to check on Ms. Patton. They hurt her to get to me," she said as she tried to push past his arm. Not to mention all the blood she needed to clean off the wall. The night had turned into a real mess. Just the way Bacchus liked it, of course.

"We need to get inside before anyone comes to check on the noise. I'll check on your neighbor after we talk, but it looked worse than it was." His voice held a hint of something new, something other than his usual rigid seriousness. The tone was softer, almost reassuring.

How the hell did he know the older woman wasn't dead? The growling coursed through Sera's mind again, leaving a fuzzy, disorienting feeling behind and distracting her from her thoughts.

Are you growling at me? she asked Bacchus, shaking her head to clear it.

Bacchus chuckled in reply, but it wasn't the same deep tenor as the growling. *That is not me. Let's talk to him, Sera. Don't you want to know what he is?*

Confused, Sera ceased to struggle against the detective's arm, although she didn't move away either. *What he is? I don't have time for this, Bacchus. Can't you just fill me in later?*

Play nice, Bacchus urged, sending another pulse of calming energy through her body. Her shoulders relaxed. *You don't want to seem guilty after all.*

Fine. But you better help me out of this mess if you're wrong, she said to Bacchus. She snorted, ignoring Theo's questioning look.

Giving in to the god's logic, she stepped back and swept an arm toward her apartment door. "Come on in, but we'll be leaving soon."

"We?" Theo asked with a smirk as he stepped inside, before he caught sight of Nora, who had refused to let Sera return to her apartment by herself. Maybe she regretted that decision now after the near-death experience facing supernatural creatures. The second one in less than a month.

Despite the scare in the hallway, the petite blonde woman squared off with him by Sera's side, hands on her hips, one eyebrow raised, lips pursed, and a look that would reduce most men to groveling. Typical Nora. Her best friend had a flair for the dramatic. At least the gunshot didn't seem to be affecting her too severely. Getting abducted and used as bait by a crazed witch who was hunting for Bacchus may have helped with that.

"Ah, I see." A few locks of his wavy, dark brown hair fell in front of his eyes as he nodded before turning back to Sera.

Nora's huff made it clear she didn't approve of his non-reaction.

He moved farther into the living room of Sera's tiny apartment, which was just large enough to hold a two-person couch, a small chair, a side table, and a coffee table that served more like a bookshelf most of the time. Home for the last two and a half years.

The detective removed his brown leather jacket and laid it on the back of the couch, his eyes dipping to the scarf around Sera's neck. "I'm going to cut to the chase—I know you have the amulet."

Sera blinked at him, her heart constricting. "Are you here to arrest me?"

What the hell, Bacchus? Anger made even her internal voice shake. There was no way she was going to let herself get arrested tonight.

Just wait, Bacchus said, a hint of humor in his tone.

For what, your handcuff fantasy? she shot back.

"So, you don't deny it?" Theo continued to stare

intently at her, his eyes searching her face.

"Listen, despite your fancy fighting moves back there, you don't know what you're getting involved in. I guarantee, you don't want me to answer—" She stopped, her mouth popping open, as he pulled his sweater off over his head.

"I don't know what's happening," Nora leaned close to whisper, "but I like it."

"What are—" Sera's mind reeled as he continued to undress, taking off his white undershirt. An expansive, colorful tattoo spanned the breadth of his muscular chest from the bottom of his collarbone to his navel.

Recovering from a moment of pure astonishment, Sera realized she was staring at the image of a giant conch shell, as if the top had been lopped off to reveal the whorl within and the ridged piece laid against his skin like an ancient breastplate. The outer ridges curled over his shoulders and under his arms like the spokes of a wheel and disappeared under the top of his pants.

As he breathed, pearlescent shades of white, pink, and gold rippled and made the spiral pop, like a real shell across his chest. She continued to stare, the unmistakable sounds of thunder and roaring winds filling her ears.

What on Earth is happening? she thought to herself.

"Well, that was unexpected," Sera said, unsure of what else to say. An impromptu striptease was not something she'd prepared for when he had stepped into her apartment. Arresting her, possibly tasing her, sure.

She peeled Nora's tight grip from her arm.

Tell her... the growling sound seemed to say in her mind.

Tell who what? she asked Bacchus, annoyance at the mind game making her tone sharp.

That wasn't me. His soft laughter rumbled in her thoughts.

"I know you have the amulet," Theo said, "and I know about Bacchus."

CHAPTER 2

Serafina

Theo stood as stoically as he always did despite the anvil he had just metaphorically dropped on the two women. That and the fact he was now topless.

"Uh…" Sera tried to think of something to say, but she was still trying to focus her mind. It was beyond difficult to think straight with him standing there half-naked, displaying his elaborate tattoo, and she had no idea *why*.

"I know because I'm also connected with a god. Xolotl."

"Bless you," Nora said.

Theo smiled, a dimple appearing on each cheek. Well, wasn't that cute. The few times Sera had interacted with him—if his usual silent observation could be called interaction—she wasn't sure the man had smiled or made any face other than one of stern disapproval. He should definitely do it more often. The dimples made him much more tolerable.

"Xolotl is the Aztec god of death and lightning." He tapped his chest tattoo. "This is his wind breastplate. We've been working together, merged, for nearly one hundred years."

Tilting her head to the side as she processed his words, Sera couldn't be sure she'd heard him right, mainly because he'd said it so casually. Better be on the safe side in case she *was* hearing things.

"Say what now?" she asked.

Theo let out a breath and ran a hand through his mop of dark hair. The growling noise returned to her mind, and he nodded a moment later. "I don't reveal myself to mortals often, so let me just show you."

Bending his knees into a fighter's stance, he kept his gaze connected with Sera's as he held his fists before his face. His pupils changed first, transitioning from dark brown to a reddish-gold that glowed like the sun behind a thin cloud at sunset. Just as they had during the fight in the hallway.

Then the shell tattoo began to shimmer, the colors swirling together as they came to life, raising the iridescent ink from his chest. The image continued to rise out of his skin until an actual, hard breastplate made from the twisted spiral of a conch shell covered the front of his body.

Long, thick claws grew from his nails, and a deep growl emanated from his throat as he took on a predatory demeanor. A black dog with a long snout baring its teeth was superimposed on the man's face like a hologram.

Without thinking, Sera stepped in front of her friend,

who appeared more awe-struck than scared.

Sera glared at him. "All right, we get it. You've got a god friend. You can turn off the magic show."

I can't believe you didn't tell me about this, she thought to Bacchus. Daggers formed in her mind.

Only his rich chuckle replied. Of course.

As Theo returned to an upright posture, the shell smoothed back into his skin like melting butter, and the color faded from his eyes. The dog simply vanished.

"What's the deal with the giant tattoo?" She crossed her arms.

Stepping around Sera to get closer to him, Nora peered at the ink. "Can I touch it?"

"No. The tattoo is from my merge with Xolotl years ago." Turning his shirt right side out again, he pulled it over his head.

Nora sighed with a wistful note.

Seriously, how did this not seem to faze the girl? All this god and magic stuff creeped Sera out, making her long for the non-supernatural days she'd enjoyed only a few short months ago. But with everything that had happened since—and was still happening—an ordinary life might never be possible again.

"And a merge means what exactly?" Sera asked. If she couldn't go back, she might as well get educated.

"You really don't know much about this world, do you?" His expression became quizzical as he put on his sweater.

"Listen, my whole world turned upside down in a very short amount of time. You don't have to be rude about it." She scowled back at him.

He raised both hands in a gesture of surrender. "I didn't mean it that way. Xolotl told me about you and Bacchus, and I assumed Bacchus would've given you more information."

Why are you holding out on me with all of this? Anger flashed brightly in her mind as she questioned the god. She hated being caught off guard, even more so after all that had happened with the Bacchae.

You're learning well enough on your own, came his reply, mirth tangible in his words. The response was typical by now but also annoying as hell.

"Apparently not. Pretend like I don't know anything except I have a god in my head who likes to keep secrets from me," she said.

Someone's testy, Bacchus said with a tsk-tsk.

Sera rolled her eyes and took a seat on the couch, waving Theo toward the chair next to her. Whatever else the man had to share would probably be best heard while sitting. Not to mention that she still felt weak from her torture and comatose state two days ago. Oh, and that fight in the hallway didn't help either.

Nora plopped next to her, curls bouncing as she tucked her legs beneath her. Sera's best friend couldn't be more her opposite—her curly, short blonde bob haircut, bright green eyes, and tiny stature contrasted as sharply as an aged cheddar next to Sera's straight dark brown hair, steel grey eyes, and average height. Not to mention the stark personality differences.

Yet the two had been thick as thieves since the day they met in their Li'l Archaeologists summer camp, and Sera wouldn't want to go through any of this craziness without Nora beside her.

Dimples appeared in Theo's cheeks again for a brief moment before he sat in the chair. The cuteness factor of the sight had faded as her annoyance rose.

"Okay, so you've probably noticed that working with Bacchus comes with some downsides," he said.

Trying to hold back a derisive snort, Sera burst into a coughing fit as she choked on her spit. Because her inner klutz had to come out eventually. "Talk about an understatement," she managed to get out.

The god tsk-tsked again. *Am I going to have to come out and defend myself?*

"I mean specifically about using his power." Theo chuckled. "With Xolotl's power, I can shift into a dog, a giant dog who used to be uncontrollable."

"Like a werewolf?" Nora's eyes brightened with interest.

He nodded. "Gods using human bodies to shift into different creatures created the werewolf lore, much like Bacchae encounters turned into vampire mythos. But, as I said, I couldn't control the dog side of Xolotl. I used to wear an amulet like yours, but a conch shell is not as easy to hide. So, we decided to *merge*. He became a part of me, our memories combined." He tapped his chest. "And his symbol, the wind jewel, became this tattoo."

"And now you can control him?" Sera asked.

"Yes, completely."

Can we merge? she asked Bacchus. Fatigue tugged at her insides, the ever-present downside to using his powers. At least she hadn't blacked out—yet.

It's possible. Do you want a tattoo of the amulet across your chest? Bacchus flashed an image of the necklace melting into the skin around her collarbone. She shuddered.

The growling sound in her mind amplified, and Theo smirked. The pieces clicked into place.

"Is that Xolotl speaking to you?" Sera tilted her head to the side.

His mouth dropped open. "You can hear him?"

"All I hear is growling in my head, and every once in a while, I catch a word. So, if that's him, then yes, I hear him."

"That Gift is incredibly rare," he said, his eyebrows lifting toward his hairline.

"Gift? You mean like Renee having the Sight?" Nora asked, smacking Sera on the arm in her excitement.

Is this what you meant earlier tonight when you said I had talents I didn't know I possessed? Sera asked, rubbing her abused arm. Having a Gift didn't seem possible. She'd never even had an inkling of listening to others' thoughts before now. Except for Bacchus, of course.

That and more, he replied. Cryptic as usual.

"Who's Renee?" Theo asked.

"You've been following Sera around searching for the stolen amulet, and you don't know who Renee is?" Nora gave him a disbelieving look.

Annoyance flickered across his face. "I haven't been following her around. She was never truly a police suspect. Julia was the one always pushing the idea."

Nora pursed her lips. "Okay. Well, Renee is a friend of my mom's and a witch. A pretty powerful one, too, it seems. Her house is super protected by magic like a safe house, so we're headed there after this chat. She also has the Sight, which means—"

"I'm aware of what the Sight is," he interrupted, back

to his old stern self. "But I've only heard of one or two others who possessed the ability to hear other gods, and it's usually after a merge."

Sera groaned, rubbing her face with her hands. "Wait, there are even more of you merged?"

The detective grinned. "Oh, yes. Bacchus really has been keeping you in the dark."

I did tell you about the others. It's not my fault you don't listen well, Bacchus chimed in.

"You told me about other gods encasing their essence into artifacts before they faded completely into mythology, but not about this merging thing. And also not that long after an evil Bacchae witch murdered my boyfriend in front of my eyes. So, don't lecture me on not listening well," Sera snapped out loud without realizing, fuming at the god.

"Wait, your boyfriend is dead?" Theo asked, his eyes widening.

Dead. Gone. Finished. No pain. It almost hurt to not feel anything, like she was dishonoring him somehow. "Yes, and so is your partner Julia. She was working for Lorenzo Vicari, who apparently is one of the Bacchae. An ancient one. Only her plan of becoming immortal backfired. Do you know much about the Bacchae?"

"Wow. I'm very sorry to hear about them both." He sat back in the chair, shaking his head in disbelief. "Yes, I know quite a bit about them. Xolotl and I had been keeping watch on them for a few decades as they became a bit unruly. Until Bacchus fixed that, of course."

He let out a deep sigh. "Man, I knew Julia was dirty, which is why I didn't tell her the amulet was in your bag when we questioned you at the diner. But I—"

"So, you did see it!"

He frowned. "Of course I saw it. I wouldn't consider wrapping it up in a towel with the chain sticking out to be hiding it."

Sera snorted. What a know-it-all. Not everyone had a penchant for thievery and deception.

"Can I see it?" Theo asked.

"Uh, sure." She unwrapped the scarf, revealing the pinecone-shaped amulet.

Leaning forward in his chair, Theo's face got close as he stared at the amulet on her chest, and she caught a whiff of some sort of fruity soap or shampoo. Not the scent she expected him to choose. Her cheeks grew warm at the uncomfortable nearness, and the amulet burst into a crimson blaze, causing Theo to tumble back into his chair.

"I never got a good look at it in person." He chuckled. "I can see Bacchus is very protective of you."

The god beamed with pride inside her head.

"Most of the time, and very proud of it, too." Despite the sarcasm in her words, she smiled. The depth of the god's internal wrath had surprised her—and would have been terrifying in another situation—when they faced Danae, but his almost childlike demeanor had become as familiar as family.

"Let's go back to the part where you said you've been working with this god of yours for one hundred years," Nora said, her gaze thoughtful.

"Right. When you merge with a god's essence, you become god-like in many ways, including the immortal bit," he said.

"Did it hurt to merge?" Nora's eyes moved down to his chest.

The lines of his jaw moved as he clenched his teeth. "Yes."

"So, you're like, super old?" Nora asked.

Biting her lip, Sera held in her laugh. At least she didn't choke this time. Leave it to Nora to disregard any kind of personal boundaries with her questions.

He shrugged. "Depends on your point of view. I'm young compared to some of the others."

"And you're never going to die?"

"Not of natural causes," he said.

"Renee is going to flip," Nora laughed.

"Do you police the Bacchae or something?" Sera asked.

"Not exactly. We just ensure the supernatural world stays in the shadows, which means reminding the Bacchae of their place from time to time."

"So, you probably know about Danae, one of the Eternal Bacchae? One of Bacchus's original creations?"

He nodded, his eyes narrowing. "Her bloodthirsty, manipulative behaviors are well known to us, especially because she's an exceptional witch, as well. She's planning something. What that is, I don't know, but the whole god community is on high alert. Even the other Eternals on the High Council are wary of her. Unfortunately, she's very good at keeping her secrets."

"She's the one who killed them. She wants to take over the world. Make humans into Bacchae lunchmeat." Gross but not wrong.

"There aren't enough Bacchae for that kind of mission," he said, although he sounded unsure.

"That's why she's after the amulet. She knows she can restore their procreation ability, and all the other powers of theirs that have suffered since Bacchus took them away. And then she'll build an army." Sera reached up to clasp the amulet, the sharp ridges of the pinecone digging into her skin. "But we're going to stop her."

Theo drummed his fingers on the chair, looking at her thoughtfully. "You wouldn't be the first to try. You're going to need an army of your own."

"Right, I just didn't realize another god was right here in front of me the whole time," she said.

He grinned. "And I know of at least two others who usually jump at the chance of a good fight."

"You *want* to help?" she asked, surprise in her voice. Were they all going to be this easy to recruit?

"Of course. That's part of the reason I'm here."

A buzzing sound caught their attention. Nora jumped up and ran over to her jacket, hanging on a hook next to the door. She pulled her cell phone out of the pocket.

"Hey, Renee," she said into the phone then paused for a moment. "Yeah, we'll be on our way back over soon. We have some…" She glanced at Theo. "Interesting news."

While Nora finished the conversation on the phone, Sera eyed the detective, whose young face had returned to the reserved look she had grown accustomed to. She really preferred the other side to Theo, the non-stern side, but she supposed his actual age of at least a century had something to do with his demeanor.

"Does merging with a god make you like the Bacchae, then?" she asked.

A lightning bolt flashed across Theo's eyes. "No.

Bacchae were created from a god's blood, at least the Eternals were. Newer ones created by another Bacchae aren't as powerful as the Eternals, and the farther away the lineage gets from the original divine blood, the less enhanced their abilities. So, for example's sake, Lorenzo is not as powerful as Danae, and anyone Lorenzo creates is even less so.

"In contrast, those of us who have merged are like gods incarnate. On their own, the Bacchae's power doesn't compete with a god's. But against an army? Even gods have their limits."

Sera shuddered at the thought of an immortal life bonded to a god. Some people dreamed of achieving such a thing, and some actually did. But losing everyone she loved in her life again and again to old age—or worse—didn't sound like her cup of tea. Or coffee, in her case. Life was precious, and she'd lost too much already. All she wanted was to stop Danae and then carry on with her life. Oh, and do her best to keep building a better relationship with her father, too. Bacchus would move on to another human host, and life would be good. Well, *normal* anyway.

"Renee's getting nervous about us being away from the safe house and wants us to come back over as soon as possible," Nora said as she came back to the couch, leaning against the arm.

Sera sighed, finding it almost hard to believe how much her life had changed yet again.

Theo stood and pulled his jacket on. "I'll let you two fill her in. I've got to head down to the station to complete some paperwork. I'll see if anything has come in on Julia and Hiro—" he stopped short when he looked at Sera.

The shock of hearing his name out loud struck her in the gut harder than a swing from a gladiator.

No, she told Bacchus firmly when he started to ease the grief again. She wanted to feel it this time, to hold on to the raw pain. She needed to honor Hiro's memory this way. Wrapping her arms around herself, she bent over, afraid she was going to throw up.

"We still have questions. I'll give you my phone number," Nora said quietly, her voice fading as she must have walked away from the couch.

"I'm very sorry for your loss," she heard Theo's voice at the door before it clicked shut.

CHAPTER 3

Solomon

As the sun dipped below the horizon, Solomon returned to Lorenzo's mansion and headed for his room. The Mediterranean style compound hidden in the wooded hills of the District had been his home for the last few decades, and if Danae's plan failed, they would have to move on soon. Too many people would question their lack of aging.

After seeing Nora outside the witch's house early that morning, he had spent some time alone in the city, trying to make sense of his jumbled thoughts. The dark-haired girl Serafina and the god's relic were inside the row house, comatose according to Nora, and part of his job included getting them back. Or at least the amulet. The problem was Nora had stolen his heart. That much he knew for a fact.

But what was he going to do about it?

Solomon enjoyed his life as an Immortal, getting to see the changes—both good and bad—that humans made to the world over time. But he wasn't entirely convinced he wanted to be a part of the changes Danae wanted, even if it meant living without their full abilities. That plan meant the end of the human species. The end of Nora. Unless she accepted an Immortal life, of course.

His feelings for the blonde beauty had snuck up on him so quietly he hadn't realized how much she meant to him until he had lost her. He hadn't fallen in love with anyone since he was mortal, but every time he parted with Nora, he felt a piece of his heart stay with her. Only seeing her again put it back together.

Low voices coming from his maker's meeting hall caught his attention. He scanned the hallway to see if anyone else was near before making his way to the double doors as quietly as he could. He didn't need to see inside; Lorenzo's and Danae's voices drifted out as Solomon stood beside the doors.

"She will have to. She cannot face them while wearing it." Lorenzo laughed. "It is a genius plan. Genius!"

"I'll need one of the Council members to assist me in the ritual."

"Certo," his maker said. "I will have one of them fetched from their beds now. I—"

"No, not a mortal. The blood must be Eternal," Danae snapped.

"Ah. I see." A pause. "Who do you recommend?"

"Nestor."

"I will ensure he is on his jet tomorrow."

"No one can know we requested his presence, Lorenzo," Danae warned. "At least not until the binding spell is reversed, and we are freed from this curse."

Solomon almost laughed. *This curse.* The queen sure knew how to spin the propaganda. He had learned Bacchus revoked their gifts due to the overreach of Immortals like Danae, those who didn't heed the god's rules and sought powers far beyond their grasp.

But it had taken him extensive research and careful questioning to uncover that fact, and most of the other Immortals only knew what had been told to them, which was not much. It was no wonder most Immortals in Danae's employ were caught up in her visions for a new world, believing the god had cursed them.

"Not a soul will know, Your Majesty." Lorenzo's lips made a smacking sound.

Guessing the ancient Italian had kissed the back of Danae's hand, Solomon knew she'd be cringing at the touch. He didn't blame her. Slipping away from the door, he continued to his private room, a chill spreading through his bones.

As one of the members of the High Council and an Eternal—those with Bacchus's own blood coursing through them—Nestor ruled the Immortals inhabiting South America, while Danae controlled all of North America. Their proximity meant it wouldn't be unusual for the two Eternals to meet, but it was far from normal to keep it hidden.

Determined to get some rest despite his turbulent thoughts, Solomon peeled off his clothes and lay down on his King-sized bed. The mattress and sheets were the finest available, a small luxury he requested every time they moved. Although Immortals didn't need to sleep the way humans did, relaxing for an hour or two rejuvenated their minds and bodies faster, and Solomon preferred to do so in finery he never knew existed as a black child in the pre-Civil War South.

A handful of minutes later, a knock sounded at his door. Solomon groaned as he pushed himself off the bed and answered the door, still nude. Modesty wasn't really his thing.

"Her Majesty requests your presence in her chambers," the Immortal guard stated. She looked Solomon up and down hungrily and gave him a wink. "And now I know why."

Letting out a sigh, he dressed again. This time he wore sweats, an undershirt, and house loafers, assuming, like the guard, that Danae's request would involve bedroom activities. She enjoyed watching him undress or else he wouldn't have bothered. At least she didn't require more formal attire for such occasions. He followed the waiting Immortal to the queen's guest quarters.

She sat on a cushioned stool in front of an ornate vanity mirror, brushing her hair. Her dark brown strands had a natural wavy curl to them and tumbled to her waist. For a few minutes after the guard left, she continued the methodical brushing, her eyes locked on her own in the mirror. Whatever inner dialogue she was having, Solomon knew to wait until she addressed him.

Finally setting the brush down, she stood and faced him, the scent of her arousal drifting across the room like an expensive perfume. The sapphire silk robe she wore fell to the floor silently as she slipped it from her shoulders, leaving her naked save for the ruby-red collet necklace she wore. A replacement for the amulet, he guessed.

Solomon couldn't help but marvel, though he had seen the sight many times at this point. Her nearly flawless skin was olive-toned, indicative of her Mediterranean ancestry, and her hips and breasts rounded just right for a man's hands to hold—or a woman's, should the need arise. He met her eyes, a bright blue at the moment due to her desire, though at times they turned dark and murky like a raging storm at sea.

"Tell me, did you like what you heard?" she asked, her voice soft despite the threat of her words.

"Your Majesty?"

"I know you were listening at the end of our conversation. You're not as stealthy as you'd like to believe, at least not to an Eternal." She moved toward the bed.

Only catching a glimpse of her back before, now he could clearly see the raised lines he had felt beneath his hands, lines that crisscrossed the entire length and breadth of her back in the light of the room. He had no knowledge of where or when her whippings had occurred, but he had seen those marks many times as a mortal slave in the South. He had his own to compare, though on much darker skin than the queen's.

He resisted the urge to touch the scar that ran through his eyebrow. Not taking his eye had been a gift, his owner had said, but Solomon was sure it was merely poor aim. Or dumb luck. After two hundred years, the crack of the whip still resonated in his mind.

"My apologies, Your Majesty. I was on my way to rest."

Half-truths were still truths.

She climbed into the bed on hands and knees, graceful and cat-like as she settled into place before looking at him expectantly. Solomon stripped himself of his clothes once again, feeling her gaze take in the view, then slipped into the bed beside her. Loafers and sweats had been the right call.

"Do you know why I'm inviting Nestor here?" she asked.

"It's none of my business."

"No, it's not. But I would like to change that by having you become one of my advisors." Her eyes moved around his face, then settled on his lips. She reached a hand up and gently stroked the curve of his lips with a fingertip. "A secret advisor."

Despite his disagreement with her plans, he found himself rising to the current occasion as she touched him. She was difficult to resist in such a state.

"Of course, Your Majesty. But I'm afraid I won't have much to advise." He wasn't the humble sort, but Solomon didn't know how he could assist her any more than Lorenzo did.

"You and I come from a similar background, unlike most of the other entitled imbeciles who call themselves Immortal." Her lip curled up in disgust. "We know what atrocities these mortals are capable of. You must feel the same hate toward them as I do."

He didn't, but now wasn't the time or place to correct her.

"I need another Eternal present to complete a ritual that will allow me to bind Bacchus's power within the amulet until I'm ready to restore our powers. We will have an opportunity shortly to get it from the girl, but I need to ensure Bacchus does not attempt to destroy himself when I do."

The pieces of the earlier conversation fell into place. When the two bodies were found, Serafina would be called in for questioning, and she couldn't possibly expect to wear the amulet in front of the police.

"How will you get past the witch's protection spells?" he asked.

The corners of Danae's lips pulled up in a rare smile. "Her magic won't hold up against the essence of an Eternal."

"Why not just use your own blood?" he asked.

A delicate hand trailed down from his lips to his chest, where she pushed him back against the pillows before straddling him. Her hands ran up and down his chest, raising goosebumps as her nails scraped along his dark skin.

"I need an Eternal's dying dust, and I don't plan on dying anytime soon."

She leaned down to kiss him, her hair falling across his cheeks and chest. Hidden from her gaze as her lips met his, she couldn't see the shock flash across his face. Before his thoughts could affect him further, he pushed them away, needing to be in the moment to please the queen. Despite his new advisor title, his life could still be forfeit if he failed in his bedroom duties.

Gripping her hips, he held her to him as he rolled over. He took her wrists in his hands and held them above her head. Hunger radiated from her eyes. He knew this was the only time and place she liked to be dominated, and he had no problem satisfying her desires. At least for now.

CHAPTER 4

Serafina

"Are you okay?" Nora's voice broke through the grief with its loving tone, like the brilliance of a rainbow after a furious storm.

Nodding, despite the blatant lie, Sera wiped away the tears running down her cheeks. Breaking down again felt imminent, so she stood from the couch without speaking and picked up the duffel bag stuffed full of her clothes and other daily necessities.

She followed Nora out the door in silence and locked her apartment behind them, not sure when—or even *if*—she'd ever see it again.

A fresh pang shot through her heart. Her apartment was one of the last normal parts of her life, and now she was saying goodbye to it for the foreseeable future.

She avoided looking behind her where the fight had occurred in the hallway as she headed for the steps, then out the building's front door. The crisp fall night air felt soothing against her puffy eyes.

Theo had said he would take care of the blood and her neighbor, and she would have to trust him. She was too tired, emotionally and physically, to even care otherwise. Although if Ms. Patton hadn't survived... Well, she didn't want to think about that possibility.

After throwing her bag into the back of Nora's white Honda Civic, she let out a sigh and slid into the front seat of the coupe, shivering from more than just the cold.

"It's hard to believe this whole other side to life exists," Nora said. Glancing over her shoulder, she pulled the car out onto the road.

"You're telling me. Try living with an ancient god talking in your head," Sera said, holding her hands in front of the vent for heat. With all that had occurred that night, she hadn't thought to put on gloves.

Nora smirked in her direction.

I think I've been helpful so far, Bacchus quipped.

You've done all right, she thought back. If she let his ego get any bigger, her head might explode trying to contain it.

You'll be singing a different tune when I get through with you, he said.

"Get through with me?" Are you planning on using me for revenge then dumping me? Sera choked back a laugh, resulting in a coughing fit as she inhaled her own saliva. Yet again. Maybe it served her right for talking back to a god.

Nora glanced over. "Is he talking in your head now?"

"The real question is when is he not." Ignoring his

grumbling, she asked, "How do you think we should tell Renee?"

"She's already aware of the supernatural world, even if it's not as much as we just learned. It shouldn't be too hard for her to accept this news, especially because Bacchus did tell us others existed."

See? he asked, though she knew it was more of a rhetorical question.

Sera rolled her eyes. *Yes, you were right. Happy?* She could almost taste the smugness he emitted as she admitted defeat.

"Good news, you didn't miss much at school," said Nora. "You know how everyone checks out mentally after Thanksgiving. Dr. Davis has been up my ass about…"

A common feature of their relationship, Sera let her best friend continue to talk without interruption for the rest of the drive. It was comforting to have that sense of normalcy, and she couldn't be more relieved to have Nora by her side while Sera's world continued to crumble.

The last time she had needed this kind of support, she had been five and had just lost her mom in what everyone thought was a freak caving accident. She now knew her mom had been a witch like Renee until Danae had killed her. Almost killed Renee, too. She turned to stare out the window, needing a distraction.

The familiar landmarks of the District continued to roll by as they drove the short distance from downtown to Capitol Hill. Short distances could take outrageous amounts of time with the volume of people living in or commuting to the city for the day. It could be infuriating.

Driving at night, however, provided a different ambiance of the city as the multi-hued lights cast their glow upon the streets and sidewalks, a view that never failed to send thrills of excitement coursing through Sera's veins. She wondered if the excitement had always been due to her ability to sense the world of the supernatural.

How many fabled creatures walked these streets, unknown to the humans beside them?

As they passed the National Mall, the Washington Monument lit up the sky like a lighthouse, calling the tired and poor to the city just as the Statue of Liberty did for New York. Although the topic was always a point of contention in any social group, Sera loved that the city still had height restrictions on buildings, which meant she could see the stone monument from the roof of her apartment building. Her rooftop wasn't nearly as fancy as some of the newer buildings (not even close), but the landlord had thrown a few plastic Adirondack chairs up there amongst the AC unit and backup generator for the tenants to enjoy the space.

Yes, she would miss her tiny sanctuary.

They found parking on Renee's street in Capitol Hill, a stroke of luck thanks to it being Tuesday after the Thanksgiving holiday. The bar-hopping street near the green Victorian row house would be a ghost town.

Sera trailed her fingers along the purple bike chained to the low, wrought-iron fence as she followed Nora toward the front door. Enjoying such simple things as a bike ride seemed like a far-off luxury. Even returning to her graduate classes felt like a mockery of her once-normal life. She would take boring over this mess any day.

She dropped her hand and climbed up the short flight of steps to the door, stopping beside Nora. The unlit neon OPEN sign was barely visible in the front window.

"Ready?" Nora's finger hovered over the doorbell as she looked to Sera for confirmation.

She nodded, and Nora pushed the button. The doorbell chimed inside.

A few moments later, Renee's concerned face appeared behind the opened door. "You two had me worried about how long it was taking."

Holding on to her black shawl with one hand, she ushered them inside to the small foyer where they removed jackets, scarves, and boots.

"Sorry to make you nervous, but trust us, it was worth it," Nora said as they followed the silver-haired woman down the hall.

The old, wooden floorboards creaked beneath their feet as they reached the library, the room so filled with books that the woman had started to create towering piles of texts on the floor next to the massive cherry bookshelves. Sera inhaled, letting the welcome scent of so many unread pages, warmed by the fireplace, soothe her soul.

Renee had already poured steaming cups of tea and placed them by each of the purple wingback chairs. She had obviously prepared for a long story upon their return. They all sat and took a few sips of tea, although Sera—or perhaps it was Bacchus—longed for a stronger beverage. Preferably a Merlot.

"All right, one of you is going to have to talk." Renee gazed at them over the cup she held with both hands, elbows resting on the arms of the chair. Lavender-framed glasses hung from a strand of clear crystals around her neck.

When they first met, Sera had assumed the crystals were just a pretty decoration, but now she was fairly sure they were some kind of defensive ward, like the one the woman had made for Sera before she wore the amulet.

"Okay, try not to drop dead from a heart attack, but remember how Bacchus told us that other gods existed?" Nora grinned at the older woman.

"Of course. It's hard to forget such a detail."

Sera rolled her eyes skyward as Bacchus chuckled inside her head. *Neither of them had witnessed two brutal murders and been tortured just a few days before, okay?* she thought to him.

Sympathy flooded through her mind in response. At least he wasn't smug *all* the time.

After explaining what they had learned about the detective, Nora leaned forward. "I'm *dying* to see him turn into his other form."

Sera stared at her best friend. "How do you handle this all so well? I feel like my head is going to explode at any given moment."

Nora's green eyes twinkled. "You know I love adventure."

"I'd call this more than an adventure."

"That may be because it's directly happening to you," Renee said, "but Nora sees it from more of a distance."

"I did get kidnapped and used as bait by a maniacal witch." Nora gave a small nonchalant shrug before sipping her tea, although her eyes glanced warily toward the door.

"That you did. So, where is this Theo now? Didn't want to face a witch?" Renee chuckled.

"He needed to complete some work at the station," Nora said. "And see if any... news had come in."

"I'm okay. Really. I just got caught off guard back there," Sera said, catching the glance between the two other women. "Hearing his name felt like a punch in the stomach. Even part of his name, apparently."

Renee's expression softened with sympathy. "There are no words or magic that will ever make the pain easier, only time. Be kind to yourself. It's only been a few days and only one since you woke up."

Rage ignited within Sera. "I don't think I'll really be able to grieve and say goodbye until that monster is gone." She took a deep breath to control her anger.

A moment later, a calming wave rolled like warm nectar through her body. Yeah, Bacchus had definitely been more helpful than she gave him credit for.

"Hey, girl, tell her about your Gift," Nora said, placing a gentle hand on her arm.

"Yeah, I guess I have one, too." Sera gave a half-smile. "Must be from my mom being a witch and all. I could hear the god Xolotl speaking inside Theo's mind. Mostly growling, anyway."

The older woman's head jerked back with surprise. "I didn't see that one coming!"

"A little psychic humor?" Nora asked with a smirk. The phrase had become the witch's joke ever since they started seeing her regularly during the fall semester.

Renee laughed. "Unintentionally this time. You're right, though. Your mom was a telepath and could communicate with us without words. Very convenient. Can you send a message or only receive one?" She tilted her head as she looked at Sera.

"I don't know, we didn't try. We got distracted by talk of the deaths." Sera looked down into her tea, watching the leaves settle. "How would I even try?"

"Envision a thread connecting your mind with another," said Renee. "Go ahead, try it now."

Sera closed her eyes and tried. She couldn't seem to connect or sense Renee or Nora, and after a few attempts, opened her eyes again.

"I didn't even have to try with Xolotl, his thoughts just came through." Sera tilted her head to the side. "I wonder if it's similar to how I sensed Solomon and Alexander when they were nearby."

Renee chewed on the end of her glasses. "There are a few possibilities. Your Gift could still be developing, or it only works sporadically. Or it could be that you can only communicate with immortals."

Bingo, Bacchus said, snapping his fingers.

What? Why didn't you speak up before? she asked, although she had a feeling she knew what the answer would be.

This game was fun to watch, he said. Yep. Exactly as she figured.

Sera let out an exasperated sigh. "Bacchus said it's the last, that I can only communicate with non-mortal creatures."

"Did he know all along?" Nora asked.

"Of course he did. He's insufferable sometimes."

Nora shook her finger at Sera, but she was pretty sure the gesture was meant for Bacchus.

Renee nodded. "Okay, so your telepathy Gift only works with the non-mortal folks. It makes sense that you didn't notice it until now—you were probably never in such close contact with them before."

"That I know of." Sera scrunched her nose at the thought of being around supernatural creatures in the past without even knowing. Her skin prickled in response. Maybe it was time for that glass of wine.

"Going back to the new god, did Theo say why he approached you with this revelation?" Renee asked.

"He's going to help me build an army to defeat Danae." Digging her nails into the skin of her palm when she said the creature's name, she nearly drew blood.

Creases formed on Renee's forehead again as she frowned. "I still don't like this plan of yours."

Sera simply returned the witch's gaze. Arguing wouldn't help.

"When do you think you are going to leave?" Nora asked.

"Immediately. The sooner we can stop her, the better."

"What about the end of the semester?" Nora asked. "You have finals to give and your own to take."

"How can I even think about going back and pretending like everything's okay? I don't even know what those monsters did with Julia and Hiro after I left." She allowed the tightness to form in her chest, letting it constrict around her heart like a snake would bind its prey. Honoring Hiro meant feeling this pain, no matter how difficult.

"You ever hear the phrases, 'practice makes perfect,' or, 'you fake it till you make it?' That's what you're going to do." Nora reached over and squeezed her hand. "And I'm going to be there to help you. So is your invisible best friend."

She's right, you can't avoid your life, Bacchus said.

Realizing they both spoke the truth, Sera sighed. A phone buzzed on the side table next to her.

Nora picked it up, reading the message. "It's Theo, he says he's stuck at the station, but he wanted to give us a heads up. They—" Nora stopped, gazing up at Sera, her eyes filled with sorrow, but also fear.

"What?"

"They found Julia and Hiro."

CHAPTER 5

Serafina

Someone must have tied an anvil around Sera's heart and dropped it into the deepest part of the deepest ocean. Or was it tossed into a fast-flowing river? Was her heart stopping or beating too fast? She couldn't tell, but either way, she was drowning.

A bright red glow filled her mind, encasing her entire being in love, driving out the pain. Her heart, which had been beating its way out of her chest, slowed to its usual rhythm, her breath returning to normal.

Sera opened her eyes to find Nora's face directly in front of her, her friend's hands gripping Sera's shoulders and shaking her lightly.

"Jesus, girl!" Nora breathed a sigh of relief.

"I'm sorry I just needed a moment."

"A moment?" Dropping her arms, Nora sat back on her heels from her kneeling position in front of Sera's chair. "It's been like five minutes. Okay, maybe just one, but you weren't responding. At all."

Sera rubbed her face with her hands, trying to clear her thoughts. "Did Theo say anything else? Where? How?"

"Just that he'd swing by before classes tomorrow to fill us in and prepare us," Nora said.

"Prepare us?" She tensed. She already knew how they were killed. Maybe he was going to update the others, rightly assuming she hadn't told them all the details yet, and probably couldn't. Not yet, anyway. But where were they found? Did anything else happen to them? She swallowed the bile rising in her throat.

"That's all he said."

"You girls need to get some rest," Renee said. "Eleanor, you're welcome to stay here as long as you'd like."

Nora's curls bounced as she got to her feet. "You know I appreciate the offer, but there's nothing like sleeping in my own bed again after a few nights away. I'll be back around seven."

As Nora leaned down to hug her, Sera breathed in her familiar oatmeal scent, courtesy of her ridiculously expensive shower gel. She would definitely sacrifice herself before letting the Bacchae get their hands on her best friend. Not even Bacchus could stop her wrath if they tried.

A feeling of mirth drifted through her mind.

Once Nora left, Sera headed upstairs to the guest room that had become her new home. The room was just large enough to hold a full-sized bed and side table adorned with a vase holding a few white snowdrops. Once she turned off the light, the room would be enveloped in complete darkness due to the lack of a window. She welcomed the dark and sleep right about now, if only to cease her chaotic thoughts.

She knew Renee didn't mind her staying there, but Sera hoped it was only temporary like she kept saying it was. Someday, she'd like her life to return to normal. Whatever her new normal would be, anyway.

But first, she had a Bacchae witch to take down.

* * *

THE DOORBELL TO RENEE'S row house rang early the next morning, earlier than they had expected Nora.

"I'll get it," Sera called out as she came down the stairs from the guest room, knowing from the scent that Renee was busy cooking breakfast for everyone.

When she opened the front door, Theo's dark brown eyes met her grey ones. It was hard to get over how young he looked, despite being over a century old. The first time she had met him, Sera thought he had just joined the police force and wondered how he had already become a detective.

His ash-brown hair fell in tousled waves toward his chin, though pushed back behind his ears in the front, adding to his youthful appearance. The darkness to his complexion hinted at some Latino background. Maybe that's why the Aztec god chose him.

"Are you going to let me in?" He cocked an eyebrow at her.

"Yeah, sorry," she said as she stepped back. "It's just weird looking at you."

"It's not every day I'm insulted first thing in the morning."

"No, I mean, you look younger than I am, but you're old. Really old." Sera shut the door after he walked in.

"I'll take that as a compliment." His eyes flicked around the foyer, taking in his surroundings.

Always observant, Sera thought.

"Are you aware you're being watched?" He nodded his head toward the door.

She froze. She expected it, but the confirmation still terrified her after what she had gone through, even with Bacchus by her side. Or in her head. She wondered how long they had been there. "How many?"

"Just two, which means they aren't planning on confronting you anytime soon."

"Do they know who you are?" she asked.

"No. I've always kept myself hidden."

Good. Chances were they wouldn't immediately know her plan yet. Relief flooded through her like water through a broken dam.

"Come meet Renee." She turned and led him down the hallway to the kitchen.

Because the u-shaped kitchen in the narrow row house was barely large enough for two people to move around comfortably, let alone three, Sera stopped in the even tinier dining room. Renee had her back to them, finishing up the last batch of cinnamon-scented waffles. A plate stacked high with the fluffy breakfast cakes already graced the two-person table set against the wall just outside the kitchen.

"Renee, this is detective Theodore Pratt and the Aztec god Xolotl," she said when the other woman turned around.

Renee's face lit up with her usual warm smile. "You're welcome in my home, both you and your god friend. Please help yourself to some food. Coffee?"

Theo dipped his head in greeting, and a low growl resounded in Sera's mind. "No, but thank you for the offer. I've found coffee to be more draining on my senses, rather than a boost."

Renee nodded and turned back around, pulling more golden waffles off the iron and onto her plate.

Holding back a snort, Sera poured herself a cup. Coffee was life. She sat at the table and turned so her back was against the wall, facing him.

"Is Ms. Patton okay?" she asked.

"She's fine," he said. "I applied a salve to her wounds, and she fell asleep on her couch. All while still under the Bacchae's *influence*."

Relief washed through her and eased her guilt at the woman's involuntary involvement. On to the next problem. "So, the police found them?"

Renee walked over and placed a comforting hand on Sera's shoulder.

Are you sure you want that information? Bacchus asked, his tone soothing.

Yes, she said as firmly as she could muster.

Shall we get wine first? he asked.

Deciding to take his question as rhetorical, she stayed put, waiting for the hammer to drop.

Theo's lips tightened as he nodded, his eyes fixed on hers. "In the Anacostia River. Normally, Lorenzo does a better job of hiding bodies. He wanted them to be found. Quickly."

Sera swallowed the lump forming in her throat, trying to focus on calmer thoughts. It didn't help a whole lot. "Nora said you needed to prepare us for something?"

"I wasn't assigned to this case because Julia was my partner, but the detectives involved are going to question you about both."

"I assumed they'd ask me about Hiro." She fought the urge to gulp as she said his name. "But why Julia?"

"You're a potential suspect."

Coffee splattered across the table and her lap as she choked. "I'm a *what*?!" she managed to get out.

"Significant others can be considered potential suspects in a murder case. It'll help that you aren't married. However, Julia had questioned you about the missing amulet. It doesn't look great that two people connected to you in some way are now dead. Not to mention, you haven't gone to classes for a few days."

She wiped the coffee from her chin with a napkin. He sure didn't mince words. "But why me? Why would they think I would kill either one of them?"

"That's why they're going to question you. I'll do what I can to help redirect the focus, but it's going to work in your favor to be as honest as you can, considering the circumstances."

Sera barked out a laugh. "Honest? So, you want me to tell them that I'm wearing the missing amulet? That Bacchus, the ancient Roman god, is alive and well and works through me? That Lorenzo Vicari is an immortal demigod, a supernatural *creature* called a Bacchae, and that his boss is the one who murdered your partner and my boyfriend? That my boyfriend was actually going to propose to me sometime soon? Oh, and let's not forget that the Bacchae witch who killed them both wants to take over the world and make humans her breakfast, lunch, and dinner?"

She was losing control, and she knew it, as tears gathered in her eyes. A warm hand gently squeezed her shoulder.

Ugh. She hated crying in front of people, and Renee had seen it far too often in the short time she'd known her. She was tempted to let Bacchus intervene, but he wisely pretended to be too busy drinking wine in the corner of her mind to notice.

Theo's expression softened. "You're going to tell them Lorenzo abducted you to question you about the amulet two nights after it went missing. The abduction is already on record due to the break-in at your apartment, which also works in your favor, even though you and I know it wasn't Lorenzo's men who broke in."

"Wait, how do *you* know that?" She wiped her wet face with the back of a hand.

"You would have had to invite one of them in, and I know that didn't happen. Do you know who broke in?"

"A man named Leif Karlsson," Renee said as she walked back toward the waffle maker. "He's a witch from my old coven. He helped take powers away from the Bacchae before he disappeared with the amulet."

Theo nodded at her. "Ah, I've heard of him. But the good news is the police probably haven't. So, continue to direct blame toward Lorenzo."

Renee poured new batter into the griddle. "You'll want to keep an eye out for Leif. He's already caused us trouble by kidnapping Nora to try to get the amulet back."

"She seems to be handling that event well."

Renee chuckled. "Eisler women handle most things well. But I know she also hides behind her confidence sometimes."

Theo looked pointedly at Sera's neck. "Speaking of hiding, you're going to have to remove that."

Sera's jaw went slack. "Remove the amulet? With evil Bacchae after me? And a few witches? Are you insane?"

"You can't risk the detectives seeing it on you, even wearing all the clothing in the world. If they decide to bring you in, you'll be caught with it on your person. Then they'll charge you for the theft as well as the murder of Julia. I'm sure they'll find a reason to add on Hiro's murder, especially if Lorenzo gets involved behind the scenes."

Even though Sera and Bacchus knew the detective was right, the god's anger threatened to boil over the surface of her mind.

"It'll be safe here. The house is secure," Renee said, reaching out a reassuring hand to squeeze Sera's shoulder again. "And we'll make sure you're well protected."

"What's going on?" Nora asked.

Coffee splashed everywhere again as Sera jumped, startled from the unexpected voice. That girl was sneakier than a ninja, although neither Renee nor Theo looked surprised at her appearance.

Muttering a few obscenities under her breath, she gave up on the cup of deliciousness and set it down. She dabbed at the spots on her pants with a wet napkin. At least it hadn't been red wine.

"I'm a suspect, and I have to remove the amulet," Sera said, scrunching up her nose. "Or, I could just leave. Head to wherever these other gods are and convince them to join the fight."

"Not unless you want to be arrested when you return," said Theo. "Danae's territory includes the United States, so you'd have to return to fight her."

"Territory?"

He sighed. "Bacchus, you really need to bring her up to speed."

Remind him we've been busy, Bacchus said.

Are you going to tell me what he meant? she asked.

We have plenty of time for those details later, he replied. *For now, let's talk about keeping you out of jail. Breaking out is always an option, but it won't help either of us.*

Sera groaned. "Okay, so I can't just up and leave yet. But I need to get help to take Danae down. What do you suggest?" She looked at Theo expectantly.

"Return to school, say you've been sick. It's not a great cover story from a seeming-innocent standpoint, but you have two alibis right here." He nodded toward the other women. "In a few weeks, it'll be winter break, and the focus will be fully on Lorenzo."

"How do you know?"

"I'll make sure it happens," he said.

"Can't you just make it happen now?" Nora asked, grabbing a plate and a waffle. She sat in the chair across from Sera.

"The case needs to go through due process, which takes time. I'm just going to correct the course and speed a little bit." He looked down at his smartwatch when it beeped, scrolling through a message on the screen. "I've got to run, but we need to connect again soon."

"Wait. That's all the preparation you've got?" Sera didn't feel nearly ready enough to face other people, let alone cops.

"You'll do fine, you play dumb really well." Theo winked at her and raised his hand to Renee. "It's nice to meet such a Gifted witch in this day and age."

Renee smiled and gave a quick wave.

Ignoring Bacchus's roaring laughter, Sera glared after the detective as he left the kitchen. She turned her eyes on Nora, who was snickering through a mouthful of waffles. "Did he just insult me or compliment me?"

"Definitely both," Nora said.

"I guess I had it coming after I accidentally insulted him when he got here."

One of Nora's eyebrows quirked up. "How'd you do that?"

"I told him it was weird seeing him because he looks so young, but he's actually really old."

Nora burst out laughing, while Renee chuckled over her cup of tea in the kitchen.

"It's true. Anyway, he said we're being watched."

Nora rolled her eyes. "Yeah, Solomon was here the other day when you were still passed out. He tried to tell me he wasn't involved at all."

Renee furrowed her brow. "You didn't tell me about that. I saw the Bacchae, but Nora, you need to be very careful. You may have a crystal ward, but we don't know what kind of magic Danae will bring next."

Nora waved her hand like she was swatting away a fly. "He won't hurt me."

"You may think that, but he's a Bacchae, and his loyalty

belongs to his maker. I want you to come straight here after classes today. I'll teach you some things to use against him or any others, should the need arise."

Green eyes glittered with excitement. "You mean magic?"

Renee smiled. "Yes, magic. It's about time I start passing on my knowledge. You may not have a Gift, that we know of anyway, but that doesn't mean you can't learn to use magic. A Gift just makes it easier."

Her friend's squeal threatened to pierce Sera's eardrum. At least she wasn't holding coffee this time.

"This is going to be awesome! How about I skip school and just learn magic all day instead?"

"No way, lady. I need you by my side today," Sera said with a firm shake of her head. Fear snaked its way up her throat as she reached up to touch the amulet.

It was time to part with the god.

Goodbye for now, she thought to Bacchus, unable to hide the sadness.

I may not be with you physically, but I'll still be able to feel you. Should harm befall you while you're away, I'll let the witch know. A warmth filled her bones like a gentle hug.

Taking a deep breath, she reached behind her neck to unclasp the golden chain. She stared at the crimson, pinecone-shaped pendant in her palm. The design was so delicate, it was hard to believe a god's essence filled the inside. Especially a larger-than-life god like Bacchus.

Her neck felt bare and cold without the touch of the metal. Not liking the sensation one bit, she shivered, feeling unprotected and vulnerable. She hadn't realized how much she relied upon the god's strength and reassurance until that moment.

Renee handed her a leather thread, hiding a crystal ward within a small pouch. Sera tied it around her neck. A replacement amulet.

"It's not foolproof, as we've learned, but it'll give you a few extra moments, possibly even minutes if we're lucky, to get out of harm's way. Come right back here if anything happens. Be safe today, okay, girls?" Her caring tone held a note of concern.

Sera rubbed her arms, now tingling with goosebumps. The woman had the Sight—was she sensing something coming their way?

CHAPTER 6

Solomon

Nestor laid on the table in the cell where Serafina had been held just a few days prior, his long dark blond hair falling off the edge. Having a chamber dedicated to the art of torture within the walls of the mansion came in handy these days.

Solomon stood across the room, next to the skeleton of a long-forgotten previous occupant. Lorenzo kept it there as a reminder of what was to come to any new occupant should he or she choose not to obey the Italian's demands. Although the bones no longer attracted rats, Serafina's recent visit left a dark stain on the stones, tempting the vermin out of hiding.

Ignoring one bold rodent inspecting his shoe, Solomon watched the other man struggle against the chains that bound him. The ancient Immortal was no match against the silver-plated manacles. The smell of smoldering flesh permeated the air as the metal burned into his skin. Danae and her ever-present bodyguard looked on, impassive as ever.

Bacchus had created the Immortals with this limitation, an allergic reaction to silver that muted their supernatural powers. It had been the god's way of keeping the Immortals under control over the centuries, and Danae used it to her advantage now. Never having been on the receiving end of long-term exposure to the metal, Solomon could only imagine the level of pain the Eternal was in.

He did his best *not* to imagine.

"The Council will have you skinned alive for this," Nestor hissed through his extended fangs. His vertically-dilated eyes blazed red.

The way Nestor had been challenging Danae since his arrival, Solomon couldn't be sure the Eternal knew he was about to die. If he didn't, he was more a fool than Solomon thought.

Danae gazed back at him, calm and collected. "The Council will be mine once they learn I've restored all of our powers and have the amulet. I will be their queen."

Nestor barked out a laugh, his fanged open mouth reminiscent of a striking snake. "You will never be anyone's queen. They will thank you as they rip the skin from your body and display it on a wall. You'll die a slow death as a traitor to our kind."

Crimson flames ignited within Danae's eyes. She tilted her head to the side. "Do it."

The silent Immortal always at her side stepped forward

and plunged a long silver knife deep into Nestor's left breast. As the blade struck his heart, a glass-shattering screech erupted from the Eternal's throat, and his eyes strained to pop from his head. Steam rose from his body, and he shook violently beneath his restraints.

This would be the first time Solomon had ever witnessed an Eternal's death. In fact, he wasn't even sure the last time an Eternal had died. The longer an Immortal lived, the longer it took for the body to disintegrate, and he had no idea what to expect with an Immortal as old as this one.

The Eternal's skin lightened to an ashy grey as it melted toward the table beneath him. Muscles shrank beneath his flesh. His skin pulled away from the bones, dripping like hot wax to the floor and evaporating as it touched the stone. Minutes later, the skeleton that remained began to crumble.

Danae chanted a few words in a foreign language and held up a glass flask. As Nestor's body dissolved into glittering dust, a mystical wind swept the particles into the vial like a maelstrom. When all the remains had vanished, she put the stopper into the top of the flask. Swirling golden flecks floated around the inside, dancing in a wind that didn't cease.

She looked up at Solomon. "The girl will be out of the house later today, and I will ensure the witch will not interfere. That is when we will make our move."

Solomon nodded, although the skin on the nape of his neck rose. It was really happening. The god would be hers in a matter of hours, and he still wasn't sure how he felt about that. Was he ready to rebel against his own kind?

"Leave the room. Both of you. I need to prepare." Danae turned toward the worktable that held various instruments of torture as well as a bag that Solomon had carried down to the cell, assuming it held items she would need for the ritual.

As they left the cell, Danae said something in the ancient language she used with her personal guards. The other Immortal who rarely left the Eternal's side nodded to her as she shut the door behind her.

Not being able to understand them irritated Solomon to no end. He wanted to ask the other Immortal what the queen had said to her, but a vow of silence prevented them from speaking even to each other about the things they witnessed. That, and the bodyguard didn't have a tongue. He still didn't even know her name, just that her sleek black hair, light brown skin tone, and the slight tilt to her eyes indicated an East Asian descent. Her every movement revealed a background as a fighter.

Lethal was most likely an understatement.

"I'll be upstairs if she needs me," he said.

The Immortal shook her head and pointed down as if to say, "Stay put." She bent a knee and put her foot against the wall behind her, leaning back against the stone.

Well, that wasn't ideal. He ran a hand through his cropped hair, assuming Danae had something to do with the bodyguard's command. He had hoped to have a few moments alone, at the very least, to alert Nora to Danae's plan. Chances were the guard would alert Danae to any calls he made or texts he sent.

He fought the urge to clench his jaw. The bodyguard would sense that as well.

* * *

TWO HOURS LATER, SOLOMON eyed the dark green row house from the back seat of the SUV. The queen's technology team had already hacked into the witch's phone contacts and sent her a false message from a friend asking for immediate help. She had left a minute earlier.

The GPS tracker Solomon had placed on Serafina's phone confirmed she was still at the university, Nora having gone with her, and that detective who had started hanging around was nowhere to be seen.

It was time.

Opening the door, he stepped onto the sidewalk before turning around and extending his palm. Danae's small hand fit within his as she placed her foot, encased in her signature red stilettos, on the ground and slid from the vehicle.

Dark hair tumbled in waves around the delicate features of her face, and her full lips were marked with a bright red lipstick that matched her heels and collet necklace. All three accent pieces complimented her lighter, olive-toned skin. She wore black leather pants that were more a second skin than pants and a chunky black, tunic-length sweater that only made her appear even more petite than she already was.

A deadly weapon disguised as a pampered teenaged girl.

"Make sure there are no distractions." Danae didn't bother to look at him before walking to the front gate of the row house. She pushed the iron gate open with a delicate hand and approached the steps.

From where he stood, Solomon could just barely hear her chanting in the same foreign language she'd used before, her gaze focused on the door in front of her. As she raised her arms in front of her, a forceful, unnatural wind whipped through the front yard of the house, stirring the fallen leaves and nearly tugging the potted flowers from their beds.

Goosebumps rolled across his skin as the wind rose around her like a tornado, pulling her hair upward, then whooshed across to blow against the front door. The breeze ceased suddenly and without a trace as if it had never existed.

Danae ascended the steps and turned the door handle. She walked inside the house, no longer barricaded by the witch's magic or the need to be invited in.

Glancing up and down the street, Solomon's enhanced vision and hearing didn't pick up anything out of the ordinary. A bright flash of light drew his attention back to the house. He took a step closer but stopped as Danae returned to the door, a triumphant smile on her face.

She held up her gloved hand, opening her fist to reveal the amulet, the crimson pinecone pendant flashing as it caught the light.

"He's mine." She practically skipped down the steps and through the front gate.

"Excuse me, are you Ms. Colette?" a woman's voice asked behind Solomon.

Letting out a curse, he spun around. His superior senses were getting worse. A middle-aged white woman approached Danae, clutching her purse to her side, as she eyed him with suspicion. He was used to the look she gave him, having seen it more often than not throughout his long life.

But Danae wasn't as forgiving. She grasped the woman around the throat, lifting her from the ground with one hand. "You're wise to fear him, just not for the right reason."

She brought the woman's gasping face directly in front of her own, her fangs bared as she hissed, "But I assure you,

I'm far more terrifying than he."

The woman's gurgling scream didn't last long after Danae dragged her inside the SUV.

CHAPTER 7

Serafina

Being back at school, a normal place filled with normal people, made Sera's heart ache. The white laminate floors and fluorescent lighting mocked her with their bright cheeriness. Students and faculty strolled down the halls, some casually and some with urgency, talking in small groups and laughing with one another.

They didn't know the supernatural world existed. They didn't know that an evil force threatened their very existence. Of course they'd continue to feel happiness, frustration, and boredom. How lucky they were to be so ignorant.

Despite not having Bacchus or wine to suppress her feelings, the rest of Sera's body felt numb and emotionless by the end of the day. She simply went through the motions of what was expected of her.

In her Greek mythology course, the last class she taught for the day, Sera kept hearing the students whisper as they tackled a worksheet. Usually, she wouldn't mind the sound while she graded; she used to do the same in her undergraduate classes. But today, the tone was different, more urgent, and the students' eyes kept flicking in her direction. Anxiety blossomed within her until she couldn't take it anymore.

"Okay, does someone want to tell me what's going on?" She kept her tone light and tried to smile despite her racing heart and sweating palms.

The students exchanged a round of nervous glances. A moment later, Mary, one of her favorites in part due to the curls so reminiscent of Nora's, approached her desk and handed her a cell phone.

The blood drained from Sera's face, from her entire being, when Hiro's smiling photo stared back from the screen, followed by the news story that his body had been found in the Anacostia River. Seeing it in front of her somehow made it more real than it had been coming from Nora's mouth.

"I'm so sorry, Ms. Finch." Mary's voice was quiet and full of sorrow.

The phone shook in her outstretched hand as she handed it back. The movement seemed to happen in slow motion. Surreal somehow.

"Class is dismissed."

For once, the students didn't say a word as they packed up their things and left. Most of them whispered some sort of condolences as they walked by her desk, but Sera could only stare at the pen she had laid down in front of her when she had taken Mary's phone. The pen had been a freebie from the hotel she and Nora had stayed at during their end-of-summer beach trip to Salerno a few months ago. A lifetime ago. Her life had been ordinary then, and no supernatural creature had murdered her boyfriend.

When the last student left the room, she turned to the side and vomited into the trash can, losing the little bit of food she had been able to eat that day. As she wiped her mouth with a napkin, a man cleared his throat behind her. She took a deep breath to try to stop her body from shaking before turning around.

"Serafina Finch?" An older gentleman with blotchy red and white skin addressed her. He looked every bit the old school cop, from the fedora sitting atop mostly grey hair to the tie showing beneath his rumpled trench coat that was struggling to cinch around his protruding waistline. His pants were too long for his short stature and bunched around his ankles. Beside him stood a younger black woman.

"Yes. Can I help you?" Sera asked, her stomach clenching once again, only this time from dread.

"I'm detective Robert Bernard. You can call me Bob, and this is my partner Tiana Williams. No relation to the Disney princess." He chuckled.

Tiana rolled her eyes. It probably wasn't a new line to her. She couldn't have been more his opposite. Tiana was at least twenty years his junior, tall and slim with ebony skin and tight-fitting clothing accentuating her fit figure. She held a red leather jacket in one hand, and her Afro blow out suited her chic style.

"May we speak with you a moment?" Robert asked.

Sera nodded but remained silent, waiting for him to lead

the conversation. She didn't trust her voice just yet.

Removing his hat as he walked in, Robert pushed his coat back to allow him to sit in one of the student desks, though it was a tight fit. Tiana sat with one leg on the corner of another table, leaving the other foot on the floor. She swung the free leg beneath her.

"Our condolences for the loss of your loved one. We had hoped to get here before the story broke, but..." his voice trailed off as he spread his hands.

Sera nodded again, her throat tightening.

"From what we've gathered, Hiro has been missing for several days. Is there a reason you didn't report him missing?"

Opening her mouth to speak, she croaked instead. It was probably due to losing her lunch in the trash can, but she could use it to her advantage. She cleared her throat and tried again. "I've been really sick since Thanksgiving, only now getting back to classes."

Robert nodded and made a quick note in his pocket-sized journal. Old school. "Did you attempt to contact him at all since Thanksgiving?"

Tears already spilling from her eyes, she lowered her gaze to her lap and shook her head.

"I know this is hard to talk about, Serafina, but the sooner we can figure out what happened, the sooner we can bring the killer to justice. We don't want another cold case. Did anyone visit you while you were sick who can vouch for your whereabouts?"

Sera sniffled and wiped her nose with her napkin. "Yes. I was staying at a friend's house—Renee Colette. She and Nora took turns taking care of me."

"Nora?" Tiana asked.

"My best friend. Eleanor Eisler. She's a graduate student here, too."

"Did they ever leave you alone in the house?" Robert asked.

"I honestly don't know. I was asleep most of the time," Sera said.

Tiana eyed her from head to toe. "You must have been very sick."

Sera nodded.

"Did you see a doctor?" Tiana asked.

"No, I—" She was cut off as Nora came running into the room.

"Sera! Oh, babe, I just saw the news." She rushed over and enveloped Sera in a tight hug. They had agreed to pretend like they didn't know, just like everyone else. Ever the dramatic, Nora played her part well.

Giving in to the grief that wanted to consume her for days, Sera didn't have to fake the sobs racking her body as she held onto her best friend. Without Bacchus there to suppress it, she felt like the pain would rip her asunder.

"We'll leave you two to grieve in peace for now. We'll come by again tomorrow." Robert's gruff voice said, loud enough to be heard over her sobs.

Nora continued to hold her, whispering soothing words into her hair until her body began to quiet. When Sera finally pulled herself away and reached for tissues, the detectives were gone.

"I'm so sorry, your shirt is soaked." Sera pointed to the wet spots on the front of her friend's shirt then blew her nose. At least she hadn't attempted any mascara.

A sympathetic look crossed Nora's face as she sat on Sera's desk. "You know I always win at wet t-shirt contests."

Despite the lingering pain that had settled deep into her belly, Sera laughed. Nora always knew how to make her smile again.

In high school, other students had teased the two girls for their close relationship, calling them lesbians, as if that were a bad thing. While Sera had been embarrassed, mostly because she didn't want her friend's cheerleader reputation to be tarnished somehow, Nora had just turned her haughty glare on the bullies and said, "If only I were so lucky to call Sera my girlfriend. Fortunately for you *boys*, she's not into girls." She had done a characteristic flip of her curly hair as she turned and sauntered away. Sera had suddenly been pursued relentlessly by her one-time bullies.

Nora may not have had a Gift, but she had a magic all on her own.

"With Bacchus there to help before, I forgot how much it really hurt," Sera said.

"You need to let yourself feel it. It's all a part of the healing process." Nora handed her another tissue.

"Not yet. Not until after I take her down."

"There's going to be a funeral, and people are going to expect you to cry," Nora said.

"Everyone grieves differently. Some people just go numb. It's how I felt all day until Mary showed me the news." Sera pushed her hair back behind her ears. "I just can't believe he's gone."

"I know, babe. Let's go fill our bellies full of comfort carbs." Hopping off the desk, she pulled Sera to her feet.

* * *

THE MORNING GRIND HAD been their meeting point since they moved to the District for graduate school. Sera loved the tiny diner downtown, her home away from home, and it was one of the only places in the city open twenty-four hours a day. Studying and late-night gossip fests had been had aplenty in their usual window booth.

Light was fading rapidly due to the winter solstice being only a few weeks away, as well as from the impending storm. To avoid any parking hassles in the rain, they took a city bus from the university, shoving themselves in with the evening commuters. Sera didn't mind the crowd on cold, grey days like this one. The extra body heat helped warm her up again.

Unable to find any open seats, the two women stood, holding onto one of the metal poles. They swayed with the motion of the bus until they reached the diner's block. Dusk descended as they walked arm in arm to the front door, huddled together against the chill of the gusting wind.

The bell above the door dinged as they entered.

"Hey, girls. Coffee?" Cheryl's familiar voice greeted them. Hers was the kind of voice you expected to hear coming from a headliner in a dimly lit and smoke-filled jazz club. She sat at the bar top attached to the kitchen, her usual perch when it wasn't busy. Her dark skin was a stark contrast to the white countertop she leaned against.

"Always," Nora called out as they unwound their scarves and hung up their coats. They sat at their usual booth against the window.

They had made it just in time—freezing rain pelted the sidewalks outside, causing people to rush for cover or pull

STEPHANIE MIRRO

out their umbrellas. Carrying a small umbrella around this city was always a smart idea; the weather was wildly unpredictable. People had places to be, however, so only one or two made their way into the diner to ride out the storm.

Rubbing her hands together, Sera blew onto them until the coffee arrived to finish the job.

"I didn't get to ask earlier. Did you guys discuss where you're going to go first?" Nora asked.

"No. We only talked about today. It feels so weird not to have *him*, even though I've got this one." She avoided the god's name even though the diner was almost empty. Her hand reached up to touch the leather thread.

Cheryl walked over with the fresh brew. "Here you are, darlin's. What else can I get you tonight?"

"A stack of pancakes—blueberry, of course—as much bacon as you can manage to carry, four scrambled eggs, hash browns, and a few pieces of toast for good measure," Nora said before Sera could even open her mouth.

Cheryl frowned. "They not feeding you on that campus?"

"Comfort carbs."

"Why're you two girls needin' comfort?"

Nora glanced at Sera. "I'll tell you later."

Pressing her lips together, Cheryl nodded. "I'll get your order in."

Sera let out a sigh of relief as she walked away, glad the woman didn't press them for information. Cheryl would squish Sera to her massive bosom like a mother hen sitting on her eggs, and Sera wasn't sure she could handle physical sympathy from anyone other than Nora quite yet.

A low growling hum filtered into Sera's mind as if

hearing thunder from a distance. She couldn't see much outside in the dark with the rain coming down so hard.

"I think Theo's nearby," she said, tilting her head to the side to listen even though the sound was inside her head.

Nora squinted out the window. "You can hear the god?"

"I think so. I'm not sure what else it would be."

A moment later, Sera caught a glimpse of Theo's face underneath an umbrella as he approached the door of the diner. He shook off as much water as he could from his jacket and umbrella under the awning before stepping inside, the bell announcing his presence.

Sera raised a hand as he searched the room, his head nodding when he saw her. After hanging his jacket on the coat rack, he made his way over to their table.

"May I?" He indicated the spot next to Nora.

"By all means," Nora said as she scooted over to accommodate him. She threw a wink at Sera as he slid into the red vinyl seat.

She must be over Solomon, Sera thought, smirking. Silence filled her mind—she had expected Bacchus to reply. She sighed.

"That excited to see me, eh?" His brown eyes held a hint of humor.

"It's not that. It's just quiet in here today." Sera tapped her forehead.

"Ah." Theo nodded. "Well, some good news to distract you. Or at least, not bad news. You convinced Robert of your innocence with your throwing up and sobbing, as well as your alibis. He's a big softie, though. Tiana wasn't as convinced, so she's going to be the one you need to cater to tomorrow when they come back to question you again."

Cheryl walked over, balancing plates full of blueberry pancakes, mounds of bacon, hash browns, and a stack of toast. Exactly as ordered.

"New friend?" she asked, tilting her head toward Theo as she set down plates.

"Kind of." Sera wasn't sure what she would call him.

He put his hand out to Cheryl after she finished setting down the food. "Theodore Pratt, a detective with the DCPD."

Eyeing him with narrowed eyes, she shook his offered hand. "Whatchoo want with these two angels?"

He laughed then immediately grunted as Nora elbowed him in the ribs.

"No ill intent, I can assure you." Theo winced as he rubbed his side. "But would an angel inflict pain upon a man sworn to serve and protect?"

"Only if he deserved it," Nora said, already pulling pancakes onto her own plate.

"Mmhmm," Cheryl agreed. She held up her pot. "Coffee?"

"No, thank you."

Cheryl filled Sera's cup, knowing she would never turn it down, then turned away to tend to the two other tables and their sopping wet occupants.

"So, the detectives will be back tomorrow, and then what? Will it be over?" Sera bit off a piece of her crispy bacon.

"Depends on whether you can keep up this charade."

Feeling her cheeks flush with heat, she glared at him. "It's not a charade. I'm sad my boyfriend is dead."

Theo frowned at her. "I meant not knowing about the cause of his death and not having the amulet."

"Oh."

He eyed the plates of food on the table. "I'd ask if you ladies fasted today, but I saw the waffles Renee made."

Nora pushed eggs and a pancake onto Sera's plate before giving her a meaningful look. "Someone thinks I'm not noticing she's not eating."

"Unlike you, I can't eat when I'm stressed out. And not all of us are blessed with your metabolism." Sera raised an equally meaningful eyebrow at her pint-sized friend. Genetics like hers were just not fair.

Her mouth too full of pancakes to answer, Nora tapped Sera's plate with her fork.

After pushing the eggs around on her plate for a moment, Sera turned her attention on the detective. "How do I convince Tiana I'm innocent?"

"She's shrewd, so you're going to have to give her enough truth that she believes you. If everything comes out too perfect, she'll question it."

"Like tell her how Solomon and his Bacchae gang tried to jump me at my dad's house on Thanksgiving?" Details of the fight flashed through Sera's mind, including the satisfying sensation as the creature's head disconnected from its neck when she used the stop sign as a scythe. Working with Bacchus did have its perks.

"Right, but maybe without the supernatural details. Being confronted by Solomon and not calling the police again would indicate your naivete, which would be a good thing for you."

Sera's mouth fell open. He really knew how to insult a girl.

"What?" he asked.

"I'm sure I'm naive, but you don't have to be so blunt about it."

"You're really sensitive, aren't you?"

"I just don't like to tell people they're being a certain way if I hardly know them." She could feel the heat rising to her cheeks again, this time in embarrassment. His statement was kind of correct, but he didn't need to call her out on it. Especially with everything going on.

"You and I know why you didn't call the police, and it wasn't naïve," he said. "I'm saying if Tiana thinks you are, that would be a good thing. Don't assume I'm always insulting you."

Nora cut her off as Sera opened her mouth to retort. "Okay, kids, let's play nice. You got anything else for us, Theo?"

"I've been reaching out to my contacts, trying to find out which of the others will be most likely to help."

"Who are the others?" Nora asked, the eager gleam back in her eye.

"Freyja, a Nordic goddess. She hasn't merged with anyone, and I only know the last place she was seen, so we'll have to do some hunting. And Durga, the Hindu warrior goddess." He hesitated. "I'm not sure she'll join us, though."

"Why not?" Nora asked.

"She doesn't think she needs to," he explained. "Durga's still actively worshipped, although not like she used to be. She allows a human to speak on her behalf because she's not the force she once was. But she's still more powerful than most of the ancient gods who've stuck around."

"What do you mean by stuck around?" she asked.

"The majority of the gods still being worshipped spend their time on another plane of existence. Only those who are struggling for worshippers or those who enjoy being around their followers like Durga, stay on Earth," he explained.

"Okay, so where's Freyja?"

"There's a curiosities shop in Bergen, Norway that may have the torc she encased her essence in," he said. "The owner collects oddities in a secret back room. We'll have to go see it to know for sure. Your Gift will come in handy for that, Sera."

Keeping her eyes on the eggs she continued to push around her plate, Sera just nodded. She wished she could simply forget everything that had happened to her in the last week—in the last few *months*. She wanted to be as carefree as her friend, who hadn't witnessed the brutal murders of two people, including the man she was pretty sure she would call husband someday.

She wanted to go back to her classes as if nothing terrible had happened, as if her mother hadn't been slaughtered at the hands of the same immortal creature who killed Hiro, and instead, she had just died in an accident like they always thought. Or even better yet, she hadn't died at all. Without the Bacchae, that might have been her reality.

Maybe Sera wasn't cut out for this path, for vengeance. Maybe Bacchus had been wrong in choosing her. Maybe—

"Are you even listening?" Nora's direct voice cut through her thoughts like a knife.

"No, sorry." She didn't really feel bad. It had been a

long day, a long week. Hell, a long semester.

"Don't apologize. Let's get you back to Renee's and into bed." Nora waved to Cheryl for the check and some boxes.

"I'll drive you both over there," Theo said.

"That's not—" Sera started to say.

"That would be delightful," Nora interrupted.

Letting out a sigh, Sera knew better than to argue.

They paid the check and bundled up at the door before heading out to Theo's Jeep. He and Nora continued to chat while they drove, but Sera sat in silence in the back seat, staring out the window. She wasn't brooding, but it was pretty damn close to it.

At least the rain had stopped.

He found a parking spot a few houses down from Renee's, and the three of them headed toward the row house. She was lost in her thoughts until Theo's hand reached out to stop her. Confused, she opened her mouth to ask why they stopped before she saw the front door standing wide open.

Ducking under Theo's arm, she raced up the steps and into the house. She ignored his groan of frustration and Nora's voice shouting behind her.

"Renee?" Sera called out as she ran up the stairs toward the guest room where she had left the amulet.

Silence.

Bursting into the small bedroom, Sera's breath caught in her throat. She had left the amulet on the side table; she was sure of it. But now it only held the vase of delicate white snowdrops.

Stupid, stupid, stupid! She cursed herself for not hiding it or even locking it up in a safe deposit box.

Bacchus? she yelled in her mind. Only the sound of her beating heart and two sets of footsteps thumping through the lower level.

After a quick but thorough search, they found the house empty and the amulet gone, but no sign of a struggle. Despite the lack of evidence, Sera's blood ran cold, and her thoughts raced.

What would make Renee leave the house? Had she taken the god with her for protection? Or were they facing something far worse?

CHAPTER 8

Serafina

The drumming of Sera's heart drowned out whatever Theo and Nora were saying. It beat in tune with those four words repeating over and over in her mind like a bad record—*the amulet is gone*. Bacchus was gone. Her path to vengeance and healing was gone. Just... gone.

Yes, she'd questioned her ability to continue on that path, but the possibility of having the choice taken from her, like a rug ripped out from beneath her feet, solidified in her mind it was the right path. She *needed* to kill Danae to have closure; not doing so simply wasn't an option.

"Renee just replied, she's on her way back. She doesn't have the amulet, which means Danae must have gotten it somehow." Nora tucked her phone back into her pocket.

Deep growling and snarls snapped in her mind like a

dog's bite while Xolotl argued with Theo and brought her back to the present. The god wanted to rip Danae's throat out. Sera liked him.

"We're not stopping until the bitch is dead," she said.

They turned to look at her with surprise, like they had forgotten she was standing with them in Renee's library.

Nora's mouth hung open. "You can't be serious," she started to say, but Sera held up a hand to stop her.

"I'm not quitting just because I don't have a god's powers. We know this was Danae's work, and we still have Xolotl and my Gift. But we have zero chance of getting the amulet and Bacchus back until we get more manpower—er, god power behind us." Despite the current murky situation, the path before her was suddenly clear, her mind sharp. She would do whatever it took.

"In a few weeks, the semester will be over, the investigation will be on Lorenzo or at least off of me, and we go to Norway." Sera looked at her best friend. "Well, Theo and I go to Norway."

"Oh, hell, no. You're not leaving me behind." Nora planted her hands on her hips.

"If you want to be a part of this…this quest," Sera nearly snorted at her choice of words, "then you need to stay here and have Renee teach you some magic." Yes, this was her life now. Quests for vengeance and learning magic spells. Maybe she would even follow the yellow brick road home at the end.

Nora opened her mouth then closed it again, studying Sera's face. Finally, and with a dramatic sigh, she said, "But I really wanted to see Norway."

"I'm sure you'll have plenty of opportunities in the

future if we succeed. But we're not sightseeing. This is a get in, get out mission." Sera groaned internally. Did she really just use the word *mission*? What, was she a secret agent now? This was getting ridiculous.

"You're assuming you don't get arrested," Nora said.

"I have faith in Theo's ability to get me out of their crosshairs." Well, she wanted to have faith. But at that moment, she just needed some small hope to hold onto.

"Just now, huh?" he asked. Humor lit up his dark eyes, but his intense stare continued. She could tell he was in.

Sera rolled her eyes. "Don't make me regret saying it out loud."

The front door opened and closed, and a moment later, Renee joined them in the library, out of breath. "Are you three okay?"

Nora ran over and hugged the woman tightly. "Yes, we're just glad *you're* not hurt! Where were you?"

"I got a phone message from an old friend needing my help," Renee said. "Turned out to be a false alarm, Danae from the sound of it."

She turned to take Sera's hands in hers, her expression dark with sorrow. "I am so sorry. I told you he would be safe here, and he wasn't. I completely underestimated her magical abilities. I don't know any other witch who could have broken the enchantments here."

"Don't apologize, this isn't your fault," Sera said, squeezing her hands back. "I'm not even sure what Danae thinks she's going to do with the amulet. Bacchus threatened to destroy it and himself if she tried to use his power. I just hope he can take her down with him if he does."

"That would certainly make things easier." Renee gave

a quick smile.

"Less fun, though," Nora said with a huff.

The ring of Sera's phone interrupted their conversation. When she saw who was calling, her heart sank like it had been thrown into the ocean attached to a fifty-pound weight. She looked up at Nora, tears already pricking the corners of her eyes.

"It's Hiro's mom."

* * *

THEO HAD DONE HIS JOB well behind the scenes and gotten Hiro's autopsy prioritized. The funeral would be held that Saturday in Seattle, the city where he had grown up and where his parents still lived. Despite making his home in the District, with no plans to move back to the Pacific Northwest, his family felt it was only right to have him close to them, and Sera couldn't argue.

She was browsing for flights at her cubicle desk in the graduate student office the next day, trying to find one that wouldn't bankrupt her, when murmuring from the other students and faculty caught her attention. The two detectives she had met, Bob and Tiana, spoke with one of the teachers' aides, who pointed toward Sera from across the rows of low-walled cubicles. Everyone watched as the two detectives approached her.

Just before they reached her desk, she wiped her sweating hands on her pants. At least she had been questioned in private the first time. Lucky her.

"Ms. Finch," Robert said with a tip of his fedora. "Is there a more private place we can talk?"

"Of course." Without offering to shake their hands just

in case she was clammy, she led Robert and Tiana down the hall of cubicles toward the conference room. She did her best to nod politely as gawking faces turned their way.

She closed the door behind them before taking a seat across the large table. The room wasn't as private as she would have liked, what with the giant floor to ceiling window looking out over the entire department, but at least no one would overhear the conversation.

"I know this may be difficult to discuss, but can you think of anyone who would have caused Hiro harm? The wounds were…" Robert paused, thinking through his words. "Significant."

Sera swallowed hard as the image of Hiro lying on the ground at Danae's feet, his throat slit and eyes forever opened, flashed through her mind. She shook her head. "Hiro treated cancer patients for a living, and he was amazing at it. His patients and their families loved him. I can't imagine anyone harboring resentment against him personally."

She wiped away a tear from her cheek. "I just keep coming back to Lorenzo Vicari, though."

Tiana and Robert exchanged a glance.

"Why Vicari?" Tiana asked.

"After the amulet went missing, Lorenzo had his henchmen abduct me, thinking I had somehow stolen it," Sera said. "I told the previous detectives this information after someone broke into my apartment."

"They abducted you?" Tiana's impassive face seemed unconvinced. Her full mane of black hair was pulled back into a ponytail with a decorative ribbon, emphasizing her sharp cheekbones.

"Right. Lorenzo was furious when I said I didn't have it. Because I don't. How would I steal an amulet from a museum?"

Get it together, Sera. She sniffled and pulled out a tissue. "I can't help but think he killed Hiro because of the amulet. Because he thought I had it, and he wanted it. He's obsessed with it."

"Well. You've given us quite a bit to look into," Robert said as he scribbled in his pocket-sized notebook.

"I'll be in Seattle for Hiro's funeral, but feel free—" Sera stopped when Tiana opened her mouth.

"Ah, it would be in your best interest to stay in town and not plan any trips while we're conducting our investigation." Tiana's dark eyes held sympathy despite her reserved demeanor.

"Wait, I can't go to Hiro's funeral? Are you serious?" The air left her lungs like a quickly deflated balloon. This couldn't be real. They must have thought she was some sort of flight risk. Was she really that much of a suspect? What the hell was Theo even doing to help her? Maybe she *shouldn't* have placed her faith in him.

"It's up to you, but it may not look good for your case." Tiana spread her hands helplessly.

"What do I tell his mom? 'I can't go because I'm a suspect'?" Sera felt like she was losing control as her voice raised in anger, not caring if anyone outside the room heard.

"It's up to you, but you're not an official suspect, just a person of interest until we can rule you out." The detectives stood, and Robert tucked his notebook into his trench coat pocket. "We'll be in touch. We want to get you back to your normal life as soon as we can."

Sera snorted, her thoughts dark and angry. "Normal, yeah, okay. Like I can return to normal after my boyfriend was murdered—" she cut herself off, she was about to say in front of her eyes. A slip up like that would definitely land her in jail.

The two detectives regarded her with silent sympathy before leaving the room.

Sera took a deep breath before following them out and back to her cubicle desk. She ignored the questioning eyes on her, though she knew everyone would be gossiping about the visit later. Sweat ran down her back and forehead. When did it get so hot in the building? She needed to get out of there.

After throwing her coat, scarf, and bag over her arm, she almost ran for the door. She didn't slow her pace until the blast of cold air from outside hit her face two flights of stairs later. Sitting on one of the steps leading down to the busy sidewalk, she breathed in deeply, trying to calm her racing heart.

Why didn't Theo warn her that they wouldn't want her to leave the District? Technically, they never said she *couldn't*, just that she *shouldn't*. Maybe she should just ignore the warning and take the risk. The thought of missing Hiro's funeral made her shake with fury, like Danae was winning one more battle. Sera clenched her fists, digging her nails into her palms.

Was she even allowed to visit her father in Virginia? She rubbed her face with her hands.

Shit. I need to call Dad before he sees the news, she thought.

Sera dug around inside her bag for her phone. She pulled up his contact image and listened to the ring until he answered. "Hey, Dad. I need to tell you something."

Tears streamed down her face as she told him what had been shared on the news, although she was thankful he hadn't seen it himself yet. She ignored the passersby who looked at her with curious concern.

This is so much harder without Bacchus numbing my pain.

It was a quick conversation, in part because of their reserved relationship but also because her voice kept breaking. After ending the call, Sera tossed her phone back into her bag. "Are you here with good news or bad news?"

Theo sat down on the step next to her. The distinctive growling sound had alerted her to his arrival before he approached.

"You're getting good at that," he said, his eyes on the cars driving by. "I'm here to drive you back to Renee's."

"I'm not going to say 'no' with you here already, but you really don't need to be my personal chauffeur," she said. "Metro and I get along just fine."

"Metro doesn't get along fine with anyone."

"You just have to lower your expectations," she said. "By a lot."

Theo nodded, then stood back up and offered her his hand. "Fair enough. You ready?"

Noticing for the first time how cold she was, Sera pulled on her coat and scarf. She grabbed her bag and ignored his hand as she stood.

Without another word, Theo tucked his hand back into his jacket and walked away.

Shit. She sighed and scrambled to keep up with him. She didn't want to be rude, but she still wasn't ready for physical contact with people, especially without Bacchus there to

STEPHANIE MIRRO

control her fluctuating emotions. Even such a minor gesture of help made her insides heave.

They climbed into his Jeep and drove in awkward silence. Sera could hear the intermittent growling coming from inside Theo's head, but she tried to focus on the road outside the window. What were the rules of etiquette when it came to reading someone's mind? She didn't even know if she could read his personal thoughts because of his merge or just the conversation he had with Xolotl.

"You said you knew one or two people who had my Gift, right?" Sera asked.

"I knew *of* them, not personally," he said.

"Did you know anything about their Gifts other than their ability to talk to gods?"

"No."

They drove in silence again until he parked the Jeep a few car lengths down from Renee's front door.

"Listen, I'm—" She stopped, mouth still open as Theo got out of the car without waiting for her to finish.

How rude! Pushing her own door open, she jumped out after him. "Hey, I'm trying to explain—"

He stopped and faced her, his expression angry. "I've done nothing but try to help you. I didn't kill your boyfriend, so stop acting like I'm the bad guy." Without waiting for her to respond, he turned back around and approached Renee's door, ringing the doorbell.

Sera's face flushed with heat, both from her own anger and embarrassment. He was right, of course, but she was trying her best. Well, if she was honest with herself, which she really didn't want to do, she wasn't trying her best. She *was* letting her emotions get the best of her. But couldn't the man cut her some slack? Surely he'd lost someone he loved in the last one hundred years.

Renee answered the door and ushered them both inside and out of the cold. "How did it go today?" she asked as she walked them toward the kitchen.

Something delicious smelling wafted down the hallway, and Sera's stomach growled in response.

"Hopefully okay. I told the detectives about Lorenzo and his obsession with the amulet." She took a quick glance at Theo, but his face remained expressionless.

"Oh, obsession, that's a good word." Renee pointed to the table for them to sit and continued to the tiny kitchen just beyond. "I've made stew. I know Sera's hungry, but what about you, Theo?"

"I'm fine, thank you. But the smell reminds me of home."

"I'll take that as a compliment," Renee said as she winked at him.

He smiled at her. "It is."

"Do you think they'll take the bait and look into Lorenzo instead?" she asked, filling a bowl with stew. She placed the steaming liquid down in front of Sera, along with a spoon.

Having trained her tongue to handle hot beverages so often she couldn't even burn it anymore, Sera wasted no time diving into the stew. It felt like days since she had last eaten a full meal. It probably had been.

"Yes, but they'll quickly realize the futility of that attempt once they see how much influence Lorenzo has over the police force," Theo said. "With any luck that'll be a dead end and a closed case."

Sera gulped down the stew she held in her mouth, wincing as she did, in fact, burn her throat. She set her spoon beside the bowl as the realization of his words kicked in. Hiro's mother would have to live with the loss of her only son, dying so horribly, and then have no closure from the case. She would never know what happened to him. The unknown would haunt her till the end of her days, just like Sera's dad with her mom's death. Hunger fled as quickly as it had arrived.

A hand pressed on her shoulder, and she looked up into the sympathetic face of her friend.

"It's sad but necessary," Renee said.

Reaching her hand up, she squeezed Renee's. "I know. So then we should be good to go to Norway?"

Theo met her eyes for a brief moment before nodding. "I'm hoping your Gift will lead us to Freyja without much trouble, and I think she'll jump at the chance to fight again. Once we have Freyja on board, we can head to India to try to convince Durga. If we're lucky, one or both of them will have leads for other gods who might be willing to help."

Yikes. Those were going to be some expensive flights. Sera would need to open a new credit card to handle all the expenses. She didn't really have the money to pay them off, but she was saving the world, so she could live with some debt. Or she'd die, and it wouldn't matter anyway. Even this situation had a silver lining.

"Once we have our own ragtag army, how do we go after Danae and get the amulet if Bacchus doesn't destroy it?" she asked.

Theo regarded her with a hint of amusement, a dimple appearing as the corner of his lip pulled up. "Before I came along, what was your plan for taking down Danae?"

"Uh, that was basically it," she said.

"Bacchus really does love chaos." He chuckled. "Renee can help us cast a spell to get a virtual blueprint of her home in California. We'll need to get our hands on her calendar, find out when she comes and goes and who's with her at any given time."

He stroked his chin thoughtfully. "My guess is she's figured out a way to keep Bacchus from destroying himself. If that's the case, then she'll have it with her everywhere she goes. Our best bet would be to get her as alone as possible and attack."

"Do you think she expects us to come after her?"

"Absolutely. But Danae is going to think she's invincible with the amulet, and we can use that ego to our advantage."

"How?" she asked.

"She'll be overconfident in her abilities, but even she will have weaknesses. For now, though, we just need to wait until you're cleared."

"Any idea how long that will take?" she asked.

"Just focus on finishing the semester," he said.

"Why don't you just go without me?"

"I can't talk to other gods unless they're working through a human or powerful enough like Durga," Theo said. "Besides, Freyja will be better persuaded to help hearing your story from you."

"I thought you said she wouldn't take much convincing."

"She won't, but it'll still take some. A sob story like yours, especially coming from you, will be enough."

Sera snorted. The man was good at insulting her without meaning to. Or maybe he did this time. She wouldn't have blamed him… Much. "Okay, so when school ends in just over two weeks, we'll head to Bergen."

The front door opened then slammed, causing dishes to shake and rattle in the kitchen. The three of them looked at each other. A moment later, a still bundled up and rosy-cheeked Nora charged into view.

"You won't *believe* what just happened."

CHAPTER 9

Solomon

Danae had requested—more like commanded—Solomon to return to California with her, to her seat of power. Now that she had the amulet, she needed to restore the Immortals' powers before she could build her army. To restore that power required magic she didn't have with her, and she wasn't patient enough to recreate whatever it was she needed.

Lorenzo had been furious, of course, but he hadn't dared say no to his queen.

Moving around often to avoid any suspicion from their lack of aging was a common practice for Immortals. It really depended on how old the Immortal was when he or she completed the transformation. Solomon had been close to thirty when he received the gift of longevity from his maker, so people didn't question him for at least a decade or two.

But because she had been turned as a teenager, Danae didn't have age on her side. So, she went to one of the few places in the world where no one's age was real—Hollywood.

Unlike Lorenzo, his maker, Solomon found that Danae had no desire to become a part of the social elite. Instead, she ruled the city anonymously, using her Immortal powers as well as her magic to get whatever she wanted. But even the queen wasn't immune to the waning of their abilities once Bacchus and the witches cast their spell two decades ago. As an Eternal, she was more powerful than most Immortals, but she had several thousand years under her belt to grow accustomed to doing things a certain way. She had found it very difficult to acclimate without those skills.

Solomon had learned all of this about her on her private jet to California, which was more than the superficial gossip he had gleaned over the last two centuries as one of Lorenzo's bodyguards. But up until this week, he'd only gotten to know Danae through a handful of phone and video calls Lorenzo had had with her.

The custom Airbus 319 was one of the nicest Solomon had ever been on and small enough to not attract too much attention from the mortal world. Just the way she liked it. Most of her staff and loyal followers lounged on recliners and couches in the main cabin, which came complete with three TVs, various gaming systems, and a blood bar should anyone get hungry.

Solomon, Danae, and her closest bodyguard, Yumiko—he'd finally learned her name—sat in a private meeting room, sealed away from any prying eyes and ears by a soundproof door. The queen reclined on a white leather couch, her hair draped over Yumiko's lap, while the bodyguard stroked the dark curls. Moments like these reminded Solomon how young she had been when turned.

Danae remained reserved on the flight, but her eyes shone with excitement, and she never let go of the amulet in her gloved hand.

"There's an energy current that runs through Los Angeles, drawing the Gifted and Others to it," Danae said. "I've been able to recruit a few into my employ, though they're not very strong. Not like the witch whose defensive ward I had to break."

Narrowing her blue eyes, she turned the amulet around in her hands, studying it. "I wonder what it would take to convince her she's on the wrong side of history. She would be most valuable to my collection."

Solomon didn't know what she meant by "Others," but he had learned that speaking her thoughts out loud didn't mean she actually wanted a response or any kind of conversation. Questions usually closed her back up. Besides, Danae's side of history meant knocking humankind off the top of the food chain. No human would be on board without a promise of Immortality, and Nora's friend didn't seem like the type to be swayed by an Immortal lifetime. But he had been surprised before.

As an image of the fiery blonde's face flashed through his mind, his lips twitched, wanting to smile. Gods, he missed that face.

"We should still have more than enough power to undo his punishment." The corners of Danae's lips pulled up slightly. "The Council won't know what hit them until it's

STEPHANIE MIRRO

too late."

An uneasy feeling settled over him at her last comment. He had no idea what she had planned for the Council, and he still wasn't sure he was totally on board with *any* of her plans. Most of the Immortals in her employ knew Danae's intention to become Queen of the Immortals, but they didn't know all of the details related to the Council takeover. Solomon himself had only learned tidbits as she continued to lower her guard around him.

Yumiko smirked in response. He hadn't figured out how she had lost her tongue yet, but based on the way she worshipped her maker, it must have occurred before Danae found her. Danae didn't like being asked questions, so he would just have to keep learning what he could when she mentioned it.

When the plane landed, their entourage transferred into five SUVs waiting directly on the runway. Solomon had been to Los Angeles a few times before in his lifetime but never in recent history. He always enjoyed seeing how a city changed over time, a pleasure he was afraid would disappear if Danae's plan came to fruition. Mortality pushed the minds of men to their farthest limits. How would cities grow if all of the great minds became Immortal?

Or worse.

Most of the Immortals Solomon had met over the years had been greedy men and women, seeking Immortality as a way to secure their fortunes. Their ambitions existed solely to gain more for themselves. Many felt entitled to their Immortality based on their elite social status and who they knew. Alexander, Lorenzo's favorite pet due to their shared ancestry, had been one such Immortal, though his father was much more humble while alive. Such a shame about the old man's heart attack. He couldn't say the same about Alexander's demise when Serafina and the god had escaped.

Gravel crunched under the tires as they approached her home, and Solomon marveled at the beauty of it. Despite her preference for anonymity in the City of Angels, her plane and home proved Danae still loved to live large. With extensive stables and fields beyond, her estate had to be several times larger than Lorenzo's property in the District. Horses raised their heads from their grazing as the vehicles passed by on the long stretch of gravel road leading toward the house.

The architecture, white walls, and red-tiled roofs of the building reminded Solomon of a Roman villa, complete with ivy climbing the walls. He didn't know if she'd had the house built or if she purchased it when she last moved. Hell, he didn't even know how long she had been in Hollywood to begin with.

Once they parked, he followed Danae through the massive double entry front doors into an open-air atrium where white Grecian columns held up covered hallways. A large, shallow square-shaped pool filled the center of the atrium, surrounded by lush greenery and artfully arranged rock formations. The arrangement of the stones provided moving water via tiny waterfalls.

Fish darted to and fro in the water, avoiding the areas where two cranes perched, waiting until hunger struck them again. Above the pool, the roof opened to the sky, which continued to brighten in the early morning light.

It was possible Danae had grown up in a similarly styled home several millennia ago. What he wouldn't give to know more about that life.

The queen stopped for a moment beside the cranes, chirping to them. Their long legs brought the birds closer to her, and they held out their beaks to nuzzle against her hand. The cranes let out a rattling, bugling sound in her direction.

Solomon knew it wasn't uncommon for animals to become familiar to people, particularly if those people approached with food. But the scene before him was unlike anything he had seen before, as if she actually communicated with the birds. A full-blown conversation from the sounds of it.

When whatever Danae sought from the birds was satisfied, she continued down the hallway, Yumiko and Solomon close behind her. The amulet's chain dangled from the queen's hand as she clenched the pinecone.

"Ensure the witches arrive by this evening," Danae said. "I don't want to waste any time. The faster we can act, the better."

Nodding, Yumiko pulled out her cell phone as she walked.

The queen continued, "And bring me a few snacks. Young ones. I want my powers to be at full capacity when the deceitful god's spell is lifted."

Yumiko snapped her fingers at another guard following close behind them. Her fingers moved rapidly as she signed a message to the other guard. The entire staff probably knew the language. Solomon would have to learn it quickly to avoid missing any vital information.

Danae stopped before a closed door, her hand pausing on the handle. "Solomon, you will join me today."

A few hours later, he leaned back against the plush

couch, arms draped over the back and side, feeling full and content. Just when he thought he couldn't consume any more blood without bursting, Danae had waved most of the mortals away. He felt powerful in a way he hadn't been in over twenty years, and he hadn't had even the slightest concern when she drained the last mortal of his blood, the young man's eyes staring lifelessly at the ceiling.

He hadn't realized how much he missed his powers until that moment, and it was the first time excitement about Danae breaking the spell crept into his mind. Perhaps her ruling the world wasn't such a bad idea after all, especially if he could convince Nora to be by his side.

* * *

NOW THAT NIGHT HAD FALLEN, Solomon stood with his back against the wall of the queen's bedroom. Danae had spent the daylight hours pacing the floor of this expansive room. He had tried to leave, as she had previously demanded in the District after sex, but she shook her head and pointed to the bed. He had stayed there as commanded, arms behind his head to prop him up, watching her move back and forth as quiet as a ghost until the witches had arrived at dusk.

A flurry of activity ignited in the queen's personal chambers as the five human witches prepared the ritual, following Danae's commands. They set about lighting incense and candles throughout the room, muttering incantations under their breath with each step.

Twenty years wasn't much to an Immortal, except these past two decades felt twice as long without their full abilities, and Solomon felt twice as old. He marveled at the idea of their restoration, tingles of anticipation prickling through his nerves.

The thickness in the air held excitement and expectation, along with a mixture of fear from the gathered witches. Failure would mean their death, after all. The queen stood in the center of the room wearing nothing but a simple white dress and leather gloves to hold the amulet, her feet bare against the cold stone floor. The human witches created a circle around her, their arms raised outward toward one another, though not close enough to touch.

Chanting in a language that reminded Solomon of the little Greek he had learned but not quite the same, Danae held the amulet out before her in gloved hands.

A brilliant yellow glow began to shimmer beneath the witches' feet, connecting them in the shape of a five-pointed star. The outline brightened like the sun before the light shot upwards, enclosing the six bodies and shielding them from Solomon's view. Whistling wind swept through the room, whipping his clothes away from his body. He held his arm up in front of his face in reflex.

A moment later, the wind and glow ceased abruptly. Danae stared at the amulet as if waiting for something to occur. The fabric of her dress settled around her legs. Just as he began to fear the spell hadn't worked and the queen's fury would be unleashed on the unsuspecting witches, a crimson light burst from the amulet, rushing upwards toward the ceiling like a bloody spotlight.

Danae grinned. "It is done."

The words didn't need to be said. A fiery warmth radiated through his body down to his bones, and his skin burned from the internal inferno. He sank to his knees, pain and pleasure writhing through every nerve. The veins in his arms surged upward against his skin as if wanting to break free.

Ah, it had been too long since he felt as powerful as he did then, like a newborn Immortal all over again. He clenched and unclenched his fists, reveling in the intensity. His fangs extended as the intoxicating scent of the witches' pulsing blood found him, a scent typically present only when spilling from open wounds. A variety of minute sounds assaulted his ears, and the once-dim room seemed brighter than it had a minute ago.

Oh, yes, he had missed this.

A roar of anger echoed through his mind. He snapped his head toward Danae as he leaped to his feet.

She laughed, a full-body laugh that resulted in her holding her stomach with one arm, the amulet still in the other.

"Oh, dear. Daddy is not pleased."

CHAPTER 10

Serafina

"What happened?" Sera asked, mentally preparing for the worst as Nora charged into Renee's kitchen.

"*Chad*," Nora practically spat out his name, "cornered me and asked me out to dinner. It took all my will power and then some not to punch him in his stupid face."

The memory of his mouth crushing against hers in the stairwell at the gala flashed through Sera's mind, the reek of stale wine on his breath turning her stomach queasy. With everything else that had been going on, she had almost forgotten the asshole professor's assault.

"We were alone, so I told him off pretty colorfully. And that toad who calls himself a man had the audacity to feign ignorance. As if you wouldn't have told your best friend what he did to you," Nora huffed as she removed her scarf and coat, draping them over the empty chair.

Theo frowned as he looked between them. "Care to fill me in?"

Flushing as she dropped her gaze, Sera couldn't help the shame that rose at the memory. She still wondered if she had done something to encourage his actions.

Before she could speak, Nora jumped back in, "Dr. Lambert *assaulted* her at the gala after she presented the Bacchic Amulet. As if she had any interest in that idiot with a boyfriend as wonderful as Hiro." She stopped and looked at Sera. "I'm sorry, hon."

Sera allowed herself a small smile despite the pain. "No, you're right. He was wonderful."

"Why didn't you report the assault?" Theo asked.

Nora arched an eyebrow at him. "You of all people should know why she didn't report it. It would be her word against his. Plus, he threatened her reputation and career in the archaeology world if she said anything."

"Sera wouldn't have been the first woman to come forward with a claim against Charles Lambert," he said. "It'd be nice to see the guy finally convicted."

"I wish I'd had that information a month ago," Sera said, crinkling her nose. "I have zero desire to get involved in yet another police case at this point. Three is enough for one year. But I hope he gets what he deserves before he hurts another girl. He'd probably be first in line to become one of the Bacchae if Danae succeeds."

"Anyway, I just thought you'd like to know he got a bit of what's coming to him." Nora sniffed the air. "What smells so delicious?"

* * *

DESPITE THE WARNING FROM the detectives, Sera flew to Seattle on Friday after classes to attend Hiro's wake the following day. Though she and his mother had never become close—it was hard to when the woman didn't hide her opinion that Sera wasn't good enough for her son—Mrs. Saito had invited her to the *tsuya* the day before the actual funeral ceremony. The gesture had surprised her as the wake ceremony was typically reserved for family and relatives and some close friends.

It was an honor she couldn't refuse.

The cheapest flight possible without missing any school was a redeye Friday night, followed by a returning one Saturday evening. It would have to do. Every fiber of her being screamed at her to go, that she would regret it for the rest of her life if she didn't. She'd risk prison if it meant a chance to say goodbye to the man who had captured her heart and died because she had been too selfish to just return the amulet. Bacchus could have found someone else.

Taking a deep breath to calm her quivering lips as she approached the Buddhist temple, Sera urged her body to relax.

I can do this. For Hiro. She smoothed the fabric of her black dress one last time before pulling the door open.

After signing the registry and leaving her *koden*, an offering to help the family with the funeral expenses, she followed a couple through a set of double doors. Yellow and white flowers graced every surface of the expansive room, sweeping into a crashing wave of lilies and chrysanthemums across what she assumed was the casket. She swallowed against the knot forming in her throat, refusing to look at the portrait standing behind the casket. A pleasant floral aroma mixed with the scent of burning candles.

She took a seat near the back row of pews while the rest of the guests filtered in. It was an odd feeling to recognize faces she had never met, faces she expected to get to know when she and Hiro married. But having dated so far away from his family and childhood friends, they were all strangers with no need to become acquainted now. The weight of that sorrow settled around her shoulders, from a loss she hadn't even known existed.

As the ceremony began and the priest chanted a passage from a book, she caught a glimpse of Mrs. Saito near the front of the room. Her black hair had been pulled back into a tight bun, allowing no veil of privacy for her tear-stricken face.

Grief washed over Sera like a tidal wave, threatening to topple her over, and a tightness developed in her chest, making it hard to breathe. Gulping down air, she closed her eyes against the anguish that threatened to swallow her whole.

The remainder of the ceremony was a blur as she tried to keep the pain at bay, focusing on minor details of whatever item or person crossed in front of her vision. Here, a stray hair attached to a jacket; there, a splash of mud on the heel of a shoe. Everyone stood, and she followed the line of guests toward the altar, the scent of burning incense wafting through the room.

Then she saw him.

Hiro.

He smiled at her from the medical school portrait

behind the casket, stethoscope around the collar of his white coat and his glasses sitting slightly askew on his nose. Just after the camera snapped the picture, she was sure he had reached up to fix the tilt of his lenses, laughing at some joke he would have shared with the cameraman.

Oh, Hiro…

She couldn't stop the onslaught of tears then, but she didn't want to either. Smiling back at him, Sera pressed her fingers to her mouth and blew him a kiss.

Rest now, my love.

A gentle hand caught Sera's elbow as she lowered her arm, and she turned to face Mrs. Saito. "Please come with me a moment," the smaller woman said.

Sera nodded, wiping away the wetness on her cheeks as she followed her through the doors to the foyer.

"They found this with…with my son, and I believe he would want you to have it." Mrs. Saito took Sera's hand and pressed a small jewelry box into her palm.

The ring.

A sob erupted from Sera's body before she could stop it. She pressed the box to her lips before tucking it into her purse. There was no way she could open it now, not without completely breaking down before the woman who had birthed and raised the man of her dreams. No.

Taking Mrs. Saito's hands in hers, Sera looked into her eyes. An intensity built behind her own as Danae's smirking face seared through her memory.

"*Goshuushou-sama desu.* I will find the people responsible, and I will kill them," Sera said.

The woman's mouth opened with her surprise. After a tense moment of silence as she searched Sera's face, she squeezed Sera's hands back. "I'm afraid I've misjudged you these past few years. Please. Avenge him."

Mrs. Saito must have seen something in her, something more than just a heartbroken girl. It may have taken the death of her son, but the woman believed in her now, and Sera would not let her down. Not anymore.

Bowing her head in affirmation, Sera stepped back and left the temple.

* * *

BESIDES HAVING NIGHTMARES of a world run by Bacchae, almost a week went by without incident. Every waking moment, Sera thought about the path ahead of her—vengeance. It was the light that kept her going in otherwise dark and dreary days.

The weather seemed to match her mood. Grey clouds released a near-freezing drizzle almost every day that week. Cold, but not cold enough for snow. She hated it, which only made her mood worse.

She had given the jewelry box to Nora, asking her to keep it until Sera was ready to open it. Not knowing when that would be, or even if there would be a when, she did her best to put it far from her present thoughts.

On Wednesday, she received a text message from Theo wanting to meet about some news he had. He suggested they meet at The Morning Grind diner since it was closer to her university than Renee's, and that suited Sera just fine. Despite her overall lack of hunger lately, she had a hankering for their pecan pie.

She had her mouth full when he sat down on the booth bench across from her. "Thanks for waiting, it's been hectic," he said.

Sera swallowed and indicated the pie. "It's fine. Want some?"

"No. Listen, good news and bad news." He glanced around the busy restaurant before continuing. "You've been dropped as a person of interest. There's obviously nothing connecting you to the deaths other than Lorenzo. The case should be closed soon, the chief of police won't pursue that thread."

Her mind didn't know how to react to the news. She felt relieved at no longer being in the detectives' line of sight, but her heart ached at the idea of the case being closed without proper justice. The internal conflict further fueled her need to get revenge. Afraid she would bend the metal fork even without Bacchus's help, she set the utensil down next to the plate.

Cheryl walked over to fill up Sera's empty coffee and eyed Theo. "You're that detective friend, right?"

He smiled. "Off duty, I swear."

"You wanna tell me what's going on with all these missing people? This city's just beginning to clear its name and now this." Cheryl harrumphed. "It ain't right."

He glanced over his shoulder at the TV on the wall near the kitchen's bar top. The local news anchor discussed a record number of reported missing persons in the area, also pointing out the raised number in Hollywood, California and a few other places. Conspiracy theories flashed across the banner on the bottom of the screen.

Foreboding settled into the pit of Sera's stomach, effectively ending her hunger for the delicious pie, even with the buttery scent drifting off of it. She had a feeling she knew what the bad news was going to be.

Goddamn Bacchae, she thought.

Theo groaned as he swiveled back around.

"I know you can't tell me, hon, but do me a favor and figure it out, all right?" Cheryl gave him a quick pat on the shoulder and walked back to the kitchen.

Sera pushed the pie away from her. "Is that the bad news?"

"Yes. Danae restored their powers. She and Lorenzo are hard at work building an army. Fast."

Her heart plunged into a murky pit. As much as she missed the god speaking in her mind—though she'd never tell *him* that—she had hoped Bacchus would have destroyed himself and the amulet to stop Danae. The Bacchae witch must have done something to prevent the god from using his powers. At least, she hoped that was the case and he hadn't decided to switch sides.

"I've booked our flights to Norway at the end of the week," Theo said.

Sera frowned. "I really need to be involved in that. My credit limit only allows so much to be charged at one time, and—"

He held up a hand. "I've got more than enough saved to cover your travel expenses. One of the benefits of a longer than average life is accumulating more than enough wealth. If you invest it right, anyway."

"I can't let you pay for—"

"You can and will. End of discussion," he said firmly. "Once we find Freyja, we'll book our flights to India. Durga is not hard to track down, and I've got a contact who can help us."

While she was thankful to not have to go into too much debt with their travels, she felt odd about letting this man she hardly knew pay her way, especially with him not really giving her a choice. She was sure Nora wouldn't hesitate to accept his offer, but Sera didn't like to feel like she owed anyone anything.

He better not expect anything in return—she sure as shit didn't have anything left to give.

* * *

TWO DAYS LATER, ON Friday afternoon, the sun was just starting to set behind the horizon as they drove by the Jefferson Memorial, one of Sera's favorite landmarks in the District. The round, white top of the open-air rotunda could be seen peeking out from behind the trees lining the roads leading around the Tidal Basin reservoir.

In a few months, the entire area would become an explosion of pale pink and white as the cherry blossoms announced the arrival of spring. The National Cherry Blossom Festival caused the memorial and reservoir to swarm with tourists on foot, bike, or paddleboat, but Sera knew a few hidden places where she could surround herself with the cascading blossoms without too many other gawkers around.

With any luck, she'd be alive to see them again.

The last couple of days had been a whirlwind as she prepared for their trip—mentally and physically—while also trying to wrap up her classes. She was pretty sure she'd be failing her own, but maybe her professors would show some pity and give her time to make up some work in the next semester.

Fat chance.

The thought of how much grading she had to catch up on made her nauseous. She had planned to do it before they left, but she couldn't focus on such mundane tasks when she had a few goddesses to track down and convince to join the fight against evil. Maybe next week. Sera nearly laughed out loud.

She decided to call her father on the drive, avoiding it until then. Since they were heading out to Virginia, she had thought about planning a quick side trip to tell him in person, but she really wasn't ready to face him just yet with all the secrets she had now. And she knew if she called him any earlier in the week, he would try to talk her out of the trip. She just might have listened, too.

He would still try, but now she was in Theo's Jeep on the way to the airport and couldn't really back out. Besides, then she would owe Theo airfare.

"Hi, Dad," she said into her phone when he answered.

"Hey, Sweetheart. I don't usually hear from you during the week. Is everything okay?"

"Yeah, I'm actually on my way to the airport. A friend convinced me to go to Norway with hi—" Sera stopped herself, cringing, "with her to, you know, get away from everything for a while."

"Not giving me much notice, huh?" His gruff voice gave away his displeasure.

"Sorry, Dad. It was a last-minute deal, and I've been all over the place getting ready to go and finish up the semester."

"Why Norway? In winter?"

Good question. One she hadn't really thought through.

"It was a really good price, because, as you said, it's winter." She cringed again. This was not going well. "But listen, I've been meaning to tell you something I found out about mom…"

A woman's voice called out in the background.

"Just a moment, Susan!" his muffled voice called back. He must have covered the receiver. "Something about what?"

Sera smiled, remembering the red-headed woman from the restaurant after their annual Thanksgiving dinner. "Ah, nothing. I'll tell you another time. I've got to go, but I hope you have a great weekend."

"Thanks, honey. Susan just got here. I'm taking her fishing. Let me know when you land, okay?"

"Promise." She paused before saying, "Love you."

A slight pause on his end. "Love you, too."

She ended the call and stared at her phone. They didn't often say the words to each other, but with everything going on in her life lately, it felt necessary to tell him out loud before anything could happen to her. She sighed and shoved the phone into her carry-on bag.

"Norway this time of year, not exactly most people's ideal winter getaway." Theo chuckled.

"Maybe for skiing?"

"Do you ski?" he asked.

"Uh, no, but I could learn. Or it's possible I'm just going for the peace and quiet while my friend skis."

"Going all the way to Norway for peace and quiet?" He pulled the Jeep into the parking lot entrance and grabbed a ticket from the machine.

"Oh hush, I clearly didn't think it through."

"Clearly. And you were about to drop some major news on him over the phone about your mom." Theo tsk-tsk'd. "What made you stop?"

"His lady friend Susan showed up. They had a date planned." Her father needed some new love in his life. Over twenty years had passed since her mother died, and he hadn't pursued anyone that entire time. She didn't know what had changed with this woman, but she certainly wasn't going to question it, nor ruin it with news of her mom.

Theo parked the SUV, and they grabbed their bags. Sera had packed as light as she could for a trip of undetermined length in Norway with a jaunt over to India afterward, but the unknown still resulted in a hefty carry-on. She drew comfort knowing Nora would never have been able to pack that light.

"I got it, I got it." She swatted Theo's hand away as he tried to help her get the bag out of the Jeep. With everything else he was doing to help her, she didn't need him carrying her bags, too.

Despite the hour, Dulles International Airport was busy as ever due to business travelers returning home for the weekend as well as students returning home for the winter break. They didn't say much to each other while they waited in the security line, nor while they followed signs up and down escalators, on and off the people mover tram, and finally to the terminal.

She hated small talk, but she couldn't stand the silence any longer after they reached their gate. "So, how long have you been working in the District?"

"Only since the end of the summer."

"What brought you here?" She followed him toward

some empty seats in the waiting area.

He glanced back at her. "Seriously?"

"Uh, yeah?"

"We heard a rumor that an ancient artifact tied to Bacchus had been found and had to check it out."

"Oh." While that made perfect sense to Sera, the man didn't need to make her feel dumb for not knowing. A perfect example of why she hated small talk.

"I've always been a cop; it helps me get information that I need. I've got friends who forge any necessary paperwork for me to get a job." He dropped his bag by an empty chair away from the crowds and sat.

Now that was interesting. "For over a century?"

Theo nodded.

"No wonder you have the stern father look down so well," Sera said as she took the chair next to him.

He snapped his head sideways to stare at her, eyes wide. "The what?"

"The first few times I met you, I thought you looked too young for your demeanor. The expressions you made always reminded me of my dad whenever I got caught doing something wrong."

Theo continued to stare at her another moment before bursting into laughter.

Not quite sure why he found her comment so humorous, she raised an eyebrow. Maybe she had kind of insulted him. She couldn't help but smile as he laughed. The sound carried a deep richness that vaguely reminded her of Bacchus.

Xolotl rumbled an agreement about the man's demeanor.

"You don't really realize how much you've aged until you hear a comment like that," Theo explained when he finally took a breath.

"Still feel like a twenty-something year old?" She guessed he had been in his early twenties when he merged with the god and became immortal. Possibly even younger than she was now.

"Most of the time. The thing about merging, and perhaps immortality in general though I've never asked anyone else, is your body and mind remain at the age you were. Even though I have the years of experience, I still feel the way I would have as a young mortal, rather than an old man with a hundred years under his belt," he said.

"I think that's common for most people, mortals I mean. Hell, even I still feel like I'm a teenager sometimes. Although, I didn't really have a normal teenage experience." Sera chuckled.

He tilted his head in question. "Why not?"

"I had to learn to take care of myself after my mom died, which didn't give me a lot of room to just hang out and get in trouble."

"What about your dad?" he asked.

"He took her death really hard. Almost personally. We haven't really been close since she was alive," she said.

"Oh, I'm sorry to hear that."

Sera shrugged. "It is what it is, and we've come a long way since then."

They sat in silence for a few minutes, watching other passengers come and go from the gates and airplanes pass by the windows on their way to the runway. The high-pitched squeals of little kids rang through the air as they played on the small, indoor playground set up in the middle of the terminal walkway. It was almost peaceful.

"You and Nora have been best friends for a while, I take it?" Theo asked.

"Since elementary school. She came up to me during a summer camp for budding archaeologists and told me we were going to be best friends." She smiled at the memory of her friend's cherubic younger face. "How could I say no?"

"I'm sure she's a hard woman to turn down."

"You'll find out soon enough," she said.

He chuckled. "I'm sure I will. Hard as it might be, I'll have to disappoint her."

"Blondes aren't your type?"

"I gave up mortals long ago. Falling in love with someone who can't grow old with you isn't what I call enjoyable."

Her hand gripped the arm of the chair. Even without the immortal part, she knew the feeling he referenced. Knew it deep in her core, raw like a bandage had been ripped off her still-bleeding heart.

He must have seen the look on her face. "I'm sorry; that was insensitive."

Waving a hand dismissively, she took a shuddering breath. "It's fine, really."

The gate agent announced their flight was boarding, and they lined up with the herd of passengers. Theo nudged her forward when they started taking the first-class tickets.

"Wait, you got us first-class?" she asked, her mouth nearly dropping open in surprise.

"I don't splurge on much these days, but being able to avoid sitting on an airplane for hours, rubbing shoulders with the guy next to you who decided not to shower that morning, is worth it." He handed their tickets to the agent, and she waved them through with a smile. "Now, we can relax in peace."

Sera followed him onto the plane and to their seats. More like personal space pods. Her heart skipped a beat from the unexpected excitement. She had always wanted to fly first-class somewhere—anywhere—but the idea seemed like a distant fantasy while pursuing a career in archaeology, a job which might help her just barely pay the bills. As she settled into her space, she may have found a benefit to this whole immortality thing.

A small partition separated their seats, but Sera found herself leaning forward every few minutes to comment about something fascinating she had learned about the airplane. She was as giddy as a little girl on her birthday. Sleep seemed like a far-off idea.

"Did you *see* the menu?" She shoved the brochure across to Theo.

He sighed. Again. She'd lost count of how many sighs had come out of the man since they boarded.

"Sera, you're going to need to calm down to be able to sleep. How about some wine?" He waved a hand to one of the waiting flight attendants and ordered a glass.

"You're not drinking?" she asked after the attendant went to fill the order.

"I don't like having my senses dulled. But I won't have any issues falling asleep. You, on the other hand, sound like you swallowed an entire bag of Halloween candy."

Leaning back behind the partition, she stuck out her tongue at him where he couldn't see it. He was right, though.

The wine helped calm her excited nerves, and after a five-course meal that may have been worthy of a Michelin star, she was ready to pass out. It had been far too long since she had enjoyed a glass of wine or such a good meal. Hell, enjoyed *any* meal.

A flight attendant came by to help convert her seat into a bed, and then she slept.

CHAPTER 11

Serafina

*D*anae's eyes burned a fiery red. No, not eyes, real flames danced within the sockets of her grinning skull. Raw terror gripped Sera's heart, but she couldn't move—her arms and legs were chained to the wall again.

The Bacchae witch smiled and held up her hand, showing Sera what she held. A curly blonde wig. Except it wasn't a wig. It was a mannequin's head. Only it wasn't a mannequin. Green eyes stared unseeing at her from a face she knew almost better than her own.

Sera jolted awake when someone touched her arm. Ripping off her eye mask, she sat up, confused about where she was and why she wore an eye mask. Her shirt clung to her sticky skin. A flight attendant looked at her with concern.

"Are you okay, ma'am?" the woman asked.

Sera squinted as she took in her surroundings, details

flooding back into her mind, though her heart continued to pound. "Yes, sorry. I forgot where I was."

The woman smiled sympathetically and handed her a warm towel.

"Thanks," she mumbled as the woman moved away, passing out towels to the other passengers.

Pressing the cloth to her face, she inhaled the soothing scent of warmed lavender. Only when she closed her eyes again, she saw Danae's flame-filled eyes, her fanged mouth grinning in triumph. Sera's pulse raced, beating a wild rhythm in her ears and drowning out the sounds of the airplane.

"I see you've adjusted well to first class," Theo's calm voice said beside her, breaking her free from the memory of the dream.

"Did I snore?" she asked from behind the towel, using it to soak up the cold perspiration that had formed on her forehead.

"I was afraid the captain would be running back here at any moment to find out who'd brought a train aboard."

Groaning, Sera kept the soft cloth held to her face in hiding. She'd been told she snored before, but she didn't realize it had gotten that bad. Maybe it was because of the dreams.

"I'm kidding. That was the guy two rows up. You did snore a little, though." He chuckled.

Sera leaned forward and punched him lightly on the leg. "Not funny, wolf man."

"*Wolf man?*" he asked incredulously.

"It sounds better than 'dog man.'" She converted her bed back to a seat as a flight attendant announced their impending arrival. The TV in front of Sera announced the local time at nearly 11:00 a.m.

"Neither sound good. Let's just leave the humor to me, all right?"

She rolled her eyes behind the partition. The dividers were coming in handy. "Did you sleep at all?"

"A bit. Another perk to my situation is not needing as much rest as I used to."

"I mean, I don't *need* twelve hours of sleep in any given night," she said, "but I'm not going to say no to it, either."

* * *

THE AIRPORT IN OSLO made her think of the future—everything from the bright lighting and the curves of architectural elements simulating waves in motion, to the checkerboard ceiling, almost waiting for a game of chess to start. Even the shops were futuristic in their white, pod-like designs, and they passed at least one wall made entirely of vegetation. Green plants from floor to ceiling. No wonder the air smelled so clean.

Sera gazed around, her mouth hanging open as wide as her eyes, as they made their way through the crowds to the gate that would take them to Bergen. It wasn't until she was a few feet ahead of him that she realized Theo had stopped moving.

"What's up?" she asked as she retraced her steps.

He nodded to the TV screen over the bar of the restaurant he stopped in front of. Sera gasped, reaching her hand up to cover her mouth. Reports of missing people and bodies turning up drained of blood came from all over the world. Someone had coined the term "Vampageddon" as a joke, but real fear was starting to spread.

On the opposite spectrum, some extreme vampire lovers were going on social media, begging to be turned. They had no idea what they were asking for.

"She's moving fast. The Council will have learned what she's up to by now. With any hope, they should help slow her down until we can get to her." The muscles on Theo's face moved as he clenched his stubble-lined jaw. Rugged was a good look for him.

Sera shook her head at the news and to clear her thoughts about the detective. Noticing other men looking good wasn't anywhere close to being on her upcoming agenda.

"Come on, let's go. Our plane should board in a few minutes." He grabbed the handles of his duffel bag and walked away.

Her skin continued to crawl as she watched the TV for a few moments longer then followed him to the gate.

A half-hour later, when they were settled into their economy seats on the plane—no first-class on the hour-long flight—Sera turned to him. "I need a distraction from the news. Tell me more about your life. Where are you from?"

Theo smiled, his dimples appearing. "Chicago. I was a kid when the World's Fair opened."

"Wow. That must have been so cool to see."

"I wouldn't actually know, we were too poor to attend. About twenty years before the fair, a fire destroyed much of the city, including our family business. My parents tried to find work in other industries, but so did everyone else."

"I'm sorry to hear that." A frown pulled at her lips. She hadn't meant to drag out bad memories.

He shrugged before closing his eyes. "I'm still alive, aren't I?"

Sera knew the feeling of being happy just to be alive. She had also grown up poor, though she was sure she'd had more than he had as a child. The house she grew up in had been her grandparents' home, and her father had inherited it when both of his parents died at a relatively early age. She had still been an infant when they moved in. Not having a mortgage to pay meant her parents had a little extra money each month to spend on treats like going to the movies.

As a child, she had hated not having name-brand clothing and new school bags every year like all the other kids, but with a neighborhood mechanic and budding archaeologist for parents, she had come to appreciate experiences far more than material things. Way more than most of her classmates anyway, especially because of her mother's early death.

"How did you and Xolotl meet?" she asked.

He smiled. "I was young and foolish once, just like anyone else. A man I met at the train station where I shined shoes offered me a job in Mexico. He promised me a fortune beyond my wildest dreams. Everything checked out. How could I refuse the opportunity to turn my parent's world around and provide them the life they wanted for me?"

His smile faded, though his eyes remained closed. "He left me high and dry and stranded in a foreign country after taking the little bit of money I had. Xolotl saved me when I collapsed on the beach, ready to give my life to the song of the sea."

Sera winced. She was really ruining what she thought would be a good distraction.

"Yikes. Did you go back home?"

"Yes. But after a while, it became obvious something had changed in me. In the dog form, I almost killed my mother. It wasn't Xolotl's fault. In that form, neither of us had control. So I left home again and made the decision to merge so that I would never have to worry about hurting those I loved."

"Wow. That must have been rough." *To say the least.* What an understatement. The poor man must have been tormented.

He made a sound of agreement.

"How many others like you are there?" she asked. "Merged, I mean."

"Half a dozen, at least. I've only met a couple, but I've been told more exist." He let out an expansive yawn. "I'm going to rest now."

They spent the rest of the short flight in silence. Sera tried to imagine living life as Theo had, never aging while everyone around him withered away to dust and bones. It wasn't a comforting thought. She also couldn't fathom a world like the one Danae wanted, turning humans into little more than slaves and lunchmeat. What good is an immortal lifetime if it meant losing your humanity?

When the plane landed a few miles outside of Bergen, she glanced at Theo. He stared out the window under furrowed eyebrows. Perhaps he was thinking of similar things.

Light snow had fallen, covering the lush vegetation in a thin layer of wintery wonder. Sera wanted to play tourist like Nora and see all the quaintness the historic town had to offer, but they were there for business. They didn't even stay in the airport long because they hadn't checked any bags. They hailed a taxi to get to their hotel, which allowed her a quick glimpse of the picturesque countryside as they followed the multiple roundabouts toward the city.

At least until they reached the darkness of the underground tunnels. Sera wasn't typically claustrophobic, but she had never been inside so much darkness and for so long. The whole drive took less than a half-hour, but it felt like an eternity.

When they exited the last tunnel, she breathed a sigh of relief and then gasped. Mountains dusted with white powder stood tall next to long icy fjords, so that the city of Bergen was surrounded on all sides. Several cruise ships and a few sailing vessels dotted the horizon as well as the docks, giving the city a taste of both the old world and the new.

"Norway in winter isn't so bad after all," Theo said.

She laughed but couldn't tear her gaze away from the window. "Not at all."

The lack of overhead traffic lights provided unobstructed views of the quaint historic buildings sitting alongside more modern architecture. Cobblestones rumbled beneath the tires of the taxi as they neared the city center.

Every detail reminded Sera of the District, only older. Her sense of adventure made her itch to go exploring.

After dropping their bags in the hotel room, they bundled up and headed back out on foot, following a map toward the curiosities shop where Theo's research indicated the goddess might be. With sunset in just over an hour so far north, they had no time to waste.

They joined the throng of people walking along the historic wharf near the hotel, where colorful wooden houses flaunted a rainbow of hues. The unmistakable scent of freshly caught fish filled the air surrounding the open-air markets, causing Sera to wrinkle her nose. She loved seafood, but she shuddered at the thought of octopuses being nearby. Her fear of the giant mollusk started when her mother read her stories of the Kraken and had yet to leave her.

As they snaked their way through the city, Sera found herself almost enjoying herself, even with the nearly constant tripping on the uneven roads and sidewalks as she looked everywhere but down. For a short time, she had even forgotten Hiro's death and the reason they were in Norway, but guilt returned as soon as she realized it, and she ground her teeth together.

By the time they located *Syros' Curios* at the end of a cobblestone alley, Sera's nose and cheeks felt numb from the cold. A small bell rang next to the door as they entered, and a voice called out in greeting above the shoppers' din. It was remarkably busy for the time of year and location, away from the usual tourist destinations.

The store had been a staple of Bergen for centuries, ever since the man who opened it had left Syros in the Aegean Sea to make a new life in the north. Sera had no idea what would make someone abandon the Aegean for a climate as cold as Norway's, but that's what she found out reading the brochure while they waited for the elderly shop owner to finish helping another customer. She pulled her scarf up over her nose, hoping to warm up her face.

"Ah, hello, welcome to *Syros' Curios*, where one can find just about anything if one looks hard enough. What do you seek today?" The shopkeeper peered at them over round spectacles as he approached, his thinning grey and brown hair falling like a curtain in front of his face. He kept trying to blow it away and failing.

Sera pulled her scarf back down and smiled. She hoped it was a smile, anyway. The numbness in her cheeks made it difficult to tell.

"I'm looking for a necklace for my wife," Theo said. "Our travel agent recommended your store." He flashed a disarming smile at the owner, playing the part of the tourist.

"A lovely piece for a lovely lady." The shopkeeper bowed before them. "Follow me." He led them past other shoppers and shelves of assorted antique items to a corner of the store where jewelry of all kinds filled glass display cases. "Let's see, how about this one here? The amethyst would go well—"

"I'm looking for something a bit more *rare*, 'a curiosity worthy of the divine.'" Theo dropped his tone and looked around the room as if someone might overhear him. According to his contact, the last bit was a secret phrase used to gain access to the hidden artifacts. He slipped the balding man an envelope. It was all a part of his act, but it worked like a charm.

The man took a glimpse inside the envelope. "I see you're a man of fine tastes. Please, come with me. Anna, I'll be back in a moment," he called out.

A woman's muffled voice answered from the other side of the store.

He waved them behind a curtain separating the shop from a storage area then down a steep stone staircase, which seemed to narrow the farther down they went. Musty air filled Sera's nose as they descended into almost total darkness until the man flipped a switch on the wall. The switch had been built on top of the stone with visible cables leading up to the floor above. Electricity must have been added in recent years.

Continuing to speak to the age of the store, the shopkeeper withdrew a small collection of skeleton keys from his pocket and unlocked a heavy-looking wooden door at the bottom of the steps.

The switch had also turned on the lights inside; it was flooded in fluorescent lights that hummed and flickered. Sera couldn't help the gasp that escaped her lips as they entered. Artifacts she recognized from her studies lined the walls and covered tables haphazardly, and she would be willing to bet money they were real. She cringed at the ill-treatment.

"I've got a few jewelry pieces over here." The man pointed to a table, which held three necklaces, but none of them a torc like they sought.

Theo frowned. "I was looking for a specific item, a torc rumored to be owned by Freyja herself."

The man paused, squinting behind his spectacles. "The torc was sold. Just this morning."

"Who bought it?" Theo asked.

The shopkeeper simply stared at him. Pulling out a 1000 Krone banknote, Theo placed it in the man's thrust-out hand.

"An American man. He had white hair, thin frame, glasses. I'm sure he told me his name." He rubbed his chin as if in thought, looking meaningfully at Theo over the top of his glasses.

"That sounds like Leif," Sera whispered, her skin

prickling with goosebumps.

Theo sighed and placed another banknote in the man's hand.

"Ah, yes, now I remember. Mr. Karlsson. How could I forget."

Growling filled Sera's mind as Xolotl expressed his anger at the witch's involvement.

She wasn't mad, not really, just baffled. Why on Earth would Leif be after the torc? He had claimed the Bacchic amulet was his when he kidnapped Nora, using her as bait to draw Sera to his house. If he found out Danae had the amulet now, he'd know it was futile to keep trying. It seemed like he was moving on to obsess over a new god. But how did he know about Freyja? Renee hadn't even known about the gods before Bacchus.

"Can I interest you in something else? I have this wonderful—"

"No, thank you. We appreciate your assistance," Theo cut the man off, his own anger barely restrained in his voice.

The man bristled and directed them out of the room, locking it behind him. They followed the shopkeeper back up the steps and into the shop.

"Please let me know if you decide on any other curiosities today," he said. Without waiting for a response, he left them to welcome a new couple into the store. Theo's interruption and their lack of buying anything else must have pissed the poor guy off. She couldn't really blame him, though he did make *some* money off them that day.

Theo and Sera headed outside, where the wind whipped against her unprotected face. She tightened the scarf around her neck. It was too coincidental that Leif had known about

Freyja and somehow beaten them to the torc without some sort of help.

"I don't understand how—"

Theo held up his hand to stop her. His eyes were closed, and he turned his raised face to the wind, his nostrils flaring. Oh, right, he might be able to track the witch's scent. Handy. A moment later, he opened his eyes, his dark brown pupils streaked with gold as they settled on the road at the opening to the alley.

"Let's go."

"You've met Leif?" She had to jog to keep up with his swift pace.

"No, but witches have a distinctive odor added to their normal scent," he said, his nostrils flaring. "I can't believe I missed it when we first arrived. It's still fresh, which means he was just here. We should be able to catch up to him before he leaves Bergen."

As they tracked the man's scent, winding through the historic part of town on foot, Sera did her best to get a good look at the snowy buildings they passed. They might be on the heels of a maniacal witch who tried to kill her once already, but that didn't mean she couldn't enjoy the scenery a little more before facing him. At the very least, the landscape kept her from thinking about the last confrontation with the man.

And besides, if he got the upper hand, this might be her last time to sightsee.

After she almost slipped and fell more than once from ice on the cobblestones, or maybe from her own klutziness, Sera thanked the logical side of her brain for thinking to pack her winter boots. Snow hadn't arrived in the District just yet.

Frosted over grass crunched underfoot as Theo led her across a field of some kind—perhaps for football or lacrosse, she wasn't sure what they played in Norway—surrounded by a track for running. She regretted not doing more research before they left. Not like she really had the time with everything else going on, but it would have been nice to know basic things about the places they were going.

"He's heading north, but we're close. If we—" Without warning, he stopped walking, and Sera stumbled into him before she could catch herself.

"Sorry," she mumbled as she righted herself, but he hadn't seemed to notice. Instead, he looked alert, his head still but his eyes darting from side to side, and his knees and arms bent slightly, as if ready for a fight.

"He's here."

Just as Theo spoke, Leif Karlsson stepped out of the woods ahead of them and walked casually toward the field.

"Fancy meeting you two here. Looking for this?" Leif held up the torc, twirling it around his index finger. "Or should I say, looking for *her*?" He smirked, pushing his wire-framed glasses back up the bridge of his nose.

Despite the weeks since she had last seen him, Leif looked the exact same, as if he hadn't changed or even bothered to wash his clothes. Or himself. At least she wasn't facing him in the humid summer of the District when his stench would have been overwhelming.

Visible underneath his coat, dingy khakis hung from his thin frame. His white hair stuck out in all directions—the pieces that weren't matted to his head, anyway. Brown pupils glared at her beneath overhanging, thick white eyebrows.

"Why do you want the torc? I thought you were all

about Bacchus," she asked, trying to ignore the queasy feeling she got from seeing him.

Leif's smirk changed to a snarl. "The queen has claimed the chaos god, but that doesn't mean I can't have one of my own. She even told me where to find this beauty." He pulled the torc into his chest, cradling it.

Sera and Theo exchanged a glance at the mention of Danae. So, she did know about the other gods, and it seemed Leif was now working for her. But how had she known about Freyja?

"I see you brought a new friend. Moving on from the boyfriend so soon?" Leif asked in his nasal voice.

Keep questioning him, Xolotl's growling voice filtered into her mind. *Rile him up.*

"You work for Danae?" she asked, doing her best not to let Leif rile *her* up with his accusation.

"Her Majesty has restored the Immortals' power and is rewarding those who prove their loyalty with everlasting life. She's promised me the same in return for killing you." He narrowed his eyes at her.

Sera couldn't stop her laugh. "Oh, you think so, huh? I wouldn't count on it. Danae has a history of not fulfilling promises."

"Stop using her name!" Leif snapped. "You're not worthy of it. She is the queen."

"Oh, but she's not *my* queen."

"She is everyone's queen," he said just before flinging something in her direction.

Instinct kicked in to duck, but whatever he threw hit the barrier from the defensive ward imbued in the crystal around her neck. Just like at his house in the Wharf district, the black stone embedded itself in the magical barrier before the whole thing dissolved like a popped bubble.

Leif grinned, displaying teeth that were spotted brown and yellow. She almost gagged at the sight. Good thing she hadn't eaten much lately. The man needed a serious scrub. He raised his arms and started to chant in another language.

As the witch cast his spell at Sera, Theo pushed her to the side, and she stumbled and fell to the ground. She looked back up as bolts of lightning shot down from the grey sky, racing toward Theo before crashing into his chest.

Sera cried out in dismay, but the static of the bolts fizzled and popped, doing no harm. Not even his jacket was charred.

Glancing from his chest to Leif, Theo grinned. "Is that the best you've got?"

Leif howled in fury and reached into his coat pocket, withdrawing a handful of stones, each a different color. He threw one at Theo, who caught it in his hand. His fist started to smoke, and his face turned to a grimace of pain, but he crushed the stone and let the dust fall into the breeze.

Sera clambered to her feet, backing away to stay out of harm's way. The two men continued to face off against each other, Leif becoming angrier as Theo blocked every attempt at inflicting pain. He hadn't even gone on the offensive yet.

"Are you about finished?" Theo asked when the last stone was thrown. "We'll be taking the torc now."

Leif's head snapped toward Sera as if he had forgotten her presence until then. Raising his palm to his mouth, he whispered a phrase and blew a kiss in her direction.

She could *feel* the magic rush toward her, but she had no time to do anything except raise her arms to protect herself as she was swept off her feet. Flying backward into the trunk of a tree, her head cracked against the rough bark. The world went all white, then fuzzy as she struggled against overwhelming drowsiness pulling her down into its depths. She focused on Theo, willing her body to stay awake.

A deep roar tore through the field as Theo launched himself at the witch, who was readying another spell. Theo's body shimmered in midair before transforming into a giant, black dog—a *hairless* dog—and landing on all four large paws in front of the witch, Theo's clothes in a shredded heap behind him.

Opening his canine mouth, he literally swallowed the magic that was intended to finish Sera.

Leif stumbled back and nearly fell as he came face to face with the beast standing before him. The dog growled, low and menacing, and snapped powerful jaws at the witch. As Leif turned to run, the dog pounced and pinned him to the ground, his long teeth inches from the man's face. He snarled, saliva dripping onto Leif's face.

The torc. Now, Theo growled, the words forming in Sera's mind.

Leif must have heard it, too, because he let go of the torc, and it fell to the ground.

Crawling over from her spot against the tree, Sera grabbed the relic.

I will rip out your throat if I see you again. The monstrous dog growled at the man before stepping off him.

"Who are you?" the witch asked as he scooted backward, his face pale as he stared at Theo.

Death. Stepping forward menacingly, he growled at Leif, who jumped to his feet and ran.

CHAPTER 12

Solomon

As he walked down the aisle between the rows of folding chairs, Solomon nudged a sleeping man's leg with his foot but received only a muttered curse and a swat in return. The strong scents of cheap booze and lost hopes stung Solomon's nostrils as the man tipped sideways onto the empty metal chair next to him, not once waking. Solomon turned to address the others gathered in the Hollywood estate's meeting room, hating this part of his new job.

"Your queen is offering you a fresh start at life, one filled with possibilities you never knew existed," he said. "Should you accept, you'll be given a warm shower, food, and a place to sleep. Every single day."

He let that last bit sink in for a moment. The men and

women gathered in Danae's Hollywood home hadn't seen any of those things regularly in months, if not years. They looked back at him with grim, dirt-stained faces, although he could see the small glimmer of hope beginning to stir in a few.

"All your queen asks in return is your loyalty and submission to her command." He pointed to the table at the back of the room where two Immortals waited with clipboards and smiling faces. They would collect signatures and blood oaths before sending the recruits to the showers.

In just two short weeks after their powers were restored, Danae had built the first wave of her army in California. Missing person reports had started to accumulate on the news, as she required all new Immortals to give up their previous lives and go through extensive training on her property. Hence why she preferred the homeless at this stage of her takeover. Despite the televised speculation saying otherwise, not a single one had been abducted.

The training they would endure included fighting with various weaponry and hand-to-hand combat, as well as how to harness their enhanced senses and abilities most effectively. Danae planned to take advantage of the almost uncontrollable nature of new Immortals when she took over, and she had no problem with any of her new recruits losing their lives in the effort. She just wanted to ensure they had a fighting chance against the mortals.

To maximize carnage, of course.

"That sounds like a pretty big ask, don't you think?"

Solomon turned to face the man who had spoken. Despite his disheveled appearance, the man stood straight and proud, his eyes sharp as he gazed back. A soldier in his previous life. He would make an excellent addition to Danae's army. Solomon would need to keep an eye on where he ended up, though not necessarily for Danae's benefit.

"Perhaps." Solomon stepped closer to the man, holding his gaze. "It's your choice: a life on the streets, always wondering where your next meal will come from. *If* there is a next meal. Wondering if this next winter will be your last as you huddle beneath your blanket next to dumpsters and bus stations."

He allowed his *influence* to wash over the soldier, loving how easy it was to do now and with no troublesome side effects. "Or a warm bed and a full belly. Fighting for something you believe in."

Although he could understand the logic behind her choice in recruits, Solomon couldn't stop the feeling of disgust as he watched them brought in. Not only did he despise the loss of their once highly selective recruitment process, he hated lying to these people who had already lost everything. And if they turned down her offer, they would become the new Immortals' next meal.

This was just the start of what Danae had planned for the world, and his resolve was quickly solidifying that this was most certainly *not* the world he wanted to live in.

The man's eyes glazed over, and he smiled. "Sign me up."

Solomon opened his hand toward the awaiting Immortals.

* * *

THE HIGH COUNCIL HAD called a conference in Paris after Danae's spell deactivated Bacchus's magic, a sensation the entire Immortal community must have felt. She had managed to put off the meeting for the past two weeks, but the Council finally threatened to come to Danae with force, a threat that had her laughing. Solomon had never seen her in such good spirits as she had been since the ritual.

But before continuing on to Europe, Danae decided to return to the District for a day or two with a small contingent to check on Lorenzo's progress. Because Solomon hadn't learned what Danae planned to do after the gathering in Paris, the quick stop on the east coast may end up being his last opportunity to connect with Nora.

Lorenzo and his new protégé, who looked vaguely familiar to Solomon, met them on the runway at Washington National Airport. If his black and grey hair was any indication, the other Immortal was of similar age to Lorenzo when he was turned. He grinned, flashing his extended fangs. A *very* new protégé, it seemed.

The ancient Italian threw his arms up in excitement when he saw them descend the stairs of the airplane. His slicked-back black hair reflected the light almost as much as his white suit. For some unknown reason, he thought the color made him look more powerful, but to Solomon, it only emphasized the Immortal's shorter stature.

"Ah! Buona sera! It is a beautiful evening, is it not?" Lorenzo swept his arm behind him, showing off the red, orange, and yellow hues of sunset as if he controlled it. Apparently, he was also in an exceptional mood. He held out his hand, adorned with several overly large rings, to her as she walked toward him. "My queen."

"I want the numbers." Danae brushed past Lorenzo as she approached the SUV parked on the tarmac.

"Sì, sì." Lorenzo kept pace with her, leaving the others to follow in their wake.

The newcomer fell into step with Solomon. "I hadn't realized you were one of them. One of us," the other Immortal said.

"Do I know you?" Solomon asked.

"Dr. Charles Lambert, though most call me Chad," the other man said and extended his hand as they walked. "We met at the gala for the Bacchic Amulet."

Ah, now he remembered. The man who, according to Nora, had tried to force himself on Serafina in a stairwell that night. Just the type to seek out Immortality and precisely the reason Solomon found himself resenting Danae's plan more each day. Weren't they better than this?

"I see you're a man who doesn't learn the error of his ways." Solomon ignored the offered hand and the accompanying sound of protest and turned his attention to the conversation ahead of him.

Straining his ears, he was able to catch the end of what seemed to have been a one-sided conversation. Two hundred new recruits in the District and the entire human council turned. Quick work, though not as fast as the queen would have liked. In most circumstances, her emotionless face rivaled that of a placid lake—still and calm, hiding complex life just beneath the mirror-like surface. But it visibly annoyed her when one of the creator Immortals weakened too much to continue without rest and replenishment.

The queen stepped into the open back door of the black Yukon without addressing Lorenzo further. Yumiko closed the door behind her before walking around to the front passenger side.

As the SUV left, the Italian's anger radiated like a furnace. Danae had commanded Solomon to ride with his maker to get a feel for his sense of loyalty to her. He already knew his maker was all for her machinations, but she needed to find out if he had his own agenda for the throne.

After unbuttoning his white suit jacket, Lorenzo muttered some colorful phrases in Italian and climbed into the back of another Yukon, Solomon beside him. Chad wisely chose the front seat.

"That woman needs to learn to show a little respect." Lorenzo shook his hand in the air. "Especially if she expects us to blindly follow her."

Solomon gazed steadily at the Italian, though his thoughts were even more conflicted after meeting Chad, a man wholly unworthy of everlasting life. "You expect your queen to show gratitude for following her commands?"

Lorenzo stared open-mouthed at him for a moment before snapping his lips shut and narrowing his crystal blue eyes. "I see you have come around to the idea of her being your queen."

He hadn't yet. In fact, he was coming to the opposite conclusion as her thirst for power grew, and the high standards for Immortality shrank. But he wasn't ready for anyone to know that yet. Any Immortals, anyway. Solomon made up his mind to slip away to see Nora before their flight to Paris. He needed to convince her he was on her side before any more damage could be done.

"Do you feel as though you're blindly following her? Or do you know what you've signed up for?" Solomon asked. He still needed to collect information for Danae so she wouldn't question his motives, as well as his maker's.

"Of course I know. And she has promised me a seat on the new Court. A very prominent seat. But until she sits on a throne, a *real* throne, she would be wise to remember who has stood by her from the beginning." Lorenzo's eyes flashed red as they bored into Solomon's. "Be sure to tell her that."

Solomon gazed back until the older Immortal's phone rang, effectively breaking their silent showdown. Lorenzo answered it, leaving Solomon to his thoughts once again, a new idea forming. It might be possible to rile the Italian up enough to go after the throne himself. That would certainly put a kink into Danae's plan and give Solomon more time to plan a rebellion with Nora.

Hell, it might even result in the two ancient Immortals killing each other. Lorenzo's death, at the very least.

He may have rescued Solomon from human slavery, but his maker had enslaved him in a different way for over two hundred years. Maybe it was time for that to change. Perhaps it was time for true freedom.

Yes, Lorenzo's death would be very *satisfying.*

* * *

DANAE SPENT THE EVENING and early hours of the morning reviewing Lorenzo's reports of his new recruits and blueprints for a newly-acquired, much larger facility nearby. Solomon knew she would be preoccupied most of the day as she visited the new Immortal training facility in McLean, Virginia. For once, she didn't require Solomon by her side, which meant he had rare time to himself. He snatched the keys to the Maserati from the wall of hooks.

As daylight made its presence known, Solomon drove to Nora's apartment and followed a car into the multi-storied parking garage. He found her white Civic on the third level, the same level as her apartment. Ignoring a reserved sign, he parked in the only open spot and waited.

An hour went by before he caught sight of her familiar blonde curls trapped beneath a lavender vintage-style hat that complimented her knee-length coat of the same color. Even from where he stood a few dozen feet away, he could see the hint of blue lines beneath her light skin. His lips curled up into a smile. Someday, he would love to taste that blood, but only if she gave it willingly.

Hoping to avoid scaring her, he approached in the open.

"Nora," Solomon said just above a whisper.

"Jesus, Mary, and Joseph!" Nora's mouth opened wide, startled despite his precautions, though she recovered fast. She narrowed her green eyes at him. "I thought I made myself pretty clear how I felt about you the last time."

"You did. And I have to admit, it stung." He held a hand to his heart, which beat a bit more rapidly in her presence. She was beyond beautiful.

Nora raised one of her eyebrows. "That was the point."

"I've been doing a lot of thinking since I last saw you, about the words you spoke to me. I had a realization, an epiphany if you will." He stepped forward, wanting to see more of her. The oatmeal scent he knew and loved drifted toward him, stronger than it had ever been before.

"I'm not interested in your *epiphanies*. Best get back into your fancy car before I show you I'm not the same woman you knew two weeks ago." She waved her hand at him in a shooing fashion before turning her back to him.

Her confidence called to him like a Siren's song to a sailor. Only he, like Ulysses, knew how to restrain himself.

Usually.

"Nora, wait—" He reached out and grasped her arm.

As she turned around, she flung liquid from a flask, the contents spraying across his face. A second later, Solomon's skin felt like it had caught fire. His flesh sizzled and popped as he stumbled backward, trying to wipe whatever she had thrown at him off his skin.

"I've been told silver water can be very effective against your kind. The rumor is clearly true." She held the flask out, ready to use it again.

Solomon threw up his hands in surrender, his wounds already healing, thanks to his restored powers, although the smell of burned flesh lingered. "I came to tell you that I'm in love with you."

She glared back at him. "Do you really expect me to believe that?"

"Yes." And he loved her even more at that moment, knowing he would have to prove it to her.

"You stood by while my best friend watched her boyfriend die and was then tortured herself, and you expect me to just forget all that because you think you love me?" Nora scoffed, her breath showing in the frosty air.

"I don't think it. I *am* in love with you. And I want to help you and Sera stop Danae." He watched her face process his words, her lips turning down to a confused frown.

"I don't understand," she said.

"Danae's vision of the future is not mine. I've seen more than I care to over the last two weeks of what her plan will mean for this world, and it's not for me. She's done terrible things to a lot of people, not just to Sera. Let me help you."

Nora stared at him, her face a mask as she hid her emotions, but he could still smell her desire for him, laced with fear. He itched to use his abilities to *influence* her thoughts, but he withheld. If he had any hopes of gaining her trust, he couldn't cross that boundary.

"There's zero percent chance of us trusting you," she finally said.

"What are you afraid of?"

"Oh, you know, the usual—falling into a trap, being deceived, seeing my friends killed, having my heart broken." She counted them off flippantly. Glaring at him again, she opened her car door and threw her over-sized purse inside. "I'm late for a meeting. Leave me alone, Solomon."

He held the door open before she could slam it in his face. "Not until you know I'm speaking the truth."

Letting her go, he watched the car until it disappeared around the corner, a smile plastered to his face. After decades of feeling next to nothing, she made him feel human again. He would prove himself to her or die trying.

* * *

THE QUEEN AND HER entourage flew out to Paris the next evening and landed a few hours after midnight on Sunday. The location for the meeting changed each time it was called to avoid showing one region any particular favor.

To honor their Bacchic origin, the High Council preferred to meet on sacred ground outside. Only in recent years, they met during the day instead of after dark. Daylight meant humans would be around, which in turn ensured the Immortals would be more aware of maintaining their secrecy from the mortal world. And the sunlight, no matter how gentle or hidden behind clouds, had been blinding due to their diminished powers. Rebellions would simply be too difficult to coordinate.

Though with their powers restored, being in the sun didn't really seem to make much difference to Immortals anymore. The change had been so gradual, Solomon hadn't even realized it was their loss of powers making the light a nuisance.

In addition to the location restrictions, Council members were allowed to bring only two other Immortals with them. Danae had brought Yumiko, of course, and Solomon, much to Lorenzo's astonishment. As one of the queen's loyal favorites, his maker had always attended the meetings. This would be the first for Solomon, and, despite his hesitations with her grandiose plan, he actually looked forward to meeting the other Eternals. Perhaps he could convince one or two to assist him in keeping Danae from following through with her plan.

Although Danae still hadn't confided much to him, he knew the majority of her new army was left behind in the United States. He wondered almost as much as anyone what she would say about the restoration of their abilities.

The gathering took place in a less visited area of the Père Lachaise Cemetery, sacred ground found in the 20th arrondissement of the city. Moss-covered tombstones and towering mausoleums had been coated in a thin layer of snow and ice from the storm that passed through Paris the day before. The height of the tombs and the surrounding trees, combined with the time of year, provided a decent amount of privacy for the meeting. Each of their bodyguards would ensure any wandering humans would continue to meander in another direction.

Six Eternals made up the High Council, five of whom were of Greek or Roman descent, while Solomon was fairly certain Danae hailed from Crete based on a passing comment from his maker a few years back. As the frost melted into muddy puddles beneath the warming sun, it became evident that Nestor wouldn't be joining them. No one else but Solomon and Yumiko knew the other Eternal had visited Danae.

Liviana and Berenice, the two other women on the High Council, stood close together, each of their brown heads styled in elaborate braided updos that must have been popular in their original times, though their heeled boots, leggings, and wool coats were much more modern. Like Danae, the two ancient Immortals had been turned as young women, possibly even in their late teens, and they glared at her as they whispered in an ancient form of Latin that Solomon had only recently begun to study.

While her face gave away nothing, he was sure Danae knew what they said, and it didn't sound pleasant. Cliques had begun long before the modern age, it seemed. He wondered what she had done, or possibly hadn't done, to become the outcast.

"Didn't you call him?" Imhotep asked, his arms crossed over his broad chest. He wore his coal-colored hair slicked back, reminiscent of Lorenzo. But unlike the Italian, Imhotep stood at least six feet tall, and his burly stature and constant scowl reminded Solomon of a minotaur. Having been one of the last Eternals created, he had been assigned to oversee Australia's Immortal activities, an assignment he made clear didn't suit his interests.

"We messaged. He said he would be here." Liviana's dark brown eyes scanned the cemetery. She had been responsible for ensuring attendance as the host territory for the meeting.

"Well, I for one don't intend to wait for him," Eratosthenes said, unlocking his arm from his partner's. He placed his fists on his hips. "Who reversed the spell?"

The Council members looked amongst each other.

"I did," Danae said. "It's about time someone did something to show the god we can't be bullied into submission."

Eratosthenes clapped in her direction before entwining his arm through his partner's again. The other man had to be at least seventy years of age and stood straight and poised, a stark contrast to Eratosthenes's youthful demeanor. Solomon hadn't caught his name, but the Eternal's partner had been changed only recently, and he often fidgeted, his eyes darting around the area. After Eratosthenes's display of approval, Solomon was sure Danae would treat them both favorably in her new world.

"That wasn't your call to make," Liviana said. "How and why did you do it?"

Danae withdrew the amulet from her coat pocket with a gloved hand and held it before the group. The sun caught the liquid hidden within the pinecone, spraying crimson light across the cemetery like splattered blood. A sensation of shock rolled through the Eternals though no sounds escaped their lips.

"I thought Bacchus had chosen an American girl?" Berenice fingered a locket lying against her chest.

Was that jealousy he smelled?

"He did," Danae said.

She was enjoying this game too much, and Solomon could sense the other members weren't going to be patient for long.

"Out with the details, Danae. Stop playing coy," Liviana snapped at the other Eternal.

"I took back what was rightfully ours, and I returned us to our Immortal glory." She met eyes with each of the Council members in turn. "I would think a 'thank you' is in order."

Berenice laughed, though it sounded more astonished than humorous. "A thank you? You shouldn't be that daft, considering your age."

She stared down Danae's narrowed eyes. "As Liviana said, it wasn't your call to make that decision. We are of Bacchus; therefore we serve Bacchus. Overruling him will have devastating consequences."

Liviana and Imhotep murmured their agreement.

"Oh, you're right about that." Danae snapped her fingers. Shadows crept from behind the trees and mausoleums, expanding into what looked like several dozen Immortals. New Immortals with fangs extended, ready to unleash their chaotic nature upon their prey.

As the four other Eternals and the Immortals accompanying them were herded into a circle in the middle of the clearing, uncertainty and anger rippled through the group, including through Solomon. He clearly underestimated her strength outside of the United States, never once anticipating such a bold move.

He glanced at Yumiko, who grinned. Either she knew of the plan, or she just approved of it. He guessed the former.

"What is the meaning of this?" Imhotep bared his fangs in a hiss, ready for a fight. No weapons were permitted within a meeting, a rule Danae had disregarded with her new attendees.

Blue-grey eyes raged with a furious storm as Danae regarded them. "We've grown weary of this democratic bullshit. The time has come for the rightful heirs of the earth to take our place at the top of the food chain and make ourselves known. We will rule over all."

Liviana's took a step back, her eyes wide. "You're mad. He didn't create us to 'rule the earth.' He—"

"Bacchus created us in his image—chaos. And chaos is what we will give them." The queen's eyes burned red.

"Chain them."

CHAPTER 13

Serafina

The giant dog padded over to Sera and nudged her with his cold, wet nose, letting out a soft whine.

"I'm okay, just dazed." Still disoriented, she patted the hairless dog on his head without thinking about who he actually was. His appearance reminded her of the dogs she saw in Egyptian hieroglyphics, like Anubis, only the one sitting next to her was much bigger. And was also Theo.

Weird.

She held out the torc, wincing at the sudden movement. "Maybe bruised, too."

The dog's body began to shimmer as he shifted back to his human form. His naked, human one. Sera's cheeks warmed against the cold air, and she turned her attention to the torc while he dressed. She hadn't questioned it before, but now she understood why he brought a change of clothes in his messenger bag.

She wouldn't call herself a prude by any means, but she may have been a bit more modest than some. Her usual beach attire included a one-piece, coverup, and floppy hat while sitting beneath a giant umbrella, but that was also due to her fair skin's love of looking like a lobster.

Boy, did it take a lot of willpower not to peek at him at that moment. Maybe she was more dazed than she realized.

A few seconds later and fully clothed, he knelt down beside her. Taking her chin in his hand, he turned her head side to side, dark eyes full of concern. "You're sure you're okay? Have you had a concussion before?"

Had she ever had a concussion? She held in her snort. The man clearly hadn't picked up on her klutzy nature yet.

"Yeah, in softball. Another girl and I ran smack into each other." Sera squinted at him. "Why were you hairless?"

Theo chuckled as he sat back, leaning his arm on his raised knee. "Xolotl's spirit animal is the Xoloitzcuintli, more commonly known as the Mexican hairless dog. Do you feel dizzy or sick?"

Sera shook her head, immediately regretting that decision as a sharp stab tore through her skull. "Brutal headache, but that's about it. Leif didn't know who you were?"

"I've kept my presence hidden from the Bacchae as well as most of the Others."

"The Others?" she asked.

"A generic term for other supernaturals like gods and witches."

"Ah." Sera nodded, then reached up to cradle her head

as more pain shot through her temples. "Why didn't his magic hurt you? Does your tattoo protect you against that sort of thing?"

"Yes, normally. But in this case, Leif used lightning against a god of lightning." Theo grinned. "It's not very effective. Come on, let's get you back to the hotel and out of the cold." He stood and pulled Sera to her feet. She groaned as bruised and sore bones screamed at her.

Theo looked her over. "We should get you to a doctor instead."

Sera waved a hand in dismissal. "No, no. I'm just a big baby when it comes to pain. And I don't have Bacchus to just whisk it all away." Her heart ached as she said his name, adding to her list of injuries. She really did miss the god and not just for his healing abilities.

After requesting a taxi from an app on Theo's phone, they made their way back across the field toward the roads of the city. Sera tucked the torc inside her small cross-body purse, not entirely sure the necklace held a goddess's essence—if Freyja was in there, she hadn't made a peep.

The sun had just about set when the taxi picked them up, and Sera closed her eyes in the dark car to soothe her aching head. She participated in the idle small talk Theo kept up to ensure she didn't fall asleep, and by the time they reached their shared room, she felt better. Like maybe her head wouldn't actually implode.

She had insisted on sharing a room to keep the costs down. So what if Theo had a fortune to his name? She didn't want him or anyone else to spend unnecessary money. They had separate beds and a private bathroom, and that was good enough for her. It helped that he had been nothing but a gentleman. The world could use more men like him.

Sera pulled off her jacket and removed her gloves before sitting down on the bed. As she lifted the torc from her bag, her bare fingers tingled. A smile spread across her face at the familiar feeling.

Now that she had a moment to really get a good look at it, Sera turned the goddess's relic around in her hands. Amber gemstones embedded in the flattened metal gleamed in the light from the bedside lamp, creating shimmering golden ovals on the wall.

"She's definitely here," Sera said as excitement fluttered like butterflies within her stomach.

"Can you talk to her?" Theo asked.

Biting her lip, she imagined a thread connecting her to the torc, then *pushed* her thoughts across the cord as Renee had taught her: *Hello? Freyja?*

A sleepy yawn filled Sera's mind before a lilting voice responded. *Well, hello, darling. Why are you waking me?*

Sera grinned, adrenaline easing the pain in her body. *Freyja, my name is Serafina Finch, and I'm here with Theodore Pratt, who merged with the god Xolotl. We need your help,* she thought back to the goddess.

Ohh, Theodore. It's been a long time since I've seen him. He's just as handsome as I remember. A gentle purr rumbled through Sera's mind.

"She's here and remembers you." She didn't think it was necessary to include the compliment, though she couldn't help but agree with the sentiment.

"Good. Let her know the situation," Theo said.

The Bacchae witch Danae has taken Bacchus's amulet and restored their ability to create new Bacchae. She wants to take over the world, Sera said bluntly.

A woman's lighthearted laughter echoed through her head. *Bacchus sure made a mistake with that one, didn't he? She's always been too ambitious for her own good. How can I assist, darling?*

Relief flooded through her body, soothing her aching soul. The witch was going down. "She wants to know how she can help."

* * *

THEO BOOKED THEIR FLIGHT to India for the next morning, although there had been one out of Bergen that evening. He had insisted they wait to make sure her concussion didn't become more severe.

After recounting the past few months and discussing the upcoming plans with Freyja, Sera lay down on the hotel bed. She called Nora, filling her in on the events of their trip so far and learned that Nora's magical training was going better than expected. Apparently, Nora had a real knack for magic, which wasn't all that surprising to Sera.

"Why don't you just wear the torc for protection until you get the amulet back?" Nora asked.

"Because Bacchus claimed me, no other god or goddess can. It's a weird magic rule, I guess," Sera explained.

"So many rules! Renee keeps telling me all the things I can't do. It's infuriating," Nora harrumphed. "In other news, Solomon came by, and I had a chance to show off my new skills."

"What!" Sera nearly fell off the bed, her heart thumping rapidly. The move earned her a raised eyebrow from Theo.

"Oh, don't worry. He thinks he's in love with me."

Nora snorted. "As if he knows what love is."

"Nor, you need to stay away from him." Gripping the phone tightly in her hand, Sera lay back on the pillows again.

"I certainly plan on it, but I can't help it if the smitten kitten follows me around." There was a pause. "But he also says he wants to help us take down Danae."

It was Sera's time to snort. "Yeah, right. More like he's trying to get information for Danae."

"You're probably right." Her tone didn't sound as convinced as her words. "Anyway, I gotta go. Let me know how India goes." A smooch came through the cell.

"Be safe." Sera set her phone down and closed her eyes.

"Are you hungry?" Theo's voice asked.

"Mmhmm, famished." She was too tired to even open her eyes to answer.

"I'm going to run over to the restaurant next door and pick up some food. I'll be back as soon as I can. You rest, okay?"

She nodded her head, relieved not to feel any sharp pains when she did. The door clicked shut a moment later.

* * *

SUNLIGHT FILTERED IN through the window and across her face, warming her skin. Sera peeked an eye open and saw Theo next to his bed, packing up both of their bags.

"Weren't you afraid I would die in my sleep?" she asked.

He chuckled but didn't turn around. "Your snoring let me know everything was okay."

Sera sighed. He had already told her on the plane her snoring wasn't *that* bad, but anyone who slept in her vicinity teased her about it. Even Hiro loved to pretend he hadn't gotten any sleep thanks to the sound. Her heart grew heavy at the thought, but instead of trying to force the grief back down, she focused on the memories. A smile came to her lips. A sad smile, but a smile, nevertheless.

The growl of her stomach rivaled Xolotl's.

"Leftover stew is in the fridge." Theo pointed to the small appliance tucked beneath the counter of the kitchenette. The two double beds took up the majority of the rest of the room's space.

Sera sat up, wincing at the soreness throughout her body, and hobbled over to the refrigerator. Not even bothering to warm it up in the microwave first, she scarfed down the stew, barely tasting anything as she devoured it. Hungry was an understatement.

"Do I have time to shower?" she asked as she finished the last of the stew.

"Yeah, it's still early. We'll leave in an hour."

Taking her time in the bathroom, Sera relished the warm water as it ran through her hair and down her body, washing away the cold and travel grime. She wasn't normally a long shower kind of girl, but she didn't normally get her ass kicked by a crazed witch, either. The heat did her body some good.

By the time she finished, the sauna-like air had fogged up the whole mirror. She used a hand towel to wipe the glass, her muscles screaming at her from the movement. Dropping the towel to her waist and turning her back toward the mirror, she looked over her shoulder and gasped. Her back, shoulders, and the top of her buttocks were one giant, mottled purple and black bruise from hitting the trunk of the tree.

"Everything okay?" Theo burst into the bathroom before she could reply.

Sera yelped in surprise and pulled the towel up over her exposed breasts. "Yes! Holy shit. I would have locked the door had I known you had a tendency to just waltz right in." She glared at him.

He ignored her sounds of protest and walked over, turning her away from him so he could get a look at her back. Warmth rose in her cheeks and ears as he gingerly touched her skin. For someone who could fight with such ferocity, he had a soft touch. Hiro's had been similar due to his training in mixed martial arts. Her heart swelled with pride at the memory of his last match, and tears pricked the corners of her eyes.

"I've got a medicinal cream that will help with the pain. Let me go get it." Theo left the bathroom, giving her a quick moment to readjust her towel and cover more of her skin, as well as take a few calming breaths. When he returned, he held a plastic tub of Vaseline.

Sera raised an eyebrow. "Really? Vaseline?"

"I just used the container. It's an old Aztec recipe for pain that Xolotl taught me. Sit down on the toilet."

She did as told, doing her best to ignore how awkward she felt being almost naked in front of a man she was just getting to know and not romantically involved with. Nora would have made the most of it. She bit her lip against the giggle wanting to come out.

Theo's hands were gentle as he applied the cream, and a soothing sensation radiated deep into her skin and the muscles beneath. When he finished, she tested out a few shoulder lifts and found the pain significantly lessened. The flight to India might not kill her after all.

"Thanks," she said, then pointed toward the open door. "Now get out so I can get dressed."

He rolled his eyes but didn't argue. After locking the knob on the inside, he winked and shut the door behind him. The tiniest flutter danced in her belly.

Oh, come on, I cannot be attracted to this guy like that, Sera groaned to herself. Guilt flooded her mind faster than a burst dam, replacing any other feelings that may have arisen.

This was new guilt, because now that more time had passed—and if she was truly honest with herself—she'd had doubts about marrying Hiro. About spending the rest of her life with him. He was wonderful. Perfect, even. Any girl would be lucky to have him as a husband and father to their children. So, what the hell was wrong with Sera? Why hadn't she felt as invested in him as he clearly was in her?

Because… Hiro hadn't really been a challenge. He accepted her exactly as she was and didn't push her to be or do anything more. He supported her dreams fully, something past boyfriends certainly hadn't done, which should be all she wanted and more. But for some reason, it still didn't feel like enough.

Hiro didn't question things the way she did, he didn't need or want to know more about the past and what made people tick. As much as she hated to admit it, he would have been the easy way out. And she didn't want easy.

The adventure of a lifetime was right in front of her, and it terrified her. She hated that it had meant the death of such an amazing soul, and anger simmered, ready to boil over, every time she thought about Danae and what Sera was going to do to her once she caught up to her.

Was she ready for this life with Bacchus? Would they merge? She had no idea. All she knew at the moment was… chaos. She snorted as she held back a laugh.

Gods, Bacchus would love this right now. She had no idea what she thought or felt just yet about everything that had occurred since she found the amulet in her bag. Not truly. But she hoped she would know once the bitch was dead.

By the time she finished pulling on her leggings and tank top, the mirror had cleared, and Sera stared at her reflection. Despite random bouts of ravenous hunger, she had lost weight in the last few weeks. An unhealthy amount. Her jawline had never looked so well defined, but her cheeks had an almost hollow, skeletal look to them. Dark circles beneath her eyes made her typically light grey irises look a shade darker. Or maybe that was just what grief did to them. Regardless, this wasn't a good look for her.

Sera took a dryer to her dark hair, which fell nearly stick-straight no matter what she tried to do to it. Straight hair had been both a blessing and a curse throughout her life. She pulled a long, grey sweater over her top and left the bathroom.

Theo looked up from his phone when she walked into the room. "My contact in India will be waiting for us at the airport in Kolkata. The good news is the Durga Puja festival occurred not too long ago, which means we will be able to find her pretty much anywhere."

"What's the bad news?" she asked.

"She's going to be even harder to convince to join us after a five-day festival celebrating her," he said.

"Is it even worth going?" Even with the medicine on her back, she groaned inwardly at the thought of another long flight.

Yes, Freyja said in her mind at the same time as Theo out loud.

"Yes. As an actively worshipped warrior goddess, she will be nearly invincible against the Bacchae."

"Why Durga, though? What about another, less popular Hindu god? They're all actively worshipped, right?" she asked.

"Durga is one of the few, quite possibly the only one, in the Hindu pantheon who works alongside a human, trying to help them. The rest are virtually untouchable, living on whatever plane of existence the gods do. Despite what their worshippers think, they ignore this world for the most part."

Theo finished zipping up their bags and set them on the carpeted floor. He looked at Sera. "Ready?"

* * *

THEY ARRIVED IN KOLKATA early Monday morning after an almost twenty-hour trip with one layover. Sera was beyond grateful for the first-class seats on both legs of the flight this time around. She was almost able to forget her bruises and sore body until she stood up to disembark the plane.

As they exited the gate, the terminal ceiling drew Sera's attention. As far as the eye could see, Bengali script adorned the surface. The beauty of it took her breath away, though she couldn't read a word of it.

"Beautiful, isn't it?" Theo asked.

"Yes, it sure is. What does it say?"

"I couldn't tell you, but they're writings from the

Bengali poet, Rabindranath Tagore."

They followed the script through the terminal and past multiple coffee shops that practically begged her to stop with their tempting aromas. As they exited the airport, varying volumes of honking horns met her ears, and a wave of moist heat hit her face. The day before, they had been bundled up and watching for ice; now, she could comfortably wear a tank top. It was almost like dealing with spring weather back in the District. At least the sun wasn't directly shining on them as the majority of the pickup lanes ran beneath the second level of the airport.

Along with the warmth, a variety of odors assaulted Sera's nose, the most easily identifiable being the delicious scent of curry. She started to wonder why the city itself smelled like spices until she spotted the food cart through a quick gap in the throng of people. Then it was gone again, hidden behind a mob of bodies.

"Has it been weird watching the world change so much over a century?" Sera asked as she eyed the airport congestion, thinking about the fact that Theo had grown up before cars had taken over the road.

He looked at her for a brief moment, amusement shining in his dark brown eyes, before returning his search through the sea of taxis. Holding up a hand to one a few car lengths down, he tilted his head for her to follow. "The simple answer is yes and no."

"That's not an answer."

"Going through it is not 'weird,' as you say. It's just a part of life. Things change. But when I look back over my entire lifetime, then yes, it is a little *weird*." He chuckled as he opened the back door of the cab and gestured her inside.

"Hello, my old friend! And my new friend!" An Indian man with dark hair and skin and a friendly smile winked at Sera in the rearview mirror as she climbed in. "I am Nidheesh. You must be Serafina. You are as lovely as a lotus flower. Teddy is lucky to have found you."

Heat rushed to her cheeks from the unexpected compliment. And *Teddy?* "Very nice to meet you, Nidheesh."

"I told you she was my business partner, Nidhi," Theo grumbled as he slid into the bench seat next to her.

Nidheesh waved his hand dismissively as he skillfully pulled the car into the traffic leaving the airport. He probably excelled at games like Tetris and Mario Kart.

"You should surround yourself with beauty no matter the reason," he said.

"Nidhi is an eternal optimist," Theo said.

"Nothing wrong with optimism in a world as dark as this one," Nidheesh said. "You should try it sometime, old man."

Sera glanced at Theo with a questioning look.

"Yes, Nidhi has known me for a long time. I go by Theo these days, friend." He reached forward and patted the Indian man on the shoulder. "Nidheesh is one of the Others I told you about, but he's not connected to any god."

"So, what is he? A witch?"

"No, he is simply immortal. No magical powers that I know of."

"How?" she asked.

"He says he'll tell me when I grow up." Theo smiled in good humor, matching Nidheesh's cheeky grin in the mirror.

"Where to?" the taxi driver asked.

"Wherever Hareni can be found these days."

Nidheesh nodded and turned the car down the next street.

"Hareni is the human that works with Durga right now. If we can convince her of the threat to humankind, she might be able to persuade the goddess," Theo explained.

Kolkata was a lesson in contrasts with Bergen, and boy was it *busy*. Whereas Bergen had been dark and stormy with winter's approach, Kolkata was still bright and filled with color. Signs and advertisements plastered over every inch of shops and apartments, which were sometimes equally as colorful as the signs themselves. Historic Indian architecture blended in with buildings displaying a strong classical European style influence due to the long British rule.

Cars, buses, and mopeds drifted in and out of lanes as if the lines on the roads didn't exist, yet it seemed as natural to them as breathing. Perhaps they learned to drive as the Italians did, concerned with what was in front of their car rather than behind it. In a city as congested as Kolkata, where people were everywhere, including chatting in the middle of the streets, it made sense.

Trying to take in the rest of the city as they drove, Sera fought the exhaustion threatening to take over. Despite the Aztec cream and first-class sleeping quarters, she hadn't slept well on the plane. Her mind wouldn't shut off, and she didn't want to have another nightmare. Compared to her new terrifying visions, her past dreams revealing Liviana's discovery of the Bacchae seemed almost harmless.

If only Bacchus were with her, he would help her see the day through. He would also gloat for a week knowing she'd had that thought.

She must have dozed off against the door because the

next thing she knew, Nidheesh had parked the cab beside a curb.

"She's inside the temple. I'll wait here with your bags," he said.

Theo pushed the door open and slid out, snapping Sera out of her groggy daze.

Before getting out of the cab, she wiped her sweating palms on her pants, suddenly nervous about the possibility of meeting a goddess. It was one thing speaking to them in her mind or through another person, but having a deity standing before her in the flesh was a whole other ballgame. Sera felt horribly underdressed in her leggings, tank top, and slip-on Toms shoes. Too late now.

After taking a deep breath, Sera climbed out of the car. She stared up at the temple, which looked more like a single-level storefront in need of a good scrub than a house of worship, then followed Theo inside.

CHAPTER 14

Serafina

Inside, the windowless temple was dark, lit only by a few wall sconces and candles. It was quiet, the only sounds being the muted traffic from the street outside. Sera and Theo let their eyes adjust for a moment before moving farther in.

The altar loomed at the other end of an otherwise stark room. As she moved closer, a statue of the goddess Durga with her many arms riding atop a tiger came into view. Each of the goddess's eight hands held an item: in one a sword, in another a conch shell. She even held a lotus flower. Sera hadn't a clue what the different objects represented, but the statue was majestic to behold.

"She's divine, isn't she?" a voice asked at Sera's side.

Sera jumped, clamping a hand over her heart in surprise.

A young Indian woman, no older than Sera, stood next to her. She wore a white silk saree with a patterned red border, and her black hair was styled into a long braid that she pulled forward over her shoulder. She toyed with the end of it as she gazed at the statue.

"Hareni, it's a pleasure to meet Durga's newest apprentice." Theo bowed to the young woman before extending his hand.

Sera stood awkwardly, unsure of how to address someone who worked alongside an actively worshipped goddess. Meeting Theo had been easy in comparison because she hadn't known about Xolotl at the time.

"Oh, stop, the pleasure is mine! It's not every day another god visits." Hareni's eyes sparkled as she took his hand and shook it. "I always love a good beard on a man. Or maybe it's a beard on a good man."

Theo rubbed his chin, which was now covered in a decent amount of hair as he hadn't shaved since they were in the District. Curious, considering he could turn into a hairless dog.

"I'm sorry we didn't take the time to clean up and present ourselves properly, but time is not on our side at the moment," he said.

"Yes, we've heard some things. Let's chat somewhere more comfortable." Hareni crooked a finger and directed them to an opening in the wall, which expanded into a hallway.

A door at the end of the long hall led them into an inviting sitting room. Two dark chocolate colored couches faced each other across a glass-top coffee table while a matching buffet table stood against one of the walls. Various fresh pastries and ice-cold refreshments waited for consumption and set Sera's mouth watering.

"Will Durga be joining us?" Theo asked as he took a seat on the couch across from the woman.

Hareni waved a hand flippantly. "We'll see. She does her own thing."

"Let me just cut to the chase then," he said. "The Bacchae witch known as Danae has gotten hold of Bacchus's amulet. She's used it to revive their ability to create new Bacchae to create an army and take over the world. Humankind, *your kind*," Theo emphasized the point, "will be kept as livestock."

Hareni pursed her lips, taking in what he said. "She's going to need a big army."

"She's already hard at work. My guess is she plans to take down the High Council and replace it with her own people. She calls herself the queen already."

The young woman's eyes glazed over for a moment before she nodded. "Durga is on her way."

Sera's pulse started to race—she was going to meet a goddess. She licked her lips as her mouth went dry. A hand on her shoulder startled her.

"Relax. She's not going to hurt you," Theo said quietly.

"I know that," she said, although she wasn't as confident as she sounded. If she sounded confident at all. "I'm excited. It's like meeting a celebrity for the first time."

He let out a chuckle and rolled his eyes.

Hearing footsteps approach, Sera turned her head to the door. Only it didn't sound like human footsteps. If it was possible, the steps were both hefty and soft at the same time.

An orange and black striped tiger padded through the

door, the animal's body taking up a significant amount of the available space. Orange eyes focused on Sera.

Holy shit.

As Sera gasped and scrambled back farther into the couch seat, Theo stood and bowed to the animal. The large cat dipped its head and chuffed, a soft puffing sound, before sitting back on its hindquarters.

"Durga, may I introduce Serafina Finch, the woman chosen most recently by Bacchus to wield his powers." He swept his open palm toward Sera.

"Uh, hi." Gulping, she waved at the tiger and climbed off the couch to stand, feeling foolish but not sure what else to do. It wasn't like she addressed goddesses in the form of giant cats every day. And right now, her frozen limbs weren't cooperating enough to do anything else.

The tiger regarded her for another moment then shimmered before her eyes, the body of the tiger dissolving into the form of a dark-skinned, eight-armed woman wrapped in a red and gold saree. Ornate gold bands adorned each of her arms and around her neck, and a gold chain ran from a hoop in her pierced nose to her left ear. A tall crown decorated with jewels sat atop her head.

Only her eyes remained as a tiger's eyes, as orange as an apricot. Fierce energy radiated from the goddess's entire being, setting Sera's heart beating like the drums of war.

Durga.

"Serafina, welcome to India." The goddess's voice sounded musical to her ears, like a thousand wind chimes blowing in the breeze.

Sera's breath caught in her throat from the sheer beauty of the sound and brought tears to her eyes. Her knees threatened to buckle beneath her.

"Th-thank you. I'm honored you've agreed to meet with us," she said.

"It is always a pleasure to meet those who are new to our divine world. Tell me, what has befallen our wine-loving friend?" Durga drifted lightly on her bare feet to the other couch where Hareni sat. The goddess's arms adjusted pillows to make room for her extra limbs and also accepted a cup of tea from Hareni. It was a sight to behold.

"Danae has him," Sera said as she sat. "She murdered the man I love, then let the police find his remains. I knew I would be questioned, so I had to remove Bacchus's amulet, and that's when she stole it."

She tried to keep her focus on Durga, rather than allow her mind to conjure up images of Hiro's death or the ill-treatment of his body. She swallowed the lump forming in the back of her throat.

The goddess inclined her head. "I'm sorry to hear of his passing. He must have been quite the man to have won over such a prize as you. Bacchus never chooses randomly, despite his chaotic nature."

Dropping her gaze, Sera picked at flecks of lint on her leggings. "I don't know about the last bit, but yes, he was an amazing, selfless man who didn't deserve to die that way." Despite her efforts to suppress them, tears gathered in her eyes.

"Do not be ashamed of your grief. It is part of what makes you human and beautiful to the divine."

When she looked up again with droplets sliding down her face, Durga's smile felt like a ray of sunshine upon her heart, warming her instantly. She wiped the stray tears from her cheeks.

"What is it you seek?" the goddess asked.

"We need your strength in the battle against Danae," Theo said, "especially now that we don't have Bacchus to fight with us."

"I understand you believe she will succeed in her plan to take over humankind, but I am not so confident in her abilities."

"She has already restored the Bacchae's powers, including their ability to create new ones," he said.

Durga considered him for a moment. "My followers are many in number; she will not find the gods so easy to take down."

"You don't think your followers will be swayed by the promise of immortality?" he asked.

"Some. But the majority are devoted." The goddess smiled benevolently upon Hareni, one hand reaching out to clasp the young woman's.

"And if your devotees are annihilated?" he asked.

Durga laughed, a dozen ringing bells in the sound. "Do you think I would allow that to happen?"

"If you don't take this threat seriously, it wouldn't matter if you allowed it or not. It'll happen." His tone was blunt.

Durga's eyes, as orange as an apricot, narrowed. "I do not appreciate your tone or insinuation I do not take the Bacchae seriously. You forget yourself in my home."

"And you forget I've merged with a god who believed he had a faithful following until the end of time," he said.

Theo and Durga stared each other down, neither willing to concede. Growls and hisses filled Sera's mind as the two gods conversed. Well, more like argued. Okay, they fought like cats and dogs. A quick glance at Hareni showed her to be enjoying the showdown much more than Sera was, her eyes twinkling as she played with the end of her braid.

After what felt like an eternity, Theo bowed his head.

"I mean no disrespect to you. I have some serious doubts about our ability to stop Danae without your help. Please. Join us," he said with a slight pleading in his voice.

Durga turned her head and regarded Hareni for a few moments before returning her gaze to Sera and Theo. "I am sorry, but my place is here with my worshippers. I have every faith in your ability to put the witch in her place. Only kill her this time."

"Wait—" Before Theo could protest more, the many-armed goddess shimmered once again as she transformed back into a tiger. The striped cat walked over and licked Sera's hand, her tongue like wet sandpaper. She chuffed once again before leaving the room.

Once the tiger's footsteps faded, Hareni spread her hands, a slight shrug in her shoulders. "Sorry, guys. I know you came a long way. Can I get you anything else before you head out?"

Theo shook his head and sighed, defeat written across his face.

Standing, Hareni walked toward the door. With her hand on the frame, she turned around to wink at Theo. "Keep the beard. It looks good on you."

* * *

THEY DECIDED TO FLY out immediately; there was no sense in sticking around when they had failed. More missing persons were reported in the news daily, and it was growing into a phenomenon in the United States and France. One city in Texas had its homeless population completely disappear, which some people were actually celebrating.

If only they knew what was to come.

"What is she doing with them? Hoarding them?" Sera asked as they drove back toward the airport in Nidheesh's cab. The top of a large white marble building, adorned with what looked like a statue of an angel, flashed by between the surrounding trees.

"Training them," Theo said. "New Bacchae are wildly unpredictable and usually continue to be for a few decades. It can take up to a century for them to really master control over their new, heightened senses and powers."

"Wow. Alexander was new, right? He seemed so different from Solomon," she said, although that was an understatement.

The two Bacchae were night and day. Literally, one had been an overweight, pasty-skinned white guy until Sera turned him into shiny dust. And the other was a black Adonis. She certainly didn't blame Nora for falling for Solomon, but he would die soon if Sera had her way. All the Bacchae would.

"Alexander was the last Bacchae they created before Bacchus removed the ability twenty years ago," Theo said.

A twinge pulled at Sera's heart as she thought about her mother followed quickly by a flood of guilt when she realized she had been focused solely on Hiro's death. "Yeah, Danae killed my mom to try to stop it."

Theo snapped his head sideways to look at her. "What?"

"My mom was a witch and was trying to find the amulet after Bacchus called out to her. He knew she was powerful enough, with the help of a coven, to remove the Bacchae's ability to create new Bacchae. But Danae found them." Her eyes lost focus as she stared out the cab window, imagining the scene in the cave Renee had described.

And one that old moves with an inhuman grace and speed that is simply remarkable, Renee had said. A chill ran up her spine, causing her to shudder.

"Renee was one of the witches who escaped, and so was Leif. My mom wasn't so lucky. I just wish I knew what Danae had done with all their remains, so we could give them a proper burial." Sera clenched her fists in her lap.

"I had no idea. I'm sorry." Genuine sorrow sounded in his voice.

"I lost her so long ago, but it doesn't make it any easier to learn she was killed for the amulet. I am proud of her, though, for trying to stop that monster."

"It makes more sense why Bacchus chose you," he said.

She huffed. "It's not believable that he chose me simply because I'm me?"

Dimples flashed as he grinned. "Ah, you don't want me to answer that."

Sera reached out to punch him lightly on his arm, but he caught her hand in his before the hit could land. Her breath hitched in her throat, and her body warmed in response.

Shit. She snatched her hand back. Hareni was right, it was that damn beard. Why couldn't Xolotl have picked someone less attractive and kind, someone like Lorenzo or Alexander? She shuddered. Thinking of the two Bacchae thoroughly quenched any rising desires.

"It's more believable knowing about your Gift. Let's just stick with that," Theo said with a chuckle. Either he hadn't noticed her distress at the emotion invoked with his touch, or he was pretending not to.

"So, what now?" Sera asked, looking out the window to distract herself.

Nidheesh's phone rang, and he answered it on his earbud.

"We go back home, rest up, and continue our search. I've got a lead on an African god now living in the Caribbean," Theo said.

"I'm so glad we'll be going to the Caribbean to search for a god and *not* on vacation." Sera glared at him. Meteorologists were predicting an exceptionally cold and snowy winter for the District that year, the first after several mild ones.

Nidheesh disconnected his call. "I have some bad news, my friends. The High Council of the Bacchae has been destroyed."

* * *

AFTER ANOTHER LONG FLIGHT and a traffic-jammed drive later, one exhausted mortal and one sharp-as-ever immortal walked into a witch's library. It sounded like the start of a bad joke, only Sera felt the reality deep in her weary bones.

Nora squealed with delight as she ran over to hug her. "You're back! I can't *wait* to show you what I can do!"

Sera rubbed her ear, only partially pretending to be in

pain from the shrill sound. It just didn't make sense that someone so tiny could be so loud. "I can't wait to see it, especially if it means saving my hearing."

She smiled at the face Nora made.

"Yes, Nora has quite the innate talent with magic," Renee added.

"I'm glad things went well here. We've got some bad news, though." She nodded to Theo.

"Danae has taken over the Council," he said as he leaned against the doorframe.

"What does that mean exactly?" Renee asked, her lips pressed together in a thin line.

"All of the Eternals are missing, and if the rumors are true, they're being held captive. Danae has set up her new Bacchae, created from her own blood, in their place. She's calling the new Council the 'Court of the Everlasting,'" he explained. "It means she's one step closer to making her dream a reality."

Silence filled the room as they all took in the meaning of his words and looked at one another.

"But you found Freyja," Nora said at last, ever the optimist. She and Nidheesh would have gotten along well.

"Yes," Sera said and set down her bag. Digging through it to find the torc, her skin tingled when she touched the metal with her bare hands.

A sleepy yawn filled her mind, followed by the sounds of the goddess moaning slightly as if she stretched. *Are we there yet?*

"Yes, Freyja, we're here. I'd like you to meet my friend Renee, the witch, and my best friend, Nora. Well, Eleanor, but we all call her Nora." She held the torc up toward them.

Nora's mouth fell open and Renee inhaled sharply when they saw the gold and amber necklace in front of them.

Oh my, give me to the blonde one! Freyja's once-sleepy voice was instantly awake. *Her energy is unlike anything I've felt in centuries. There's something special about her.*

Sera placed the torc in Nora's hand and watched as her face went through a series of emotions—awe, shock, then adoration.

A familiar tug pulled at her heart as her friend's expression reminded her of how she felt whenever she was around Bacchus's amulet.

Tell her to put the torc around her neck. We're destined to be together, Freyja commanded. *Danae will cower before our glory.*

"Nora, Freyja wants you to wear the torc, which means she's choosing you to wield her power. I'm not sure if you want to think through the—" Sera paused as Nora immediately wrapped the artifact around her neck. "—potential consequences…"

For a moment, nothing happened. Then Nora began to glow, a bright pink aura that shimmered around the edges with gold.

CHAPTER 15

Solomon

Solomon remained quiet in his third-row seat on the drive from the cemetery to the queen's Parisian facility, a building he didn't even know existed until now. Anger threatened to rise within him, but he managed to keep it at bay for the time being. Immortals could sense the change in his scent, and he was in an SUV full of them.

Why hadn't Danae told him her plan for the cemetery? He already knew she had planned to take over the High Council; most of her guards had known. There was no chance she had found out about his meetings with Nora. He had been followed, of course, as all Immortals were, but it had been easy to lose the tails. Once, he had even changed his plans altogether and had gone for a drive. He was sure they had loved that.

He needed to get more information and get back to Nora before he lost her completely. If he could figure out what Danae's next move was going to be, he might just be able to convince Nora of his sincerity.

In the row ahead of him, Danae stared at the amulet in her gloved hand, sitting as still as a statue. Was she trying to speak to the god?

She snapped her fist closed over the silver necklace and thrust it back into her pocket. "We need to determine who among them we can trust, if any, and whose blood we will use next. The Ordog will be pleased with our success and will welcome the next sacrifice."

Solomon frowned. Who, or *what*, was the Ordog?

"Solomon." Her girlish voice took on a different note, almost timid.

"Your Majesty?"

"Who do you think we can sway?" she asked.

"Eratosthenes appeared to approve of your actions. Until he was restrained, of course," he said.

"What about Imhotep?"

He tilted his head to the side as he considered the other Eternal. There was a difference in opinion among the Council members—some of them believed they should use their powers to help humans, and the others felt, as Danae did, that they should control them. At least from the shadows. He didn't think any of them had desired to rule their entire kind outright except Danae. Because he had gone against Jupiter's direct orders in creating the Bacchae, Bacchus had strictly forbidden them from becoming too prominent in society. No one had dared defy him.

Until now.

"Unknown. Has he chosen a side?" he asked.

"Not yet, but the activities he's about to participate in may help persuade him," she said.

Yumiko snickered next to the queen.

"What activities?" he asked.

"Blood from the Eternals will make us more powerful than you can imagine. More powerful than the few gods who still plague the earth. Dedicating the Eternals' lives to the Ordog, as well as all the humans we kill, will soon make him King of the Underworld."

"Who is the Ordog?" Solomon asked, hoping this conversation meant she was open to sharing more.

"The Christians know him as the Devil."

He was glad she couldn't see his face from his place in the backseat. "I don't understand how he will be able to help you from the underworld."

"The Ordog rules the dark magic in this world. When I have him fully on my side, my magic will be without limits and unstoppable. He and I will rule as King and Queen, and our children will become the unquestionable heirs of the earth, ruling until the end of time."

Immortals could not procreate in the biological sense, so Solomon assumed she referred to those most loyal to her, those made from her own blood. As he thought about the kind of power she would wield if she succeeded, the hair on his arms and neck raised, and he itched to rub the scar running through his eyebrow. Perhaps she had figured out a way for Immortals to conceive. He held back a shudder.

They turned off the main road and traveled a mile down a private drive lined with lush forest until they reached what could only be described as a small palace, complete with turrets and arrow slits. Green ivy snaked its way up the grey stones, wrapping long tendrils around anything within reach.

The driveway continued in front of the palace's entryway, circling around a fountain of scantily clad nymphs being chased through the water by grinning satyrs. Danae didn't seem the type to embrace her Bacchic heritage, so the Roman mythological figures surprised Solomon. Perhaps she simply enjoyed the stories. As far as he knew, that was all the creatures were. But then again, people thought the same about his kind, as well, and look how wrong they had been.

Rather than parking in the front, their SUV continued driving around the back of the house, where they stopped next to a stone outbuilding. Following the others through the main doors of the smaller, though still quite large, building, Solomon halted in shock, unable to stop the bile that rose in his throat as he took in the scene before him.

Set up like a windowless barn or a small hangar, the structure's angled roof made the room feel larger than it actually was. Tables had been set up haphazardly, holding boxes of medical supplies. Because it was lit only from the natural light filtering in through the main entrance, the room would be pitch black when the doors closed. Even to an Immortal.

Against one of the longer side walls, the four other Eternals stood chained to the stone with silver shackles, their bound wrists and ankles red and blistered from where the metal touched their exposed skin. IVs attached to their elbows drained them of their blood, collecting it into bags attached to a standing pole. Their mouths had been gagged, but they all stared at Danae with the same open hatred.

The queen walked by them, checking each bag's contents. "After these are full, make sure they eat. If they refuse—" Her eyes flicked up to meet Liviana's, "force them, in whatever way is necessary."

The Immortal who walked at her side nodded and grinned. Sadists were among some of the first to seek their kind of immortality.

This was the future Danae had planned, and this was precisely why Solomon wouldn't be a part of it. As much as he loved the restoration of his Immortal abilities and enhanced senses, he would not be a willing participant of such moral destruction. Not any longer. He would play the part to gain information to help the resistance, but he would not do anything to further Danae's plan.

His mouth ran dry, but he resisted the temptation to lick his lips. If he hadn't been totally sure before, the blood banks the Eternals had become convinced him.

* * *

TWO DAYS LATER, THEY were back in the District, and Solomon was finally able to get some time away from the Immortals—and Danae. Time was passing much too quickly; the past few decades had made him almost forget the passing of time due to the monotony of life within Lorenzo's employ. Now, he felt as though he could hardly catch his breath, let alone find time to himself.

After sending Nora a message on the burner phone he had picked up, Solomon waited for her outside her apartment. If he couldn't convince her he was telling the truth, the world would be doomed…

Although, perhaps then she would accept his offer of

Immortality, and they could—

No. If she was going to become Immortal, he wanted it to be on her own terms, not because she had no other choice.

He hadn't been sure she would answer his text messages, but a moment later, her door opened. Nora looked out into the common area hallway from her door and waved him over. Despite the early morning hour, she looked flawless in her blue pajama pants and a hooded sweatshirt. He wanted to reach out and stroke her cheek, but he knew that would be pushing his luck. Mainly because he'd be tempted to do so much more.

"I have information I know you and your friends will want to hear," Solomon said as he approached her door. He slowed just before he reached her, catching a change in her usual oatmeal scent. Something wild and untamed lay beneath it, along with a hint of winter's frost.

Eyeing him, she chewed on her lip. After a brief pause, she held the door open and stepped back. "Come on in."

Solomon hesitated; he had expected to talk in the hallway. What had changed from the last time they spoke? Whatever it was, he didn't wait any longer to see if she would change her mind. He stepped over the threshold, no invisible barrier barring his way. He had been there plenty of times in the past, of course, but she had revoked his invitation.

"Go sit on the couch while I grab some tea. I assume you don't want any." Nora turned and walked away, not waiting for a reply.

He smiled at her usual display of confidence with a predator at her back before sitting where she indicated.

The apartment living room looked the same as it usually did, pristine and tastefully decorated. Just like the woman living in it. A cream-colored sofa with pink arabesque patterned throw pillows sat against the side wall with a rectangular coffee table, vaguely reminiscent of a surfboard as was common in the 1950s, standing in front of it. Light pink vases holding succulents and other small plants graced the surface of the table as well as the midcentury modern side tables. Two windows in the back wall overlooked the city street a few floors below.

But the real centerpiece of the room hung behind the sofa. Three large canvas prints of Marilyn Monroe, Nora's idol, adorned the walls. All three were black and white photographs of the bombshell, with a splash of vivid pink for her lips.

When she returned, Nora sat on the opposite end of the three-seater couch, leaving plenty of space between them. She held her teacup with both hands. "Talk."

"Danae has taken over the Council and—"

"We already know that." Nora sipped her tea.

"They're being held—"

"We know," she interrupted again.

Solomon held up a hand to stop her. "And drained of their blood. Continuously."

Nora's mouth stayed open, her eyes widened in surprise. "*Why?*"

"As payment to a god of the underworld, the Ordog, in exchange for the darkest magic the world will have ever seen." He let that sink in. "The blood of the Eternals is powerful stuff, and when she uses it with the demonic magic provided by the Ordog, she will be unstoppable."

"Even against gods?" Nora smirked, her hand reaching up to rub the fabric of the sweatshirt around her neck.

"Yes."

She tilted her head to the side, and her gaze lost focus. "What if we had help from our own god of the underworld?" she asked after another moment.

"I don't know," he said. "Danae's plan is for the Ordog to rule the underworld and all of its inhabitants, including the other gods. If there's one stronger than he is now who can stop him, then we might be able to do something."

Nora nodded. "There is."

"How do you know?"

"Freyja told me," she said.

"Freyja?"

"The Norse goddess," she said.

"I mean, I know *who* she is. But how and when did she tell you?" The incomplete answers were maddening, and he knew from the scent drifting off her that she was enjoying it.

"Just now." Nora pulled her scarf down, revealing an antique-looking metal torc embedded with yellowish-orange gemstones. "We're besties."

Solomon stared at the woman who owned his heart. Of course a goddess would choose her, and that explained the change in her scent. He shook his head and chuckled.

Nora narrowed her eyes at him. "Why are you laughing?"

"Because you continue to amaze me," he said.

She took a sip of tea, but he could see the smile hidden behind the cup she held to her mouth.

"Have I proven myself to you? Or perhaps to Freyja?"

Solomon asked, revealing his own smile with a small quirk to the side of his mouth.

She set down her now empty cup. "It's definitely good information, but—" She stopped as he closed the space between them and took her delicate hand in his.

"Nora, I haven't stopped thinking of you for a moment. You've invaded my heart and my soul. Even if you won't have me, I won't stop fighting Danae."

She pulled her hand out of his, though he was sure it lingered. "How can you expect me to trust you again? You literally broke my best friend."

"I know, but I can't change the past. All I can do is move forward and prove to you I've changed," he said.

"Freyja tells me you're worthy of my trust, but I'm not a goddess who can see into your inner workings. You need to give me time."

His once seemingly dormant heart skipped a beat. There was hope. "Of course. Your world is my world, and I want to make it a good one, even if you won't have me again. I—"

Her soft lips found his as she threw herself at him, halting any further speech. Solomon wrapped his arms around her slight frame as he returned the kiss, their tongues finding each other hungrily. He pulled her legs around his waist before running his hands up her back to her hair, intertwining his fingers around the curly strands.

She pulled back and stared at him breathlessly, her cheeks flushed and green eyes sparkling with desire. "The world might end any day now, but if you break my heart, Freyja will rip out yours."

Laughing, he pulled her face closer to his. "Never, my

love." He gripped her hips as he stood, carrying her to the bedroom, her hands clenched in his hair. It had been far too long since he had been intimate with Nora, and he planned on tiring her out.

In her arms, he was home.

CHAPTER 16

Serafina

"I'm just so confused, Renee," Sera said while rinsing off the teacup. She handed it to Renee and grabbed the next soapy dish.

The older woman took the cup and dried it on a towel before setting it in the cabinet. "I can understand that this attraction to Theo may feel like a betrayal to Hiro, but it could also be a part of your grieving process. Perhaps you need comfort from someone who reminds you of him."

Sera stopped scrubbing a particularly stubborn spot on a plate to stare out the row house's kitchen window, though it was too dark to see anything. Comfort? Yes, it could be as simple as that. The two men had some similar qualities, that was for sure. But where Hiro had been lighthearted and fun, Theo was more reserved. To be fair, his humor did shine through from time to time.

The two women found themselves alone with the dishes that evening, and Sera had chosen to confide her conflicting emotions to Renee, who had become an almost motherly figure to her. After Nora put on the torc, she and Freyja had become instant friends, sparking jealousy inside Sera despite her happiness for her friend. The truth was she missed Bacchus and all his inappropriate comments.

She had been stewing in her dark thoughts while Nora went silent, communicating with the goddess in her mind until she went home to sleep, and Theo spent the time catching Renee up on their visit with Durga. Eventually, the detective left, presumably to do laundry or pack a new bag of clothes for whatever whirlwind adventure they would be on next.

Renee rested a hand on Sera's shoulder, startling her from her thoughts. "Or, it could be a part of Bacchus's sexual nature. He may not be with you physically, but that doesn't mean he didn't leave part of himself behind." She tapped Sera's forehead. "In here."

Returning her attention to the plate, Sera rinsed the dish and handed it to Renee before meeting her sympathetic gaze. "I hadn't even considered that." She dried her hands on a towel. "Do you really think it's possible?"

"Yes, I do." Renee placed the dish in the cabinet and hung up the damp towel. "But what I really think is that you need some rest."

Sera smiled and wrapped her arms around the other woman in a tight hug. "Thank you. I knew talking to you was the right thing to do."

Renee chuckled returning the squeeze. "It usually is."

* * *

SOMETIME AFTER MIDNIGHT, Sera woke up again. She stared at the ceiling in the dark, wishing she had Bacchus to keep her company and organize her thoughts. Not to mention help her fall back asleep. All of the travel was messing with her internal clock.

After trying without success for an hour to will herself to sleep, she rolled out of bed, groaning as she jostled her still-healing bruises. She pulled on a loose sweater and a pair of leggings before heading downstairs for a cup of coffee.

A light was on in the library. Sera peeked her head in to see why Renee was still up.

Except it was Theo.

He must have returned after she went upstairs. The glow from the laptop illuminated his face, still covered in a scruffy beard. Her pulse beat rapidly at the sight, though she pretended it didn't. It was easier to ignore now, knowing that it could just be from Bacchus's lingering influence.

He looked up from the screen when she shuffled in. "Rested?"

Despite the yawn that escaped, she nodded. "Did Nora go home?"

"Yes, she's feeling pretty confident in her ability to keep herself safe now." Theo winked.

He really needed to stop being smiley and nice and go back to the stern demeanor Sera had known before. Back to before the butterflies in her belly.

He was a lot less likable then.

"I'm sure she is. I should have known Freyja would instantly love Nora." She sat down on one of the purple wingback chairs, tucking one leg beneath her. Hugging the other raised leg, she rested her chin on her bent knee.

"I've got two leads at this point, and the good news is they're both in the Caribbean," he said.

"What's the bad news?" she asked.

Theo furrowed his brow. "No bad news, just good news."

"Oh, it's just the way you said—" She stopped. "Never mind. Good news it is, then."

"I'm booking us flights for later today." He returned his gaze to the laptop.

Sera groaned. "So, you did have bad news."

"I don't consider working fast to stop Danae's plan to be bad news." He didn't look up from his computer, which was good because it meant he didn't see her eye roll.

"How are your bruises?" he asked.

"Healing, thanks for asking."

Theo nodded, his dark eyes moving back and forth as they scanned the screen. "Good. I don't want injuries to slow us down."

Sera snorted. *He is all business.*

He looked up at her again. "What?"

"Nothing. I can't sleep anymore, so I'm going to go get some coffee. You want anything?"

Shaking his head, he returned his gaze to the computer.

She paused as she unwound her legs from the chair. "Do you ever eat? Or is that one of the downsides to being immortal?"

"One of the downsides? Most people would consider that a perk." He laughed, his dimples appearing deeper in the low lighting.

Gods, he is an attractive man. Damn you, Bacchus. At least, she really hoped it was Bacchus's fault.

"I like food." She shrugged as her stomach growled in response. Perfect timing. She needed a distraction. "Coffee and a midnight snack coming right up."

* * *

A FEW HOURS LATER, as sunlight started to drift up over the horizon, a soft scratching sound came from the back door. Renee was still sleeping, so Sera set her cup of coffee on the kitchen table before approaching the door. She pulled the blinds back. A small, dark-skinned boy, who might have been in his early teens, stared back at her.

She gave him a questioning look.

Let us in, let us in, or we'll blow your house down, a snickering voice echoed around her head.

Who are you? she sent her thought back.

Ah! So the rumors of your Gift are true. Your canine friend talked of a fight? We're in. She could almost see the grinning smile in the shadows of her mind.

You didn't answer my question, she said.

I am Eshu. So matter-of-fact, so not what she was looking for.

Sera muttered under her breath. *Damn gods.*

Technically, he had answered her question. She unlocked and opened the door.

"And who are you?" she asked the boy. He had on faded jeans, worn sneakers, and a t-shirt in near-freezing temperatures.

"Manny," he said.

"Well, get in out of the cold. You're not even wearing a

real sweater."

The boy stepped into the kitchen just as Theo walked in from the hallway, his eyes opening wide as he saw the boy.

"Who might this be?" he asked, filling a glass with water.

"Manny," Sera answered, indicating one of the kitchen chairs to the boy. "Sit, I'll get you some food. You look hungry." Starving was more like it. The kid's clothes hung loosely on his thin frame. He eyed the toast she had just made with open interest.

"And Manny is…?" Theo looked curiously at her.

"Connected with Eshu. Whoever that is." A moment after she set the toast on a plate in front of Manny, he shoved the entire piece into his mouth.

You're not very worldly, are you. It was a statement from the other god, not a question.

Sera huffed. *And you're not taking very good care of this boy. Why are you working with a kid, anyway? Have you merged?*

No, no. But everyone underestimates children… Eshu snickered like a pleased weasel.

"He's working with a kid?" Theo asked.

Sera threw her hands up in the air. "Right? He thinks everyone underestimates children. Which is probably true, but I'm also curious to know where this kid's parents are."

Manny is an orphan. No one will miss him, the god said.

The blunt statement stung Sera's heart. It may have been true, but, damn, it didn't need to be so casual.

"Well, I'm glad he showed up. One less god to track down. Eshu is still widely worshipped in the Yoruba communities, although nothing like Durga. He's a messenger between the gods and people, so he may be able to help us convince others to join us," Theo said, then drained his glass of water. "I'd watch my back, though."

Her skin prickled. "Why?"

"Show her what you took." Theo nodded at Manny.

The boy managed to look guilty with his mouth full of the second piece of toast. He held out his palm, displaying the brown leather watch Sera had been wearing before she let him in.

She gasped and grabbed her bare wrist. "How is that even possible?"

A high-pitched giggle resounded in her mind. *A magician never reveals his secrets.*

Groaning, she took the watch back from the boy. "If you're going to work with us, we need to set some ground rules. First and foremost is don't steal from your friends." She fiddled with her watch as she returned to the kitchen counter to make more toast.

Ohh, are we friends now? What are the other rules? he asked. A vision of a thin black-skinned man twiddling his thumbs flashed through her mind.

"I don't know yet, but I'll let you know when I do."

Eshu cackled.

"This is going to be exhausting," Sera said to Theo. "I'm going to be babysitting, aren't I?"

"Something tells me he is more than capable of watching himself." He grinned at her.

Looking back toward Manny, she saw an empty seat and the kid nowhere to be found. "What the hell!"

They found him in the library, somehow already fast asleep on the rug in front of the fireplace screen. Words of chastisement died on her tongue as Sera saw him curled up, looking very much like a lost little boy. Even though the room was warm, she grabbed a blanket from the basket next to the fire and laid it over him. A small bronze key hung on a thread around the kid's neck and had spilled out onto the ground next to him. She reached forward to get a better look at the antique metal.

No touching the merchandise, Eshu said with a waggle of his finger.

Sera rolled her eyes but respected the request. Well, she ignored the command, anyway.

After picking up his laptop, Theo tilted his head toward the hallway. She followed him back to the kitchen, wincing as the floorboards creaked beneath their feet.

"I feel like I'm going to be breaking a few different international laws having him here. Although it's technically Renee's house, so I guess it's her problem?" She crossed her eyes and made a face. Pulling more crispy toast from the toaster, she sat at the table and crunched on the bread.

Theo chuckled. "I'm sure she'll figure out a way to deal with it, although I'm not sure how she'll feel about the additional guest."

He was right. Sera had stayed there regularly since Leif ransacked her apartment, and that was over a month ago. Nora stayed every once in a while, and even Theo had come back the previous night. Renee had a full house on her hands. If she minded, she was very good at hiding it.

"What else do you know about Eshu?" she asked.

Taking the chair across from her, he rubbed his beard. "Not a whole lot. He's a bit of a sly fox, as you discovered."

Sera snorted over her piece of toast. "He did use magic, right? There's no way someone can actually steal a watch off

189

someone's wrist."

A smile crossed his face. At least the beard helped hide his dimples reasonably well.

"I couldn't tell you. Stealing isn't a skill I possess."

"Can he fight?" she asked.

"Yes. He's frighteningly fast and nimble. His enemies have found a knife in their sides without ever seeing it, or him, coming."

It was hard for Sera to envision a kid as young as Manny capable of committing such crimes. But even she had taken down a few Bacchae with a god's power coursing through her veins, and she definitely didn't consider herself capable of such a thing before then.

Opening his laptop, Theo returned to his search.

Sera watched him work in silence for a few minutes. "Don't you have a home here? Or a job?"

He looked up at her, amusement showing in the small upturn of his lips. "Trying to get rid of me? I took a week of vacation. I don't go back until Friday."

"No, just wondering what you *do* all day and night." She stood and started the coffee maker again.

"Research." He continued to type.

"On gods?"

"Among other things," he said.

"Are you being cryptic on purpose?" She leaned her back against the counter.

Theo sighed. "Are we playing a question game?"

"I'm just curious what an immortal does with all his extra time."

"Right now, it's work. We need more power before we can face Danae, but we're running out of time. Her army continues to grow. So, if you'd stop interrupting me, I'd like to get back to finding out who we can convince next."

Sera blinked at him. "You don't have to be rude about it."

He slammed his laptop shut. "I'm going to pick up some things at my place. I'll be back later tonight." Without waiting for a reply, he grabbed the computer and strode from the room.

Her mouth hung open in surprise. Had her questions really riled him up that much? The coffee maker beeped as it finished brewing. She sighed as she poured her cup and padded quietly into the library, trying not to wake the boy up.

Sipping on her coffee, she watched him sleep, trying to figure out what the hell had angered Theo so much about her questions.

Renee shuffled in, her slippers a soft whisper against the wood floors. "Good morning. Did Theo leave again?"

"Yes, just a few minutes ago."

Renee glanced at the fireplace and jerked her head back. She must have noticed the boy by the fire for the first time.

"And who's this?"

CHAPTER 17

Serafina

When Manny finally opened his eyes, shadows reached long fingers across the wooden floors of the hallway outside the library. The room itself had no windows due to its placement within the middle of the row house and sharing a brick wall with the house next door, but a quick glance at her watch revealed it was almost sunset. Days had gotten very short.

Sera unfolded her legs from beneath her, replacing the book she read on the stack it had come from. Renee had left an hour or so prior to gather some magical supplies, and Sera had spent the day reading and napping. If only she could enjoy it like a real vacation day.

The boy stretched and rubbed his eyes.

"Hungry?" she asked, his gaze still glossy.

He nodded.

"Good, me too. There's a burger place not far from here. Let's go stretch our legs." She stood and tilted her head toward the door.

"Theo?" Manny's second word since he had arrived.

"He went to pick up some of his things. Come on."

He didn't protest as she led him to the front door and bundled him up in some of the extra winter clothes Renee had hanging on the coat rack.

As they ambled down the street in silence, their breath puffed out in small clouds before them. Row houses of all colors faced the two-lane road, and sparse trees lined narrow sidewalks. In the spring and summer, those same trees would provide a green canopy over both directions of traffic. Canopies like that were one of Sera's favorite features of the historic neighborhoods around the District. They passed an empty public park and playground on the way to the restaurant, typical in that area of the District, especially in the winter.

The Burger Joint was busy that afternoon, so Sera got their food to go. A few minutes later, they headed back to the playground park to eat at one of the picnic tables. There was no one else there, so they had privacy to chat about their world while they ate. She brushed crispy yellow and brown leaves off of the top of the table before taking a seat.

"So, where are you from, Manny?" she asked after handing him his burger and fries.

"Santo Domingo."

She stared at him. "The Dominican Republic? How the heck did you get to the United States?"

Shrugging, he kept eating.

Sera watched him as they ate, trying to think of a way to get him to open up more. It was clear he kept himself pretty guarded. Or maybe he didn't speak English very well. But Eshu should be able to help translate if that was the case. Maybe he just didn't like her.

The streetlamps flickered to life as the sun slid behind the buildings, and a breeze ruffled the leaves around them. Two swings attached to the play structure creaked as they moved in the wind. Despite the chill in the air, it was peaceful.

Manny looked up at her, his eyes curious, and tilted his head to the side.

I'm relatively confident in our abilities, but you may want to send a message to your canine friend to join us. Quickly. Eshu suggested, his tone nonchalant despite the urgent wording.

What? Why? she asked.

You're wasting time. Call for the cavalry. Eshu sounded a trumpet in her mind.

As she realized his meaning, her blood ran cold. Her hands shook as she pulled out her phone and sent a text message to Theo with their location. *Hurry,* she sent as a second message.

No sooner had she put her phone back into her pocket than the shadows around the park began to move. Bacchae stepped into the limited light as if forming out of the shadows themselves. Sera looked around for an escape, but the park was fully enclosed with a six-foot-high wrought iron fence. The only exit was the gate they came in, exactly where the Bacchae approached.

Manny's back was to them. He kept eating his burger as five men and two women wearing sunglasses and dark wool coats stalked toward the park, faces serious.

Goosebumps spread across Sera's arms. No Bacchus to save her ass with fancy fighting moves this time.

"As much as we'd love for this to get messy," one of the men said as he approached their table, a few of the others snickering at his words, "we can avoid the bloodshed if you come along without resisting. Our queen would like to have some words with you."

Sera glared at him, though her heart threatened to beat a hole through her chest. "I have nothing to say to Danae."

Growling, he removed his sunglasses, revealing the blood-red, cat-like eyes characteristic of a Bacchae. "Her Majesty has approved the use of force to detain you, if necessary."

Her mind raced, trying to figure out how to stall the fight that was about to happen. There was no way she was going to go with them willingly. Manny continued munching on the remaining french fries as if nothing was out of the ordinary.

Seriously, kid? she thought.

"Do you honestly think she's going to win? How is she going to overpower whole governments and armies?" Sera asked the group of Bacchae.

The majority of them grinned back, though two stared at her in silence, raw hunger in their eyes. New Bacchae were wildly unpredictable and had difficulty controlling their urges to feed. Chances were, these were all relatively new Bacchae. Sera gulped.

Manny picked up his soda and drank from the straw.

Run, Eshu's voice advised her.

The boy winked before turning around and hurling the

cup at the Bacchae who had spoken to them. She was sure Manny hadn't expected the cup to harm the man, but it provided an element of surprise as he raised his arm to ward off the cup's blow.

Before any of the Bacchae had a chance to react, the first was on the ground, a few feet away from where he had stood. Manny crouched down after the kick. He eyed the Bacchae in front of him before tumbling to the left. Sweeping the legs out from beneath one of the women, he threw a handful of mulch on her face, distracting her.

The other Bacchae sprang into action. Two of the men charged toward Sera while the other three went after Manny, the obvious threat. Sera practically fell off the picnic table's bench as she scrambled to get away, but she somehow managed to get herself back upright and behind the playground structure. It provided a bit of an obstacle from the two coming after her.

Over the pounding pulse in her ears, grunts and growls came from the fight with Manny, but her mind focused on avoiding the other two. They split up, each going around the structure from the sides. Grabbing the yellow bars, she pulled herself up and over, onto a little bridge, just as the men reached where she had been standing. She hopped over their hands stretching through the bars and raced for the slide.

As she landed at the bottom of the slide, a hand shot out from beneath and grabbed her ankle. She fell face-first into the mulch as she tried to run.

Arms wrapped around her and pulled her to her feet as she spat out pieces of mulch.

"Your resistance only makes this more fun," the

Bacchae holding her said, his unnaturally cold breath freezing the hairs on her neck.

She tried to squirm away from him, her eyes darting around like a trapped rabbit. "Seriously, let me go. You're not going to enjoy what's coming next."

He laughed and dragged her out of the park toward an awaiting SUV, though she tried valiantly to stop him by kicking and flailing and digging her feet into the dirt. Eventually, he just lifted her off the ground as if she weighed next to nothing.

She caught sight of Manny just before the Bacchae pushed her into the back of the vehicle. The boy was holding his own against the four remaining Bacchae, moving like a parkour pro across the playground. One of the men was gone. She gritted her teeth, hoping Manny had killed him.

As soon as the door closed, she tried the handle, but the bastards had enabled the child lock. The two who had seized her slid into the front seats, tires squealing as they pulled away.

"Your friend fights well. Who is he?" one of the men asked.

Sera snorted in response. As if she would tell him. Her breath came out in shallow bursts as much from fear as from the chase. Just as she pulled out her phone, the SUV jumped the curb and hit a tree. She flew forward into the back of the front seat. Thankfully, they hadn't had time to get up to a speed that would have inflicted more damage.

The sound of metal groaning and tearing free filled the air. Trying to escape the awful noise, she covered her ears with her hands. Sera looked up to see the driver's side door completely ripped off, and the Bacchae yelped as he was yanked from his seat.

Deep growling and snarling filled the air and her mind, and Sera breathed a sigh of relief. Theo had arrived. She scrambled back up onto the seat from her place on the floor as the other Bacchae jumped out of the vehicle to join the fight. Theo was still in human form, but his eyes had turned a bright gold color and crackled like lightning across a brooding sky.

Climbing over the seats to the front, Sera jumped out of the SUV just as the second Bacchae dissolved into sparkling dust. The first was nowhere to be seen. She grinned at Theo, who looked at her in surprise.

A moment later, she was staring at the orange and pink hues of sunset as she found herself flat on her back, the air knocked out of her. A snarling face appeared in front of her, fangs extended. The Bacchae drew his head back to strike.

Closing her eyes, Sera prepared to die. This was it. The end.

Nothing happened. She opened one eye to see a golden haze settling around her, Theo's hand outstretched and gripped in the place of where the Bacchae's heart had once been. She let out her breath in a rush.

Theo pulled her back to her feet, his hands feeling electric under her own. She looked up into his eyes, which had returned to their usual dark brown, a thank you on her lips. But she stopped when she realized how close their faces were, and they hadn't let go of each other's hands. She could feel his ragged breath warm on her skin, and her heart skipped a few beats.

"You're not hurt?" he asked, moving his hands up to the sides of her face. Despite the ferocity he displayed in the fight just moments before, his touch was gentle.

She shook her head, unable to form words as her pulse raced.

Theo's eyes moved from hers down to her lips, tracing them with his thumb. Her breath caught in her throat, the sensation of his touch sending shivers down her body. Before she could speak, he leaned down and kissed her, his beard tickling the skin around her mouth in a not-unpleasant way. She couldn't resist. Her body melted into his, and she opened her mouth as she returned the kiss.

Footsteps pounding on the pavement interrupted their moment. They both pulled away, the sudden movement and cold air on her face a disappointing shock.

"You guys okay?" Nora's voice rang out.

"Yeah." In the safety of the near dark, Sera could sense her face flush from the feeling of getting caught doing something she shouldn't be. Even if it was due to Bacchus's influence, how could she let herself do that?

As Nora and Manny approached, Sera's heart felt like it dropped out beneath her as she caught sight of Solomon. A streetlight's yellow glow cast shadows across his face, making his features look more menacing than usual. Or maybe her hatred of the Bacchae changed how he looked. She didn't really care either way.

"What's *he* doing here?" she asked, wishing her eyes could actually shoot daggers at him.

"He's on our side. I promise." Nora smiled up at him as she reached over and took his hand. "And he knows Freyja will destroy him if he betrays us."

Sera blinked at her friend. How gullible was she? Was Solomon controlling her mind? "How can you possibly believe he's on our side?"

"He just killed two of the Bacchae attacking you guys," Nora said. "But before that, he told me the details of how Danae plans to take over."

Suppressing a bitter laugh, Sera couldn't believe what she was hearing. "He's lying to you, Nor. Don't you find it oddly convenient that he turned up right when we get ambushed, and he manages to 'help' you take down the Bacchae?"

"No, I don't. He was with me when Theo called me about the ambush. I believe Solomon," said Nora. "And so does Freyja."

"Well, *I* certainly don't," Sera snapped.

"Why don't we hear what he has to say?" Theo asked, placing a hand on her arm.

She snatched her arm away from his touch. "Am I the only one who hasn't lost her mind? This evil *creature* stood idly by while Danae murdered Hiro. She nearly drained him before slitting his throat right in front of me. I'm not going to just pretend he's suddenly a good guy now."

"You're right." Solomon's words cut through the tension. "I'm not a good guy. I've witnessed and done some terrible things. But I don't condone the destruction of the human race, and I'm going to help you stop Danae whether you want my help or not."

A battle raged inside of Sera as she glared at him, moisture pooling in her eyes. On the one hand, she couldn't imagine him telling the truth or fighting by her side after what he had done, or rather, what he had *not* done. But on the other hand, they needed all the help they could get, and if he was telling the truth, he'd be an excellent source of information. Oh, how she hated logic.

He may be a devil, but he's not the *devil. He's not tricking you.* Eshu's voice intruded into her thoughts.

Sera glanced at Manny. *How do you know?*

I wrote the book on tricks. Snickers.

Of course you did. She looked back to Solomon, her fists clenching. A gusting wind whipped her hair in front of her eyes, watering from the chilly air, unexpected grief, and guilt.

"Let's at least get in out of the cold until a decision is made," Nora said, ushering everyone in the direction of Renee's house.

Turning toward Theo to explain herself, he seemed to avoid her gaze as he followed Nora and the others, his hands tucked into his pockets. She hadn't meant to hurt his feelings if she did, but she wasn't ready to open her heart back up. Hell, it had been less than a month since losing Hiro, and the world was a hot mess. *She* was a hot mess. Now was not the time to be thinking of romance.

Sera glanced back at the SUV, still parked in the tree it had run into. The street they were on was a side street, which meant the accident had gone mostly unnoticed. The few onlookers had continued on their way when they saw a group of people standing and no injuries. No need to stay and gawk, for any of them. It was Danae's mess to clean up.

Sighing, she followed the moon's light back toward the row house. Maybe she was the one losing her mind, and everyone else was just fine.

CHAPTER 18

Solomon

The silver-haired witch arrived once they had all settled into the library, the boy sitting cross-legged in front of the fireplace while the others took a seat. Standing behind Nora's wingback chair, Solomon remained quiet as Renee looked around the room, taking in their ruffled attire and general disheveled nature. He inclined his head to her in respect as her eyes settled on his, surprise written across her face.

Although he had returned to the Virginia training facility to avoid suspicion shortly after his and Nora's rekindling, they had been communicating via his burner phone non-stop. After he'd left her apartment, she had become apprehensive again, worrying that she had made a mistake and that she wasn't ready to trust him again. He had returned to her place to talk right when Theo called. Thankfully, Freyja had reassured Nora of his utter destruction should he betray her.

But neither woman had been entirely sure whether the witch would allow him to stay or kick him out. They were about to find out.

"Does someone want to give me a quick recap?" Renee asked.

"Sera and Manny were ambushed. Theo had to rescue Sera." Nora grinned at Serafina's snort. "And Solomon is here to help."

As he laid a hand on Nora's shoulder, she reached up to give it a squeeze. He couldn't help the small smile that sneaked out with her touch.

The witch considered them for a moment before nodding. "Okay, then. Sorry I missed the action." She chuckled.

Relief settled over him. She would allow him to stay. For the time being, anyway.

"One of them got away, but it was before Solomon arrived. He's going to be a double agent," Nora said in a matter-of-fact tone.

Sensing Serafina glaring at him from her chair, he ignored it. The girl could mope and live in the past all she wanted. He had Nora on his side, albeit tentatively, and that was all that mattered.

"A double agent, huh? You aren't worried about Danae finding out?" the witch asked, her forehead creasing as her eyebrows pulled together.

"Not yet," he said. "She trusts me as one of her advisors, and she has enough distracting her after the

Council takeover. The tails she assigns are superficial, a formality. It won't last forever, though."

As Solomon provided the group with the information he had given to Nora earlier in the day, Theo made a sound of disgust when he described the captive Eternals and Danae's plan with the Ordog. Even Serafina's look of disdain softened.

"Not all Immortals are like Danae and Lorenzo. Some of us prefer to live quietly alongside mortals," he said. It took a lot of effort not to give Serafina a meaningful glance.

"Freyja wants to reach out to Hel for assistance," Nora jumped in. "Hel is the Norse goddess of the underworld. She doesn't usually involve herself in the mortal world, but if she knows the underworld is under attack, she may be more likely to help."

"How do we contact Hel?" the witch asked.

"We'll need to summon her—you, me, and Freyja," Nora said. "We'll need a good amount of space to do the spell because she rides a—" Nora arched an eyebrow as she paused— "a three-legged horse called a helhest. Odd."

"I've got one more contact I want to pursue in the Caribbean," Theo said. "I can go there while you speak with Hel."

"I'll go with you," Serafina said, without hesitation.

Theo regarded her. "Fine. We'll leave tomorrow morning if I can get us on a flight."

The detective's stern expression hinted something had happened between the two of them. Solomon inhaled and caught the astringent scent of guilt wafting off the girl. Interesting. What had caused her to feel so guilty? Perhaps Nora knew.

But did he really care? Not really.

* * *

BEFORE THE SUN CAME up the next day, Solomon took one of the Yukons instead of the Maserati, to be less conspicuous. As usual, he had a tail, which he lost without trouble. Following him was part of the new recruits' training plan, and one they rarely succeeded at. When they did, it was because he allowed them to.

Solomon returned to the witch's house with a few stolen supplies for their summoning spell. The queen planned to fly back to California in a few days after meeting with and evaluating all the new Immortals. Praise Bacchus, Serafina and Theo had already left for their flight, so he didn't have to worry about dealing with any hard feelings toward him—Renee had accepted his presence reasonably well, and Manny didn't know the details. Nor would the boy care to, he was sure.

He drove the four of them in the dark to an abandoned golf course in Maryland. Pulling the SUV onto the grass of an old fairway, he parked near a dense patch of trees, shielding them from the neighborhood on the other side. It was a frosty and dreary morning, which would help keep inhabitants from noticing their presence. Chances were most people weren't even awake that early.

While Solomon and the boy watched from the side, Nora directed the witch in setting up the spell as she received instructions from Freyja, though Renee had to make a few minor adjustments based on their supplies. Because the sun had yet to rise, they used the glare from the vehicle's headlights to guide them. The two women poured salt mixed with charcoal on the patchy brown grass in a large circle, careful to ensure there were no gaps.

"The charcoal symbolizes the underworld to call Hel forth, while the salt will keep her anchored to her realm. It also makes sure anything else that tags along doesn't get loose," Renee explained when they finished their preparation. "That's the last thing we need."

The hairs on the back of his neck stood on end as he recalled the shadowy black figure Leif had called forth during his meeting with Danae. With any luck, nothing of the sort would accompany the goddess.

"You and Manny stand over there and wait." She pointed to a spot near the SUV.

Without hesitation, he and the boy did as they were told. Solomon was sure neither one of them wanted to be closer than necessary.

After some final tweaks to their setup, Renee removed her glasses, and the two women took their places in front of the large circle, joining hands. They repeated an incantation in an old form of Norwegian, some phrase Freyja had taught them. An eerie sense of foreboding settled onto Solomon's shoulders as the light breeze fell still, the leaves ceased their rustling, and all sounds other than the chanting faded to silence. Darkness enveloped everything outside the light of the headlamps in its impenetrable embrace.

The entire summoning circle burst into a roaring inferno stretching toward the morning sky. Manny took a step closer to him, raising his arm against the intense heat.

A moment later, the fire withdrew to the edges of the circle, dying down to a more gentle, foot-high flame. The undeniable sound of a horse whinnying and hooves beating the ground at a terrible pace echoed around them.

Within the ring of fire, the grass melted into a pool of bubbling black tar. A horse, the size of which Solomon had never seen—it must have been as tall as an elephant—and as dark as a starless night, coalesced out of the pit. Missing one of its front legs entirely, it landed on three hooves in front of them, just outside the tar but still within the circle.

A three-legged horse wouldn't normally terrify him but add in the empty eye sockets and sulfuric scent wafting off the hideous creature, and Solomon couldn't help taking a step back. Fire licked the beast's hooves and burned prints into the grass as it stamped and snorted. Its lips pulled back, foam frothing at its mouth, as a figure on its back pulled at the reins with gloved hands.

Sitting sidesaddle, the woman wore a long black robe with a hood covering the top half of her face, keeping it cloaked in shadows until she tilted her head back. Oh, and what a face it was. On one half, the skin that showed was hauntingly young and beautiful, half her lips red with life. But where her lips should have been on the other side, only teeth showed, her skin mottled blue and decaying. Bits of bone peeked through beneath the sagging flesh.

Death herself had arrived.

"Freyja, goddess of the Vanir, why have you summoned me to the mortal world?" Hel's voice echoed like a hundred wailing souls, nearly bringing Solomon to his knees in agony. Beside him, the boy winced and covered his ears.

"The Bacchae witch Danae grows too powerful and must be stopped." Freyja's melodious voice rang out from Nora's mouth. "She uses the blood of the other Eternal

Bacchae in her dark magic to feed the Ordog, who she plans to name King of the Underworld. We ask for your assistance in stopping her."

The colossal horse shuffled and tossed his head, pawing at the ground in front of him. Hel sat without moving. "Where is her maker?"

"Bacchus has been taken by the witch and secured within his own amulet by dark magic."

Hel regarded them for several moments from beneath her hood, her corrupted face unreadable. "I know you would not have called me were the situation not dire. However, I am forbidden from interfering in the lives of mortals. I can release the enchantment Danae placed on the amulet, freeing Bacchus, if you summon me in its presence. That is all I can promise."

Nora bowed her head. "Thank you."

The horse reared up on its hind legs, whinnying loudly as it kicked out its one front hoof. The beast turned mid-air and dove back into the tar pit. Flames reached high toward the sky once again before collapsing and disappearing.

Scorch marks on the grass were the only signs of Hel and her beast ever being there.

Renee let out a shaky laugh, her hands trembling as she put her lavender frames back on her face. "Well, that was something, wasn't it?"

CHAPTER 19

Serafina

"Do you want to talk about what happened?" Sera asked as she watched the city landmarks go by in the shadows created by the city's street lamps. The sun had yet to rise, and they were back in Theo's Jeep headed to the airport once again.

"No."

She turned to look at him, anger bubbling to the surface. "Why the hell are you so mad at me? Because I pulled my arm away after seeing Solomon?"

Sighing, Theo turned the wheel at the next light. "I'm not mad at you. I'm mad at myself."

Sera blinked at him. That was unexpected. "Why?"

"Because I care for you." His knuckles gripped the wheel a little tighter.

She pursed her lips, not sure if she should be offended or laugh. "And that's so awful because…?" Even though she herself felt guilty, she wanted to know why *he* thought caring for her was such a bad thing.

He glanced at her. "I told you on the way to Norway. I don't date mortals. It doesn't end well."

"Well, that's good. I'm not ready to date. You, or anyone else. I'm sure we were both just caught up in the adrenaline of the fight." She turned her head away from him as she bit her lip. Why the hell did she think it was a good idea to travel with him again?

"Sure."

Facing the window, Sera rolled her eyes. "Who are we going to go look for this time?"

"Mami Wata." In the reflection of the glass, she saw his shoulders relax a little as they changed the subject.

"Mommy water?"

Theo chuckled. "It sounds like that, but it's not English. She's an African water spirit, and in Haiti, where we're going, she's sometimes called Lasirenn. That's the name she prefers to go by."

"The Siren? You've met her before?"

"Yes," he said. Sometimes getting information from Theo was harder than going a day without coffee. Almost impossible.

"What's she like?"

Theo grinned as he looked at her. "Exactly what you think a Siren would be like. Sensual and cutthroat."

Sera felt a twinge of jealousy and wondered just how close they had gotten. She refocused her thoughts on the flight. "I hope you got us first-class again."

THEY REACHED PORT-AU-PRINCE in the early afternoon and headed for the area of town where Theo believed they'd find Lasirenn—Cité Soleil. Despite its grandiose name, the City of the Sun proved to be a devastatingly poor area of the bigger capital city.

Sera had grown up poor, and she had seen real poverty in person living in the District, but none of that had prepared her for such an extreme. Her soul ached for the inhabitants. They drove past armored trucks and uniformed personnel on dirt roads that were kept relatively clear of debris and trash. But the telltale scent of a crude sewer system nearby couldn't be hidden, even from the confines of the car they rented.

Most of the stores and homes they passed seemed to have been haphazardly thrown together with corrugated metal and other scraps, some covered only with tarp. The buildings made of stone were often missing large chunks and even entire walls, replaced with whatever materials could be found.

Despite the devastation around them, children with swollen bellies played in and around just about every building, kicking soccer balls, fencing with sticks, and chasing each other in never-ending rounds of tag. When they caught sight of the car and the unknown occupants within, they followed after on foot, shouting with excitement.

Theo parked next to a home at the end of a narrow street and got out, shooing the children away in a good-natured way. Speaking to them in French Creole, he wagged his finger at a few of the bolder ones who tried to climb into the car's front seat.

He waved at Sera to follow him inside the makeshift house, the floor made up of the same dirt as outside, only inside was swept clean of loose debris. A shriek of delight split the air, and two tiny dark-skinned arms wrapped themselves around his legs. Theo leaned down to pick the girl up and swung her around while the shrieks continued. After pulling her in tight for a hug and a kiss on each cheek, he set her down and spoke in Creole.

Sera tried hard to pick up anything they were saying, but her French had never gone beyond the reading and writing skills required for her degree, and definitely had not included any Creole.

"This is Roseline," Theo said, turning to Sera. "Her mother's line has a history of Gifts, which is how we came to meet a decade back, just after the earthquake. If you think this neighborhood looks rough, you should have seen it back then."

Sera smiled at the little girl who shied away behind one of his legs. "Why were you here? Did you help with the disaster relief?"

Nodding, he looked down at Roseline, stroking her hair. "The city was in shambles, and a part of the city like this receives the least amount of aid and not for weeks later. I came to help, and Rosie's *manman* let me stay here after I tracked her down. It's always easier to make contact with people who are even remotely involved with the supernatural side of the world."

Her heart skipped a beat as she gazed at Theo in a new light, respecting him even more than she already did.

Just then, a woman only a few years older than Sera

entered the house from the back entrance near a row of kitchen cabinets. A smile lit up her face as she saw Theo. Roseline skipped over to the woman and tugged at her knee-length skirt.

Theo and the woman hugged and kissed on both cheeks before conversing. Sera caught her name and the words, "Mami Wata," but everything else was too fast to pick up. After another minute, the woman came over to Sera and took her hands, smiling warmly.

"Welcome," she said in thickly accented English. "I am Cassandra."

Sera smiled back. "Thank you for inviting me into your home."

Cassandra reached up to touch Sera's face, her eyes becoming curious. She turned to Theo and asked him a few questions in French.

"You are god-touched," Cassandra finally said to her.

She nodded. "Bacchus."

"Ah." The woman's eyes twinkled with humor. "Wine and chaos." She said a few more words to Theo, who actually blushed. That may have been a first.

"We'll stay here for the afternoon, get some rest, then head out in the evening," he said, not meeting Sera's eyes when she looked to him for clarification.

"The evening?" she asked.

"Lasirenn can usually be found among the city's prostitutes. She gathers followers from the men and women who pay for her, uh, services." Theo coughed, eyeing Roseline warily out of the corner of his eye.

A twinge of jealousy burned in her chest. "And that's how you know her?"

He met her eyes this time. "Not exactly. She came to meet me once she got word of my presence in the area." He pointed to a partition near one of the side walls. "There's a cot back there you can use to rest for a bit."

"What about you?"

"I don't need a lot of sleep, remember? I'll be outside with Cassandra and Roseline helping with chores."

"Let me help, I'm too restless to consider sleep," she protested.

Theo eyed her before conversing with Cassandra, who nodded. "All right, but no complaints about hard work, okay?"

Sera snorted. "I spend my summers digging in the dirt for fun. I think I can handle chores around here."

They followed Cassandra outside to a garden, Roseline skipping around them. As the afternoon sun drifted across the blue sky, Sera felt happy, something she hadn't felt in almost two months, since the amulet first disappeared.

* * *

CITÉ SOLEIL AT NIGHT was a completely different city, and Sera stuck close to Theo as they walked down the dirt roads. She couldn't help her instant recoil reaction every time a gunshot went off. Now she understood why Cassandra had argued so strongly against them leaving her home after they had finished dinner.

He looked down at her, amused. "You sure you want to come?"

Despite her racing heart, Sera glared back. "Don't judge. I don't have a god's powers protecting me."

Theo chuckled. "Maybe not directly, but you have me."

Thankful for the darkness, she could feel herself blushing when she thought about what it might mean to have Theo. If these feelings really had come from Bacchus, he was going to have hell to pay when they reconnected. She jumped as a gunshot echoed down the side street to their left, effectively distracting her once again.

Following the twists and turns of the streets, they wound their way through the broken city. As they neared an even more impoverished area—if that was even possible— scantily dressed women appeared out of the shadows, beckoning to them both.

Theo called back to them in Creole, gesturing with his hands as he must have been describing the goddess. The woman who answered pointed to a metal shack leaning like the tower of Pisa a few buildings down. A stiff breeze might topple it over at any moment. Theo grasped Sera by the arm and kept her moving as some of the bolder among the women approached, toying with her straight hair.

"I'd say Nora should have been the one to come, but she'd spend too much time getting to know these women." Sera grinned before the image of Solomon by her friend's side flashed through her mind. Her grin turned to a grimace, which Theo must have caught.

"You don't like her sexual preferences?" he asked.

"It's not that. I just can't understand her draw to Solomon. Besides the obvious physical attraction, I mean."

"Do you need to understand?"

Sera paused, her mouth hanging slightly open. She hadn't looked at it that way. "Well, no. But she's my best friend. I don't want her to get hurt."

"You don't think Nora can handle it herself?"

"Of course I do, but I—"

A pickup truck squealed to a stop down a street to their left, backed up, then came straight at them. The high beams flooded the area with light and nearly blinded Sera before she looked away. The men filling the bed of the truck jumped to the ground through dust stirred up from the braking tires and ran toward Theo and Sera.

Her heart jumped up to her throat as the men surrounded them, shouting in Creole and lifting their guns. She had no idea how Xolotl would defend either one of them against bullets, and she also had no desire to find out. Swallowing hard, she pressed closer to Theo, raising her shaking arms in a sign of surrender.

Theo held up his hands calmly. "English, please, for the benefit of my partner."

One of the men in front of Theo spat at his feet and replied in Creole. Probably nothing nice. Sera gulped. This was going nowhere good pretty fast.

A deep growl rolled like thunder through the area. Sera glanced at Theo just as his eyes lit with gold, bolts of lightning flashing through his pupils.

The surrounding men all took a step back but aimed their guns directly at Theo.

"Sispann!" a voice bellowed from the truck. The harsh light of the high beams flicked to a lower setting as the door opened. Another man stepped out, the muscles of his arms visible from where Sera stood. He wasn't a tall man, but as he strolled toward the group in camo pants and a dingy white tank top, his presence caused the other men to part and allow him through.

"You were warned to stay away," the man said in thickly

accented English. He took a drag of the cigarette hanging from his mouth before tossing it into the dirt, tendrils of smoke still rising.

Don't tell me we went to all this trouble just to die here in Haiti, Sera thought, clenching her fists as her fear turned to anger.

"And yet, here I am," Theo said, no hint of a threat in his tone.

The other man eyed them for another moment before breaking into laughter. He snapped in Creole at the gunmen who immediately lowered their weapons and stood at ease.

Although she didn't know what was happening, Sera let out her breath in a rush. The immediate threat was over at the very least.

"Theodore, my friend." The man stepped forward with a broad smile and clasped arms with Theo. "To what do we owe this pleasure?"

Theo returned his smile. "Nothing good, I'm afraid. My partner and I need to see Lasirenn."

The group muttered and shuffled, discomforted by the name of the water spirit. The man addressing Theo flicked a hand toward the truck, and the other men walked away, casting looks of disgust toward the leaning shack.

"The sea witch is all yours," the man said. He met Sera's eyes for the first time before appraising the rest of her, gazing for an uncomfortable amount of time at her breasts. She glared back at him. His appraisal of her body reminded her of *Chad*, a man who thought women were merely there for man's pleasure, and she wanted to slap the stupid smirk off this guy's face.

After a quick exchange in Creole between the two men, Theo shook his head, the lines of his jaw clenching. Barking out a laugh, the other man shook hands with Theo and departed. The truck backed up and sped away into the darkened streets.

Theo turned to walk toward the shack where the woman had indicated they would find Lasirenn.

Sera caught his arm to stop him. "What in the hell was all that?"

"Joseph is the leader of the gang that runs this area of Cité Soleil," Theo said as he pulled her along with him.

"And you know him?"

"If you have any intention of surviving here, you respect the gang leaders."

"What did he ask you at the end?" she asked as they approached the building.

"If I would consider selling you to him at a discounted price as a tribute." He grinned at her.

Sera snorted at the audacity of the insinuation that she was for sale and at a discount. She may not have been overly endowed, but she was proud of what she had.

The rusted metal door to the makeshift shack fell open with a bang, making her jump. A man stumbled out, his eyes glazed over. He looked drunk but didn't smell of booze.

"She's here. Let's go," Theo said and ducked through the slanted doorway.

Taking a deep breath before following him, she immediately regretted needing to breathe being so close to the sewage canals. Inside, candles and burning incense lit the tiny room, but it still took a moment for her eyes to adjust from the stronger lights outside. When they did, she saw a pile of pillows and blankets in a corner and not much else. Not much else would fit in the small space.

"Theodore…" whispered a sultry voice from the shadows.

The woman who stepped forward was almost indescribable due to the burnt umber color of her skin. Her dark pupils nearly overtook the whites of her eyes, and her closely cropped hair was as deep brown as the rest of her. The short black robe she wore hung loose, exposing the curves of her breasts, and threatened to come untied at any moment.

Theo took the woman's hand in his and kissed the back of it. "Lasirenn. Your beauty never ages."

Her deep chuckle sounded like a cat's purr. "It has been too long, my lover. Where have you been? What brings you to me again?" She stepped forward and ran her hands up his chest, gripping the collar of his jacket. Her eyes burned with desire as she looked up at him.

Theo ran his hands up her arms to her hands and slowly removed them, kissing each palm. "Not that. I've relocated to Washington, D.C. My partner and I need your powers in a fight against the Bacchae."

She pulled back from him with a hiss. "What have the wretched creatures done now?" Looking at Sera for the first time, Lasirenn's gaze wandered up and down, not unlike Joseph had outside. She met Sera's eyes last, and an unknown fear sprang into Sera's mind as she gazed back into the spirit's serpentine eyes.

A tan and brown python appeared from behind the woman, slithering its way around her shoulders and neck and draping itself between her breasts. Its forked tongue flicked in and out as it stared at Sera.

Sera's mind screamed at her to run, but her body went

rigid as terror froze her limbs in place.

"Stop," Theo's voice broke through the enchantment. "She's not the enemy."

Sera stumbled back a step as she regained control of her body. The snake was gone. She looked around the room warily, rubbing her arms against the goosebumps.

Lasirenn's lips pulled up into a smile. "No? Is she the reason you turned my offer down?"

Glancing at Theo, Sera wondered what kind of offer she meant.

"Let's not rehash the past," he said. "We need your help to defeat the Bacchae witch who thinks she should be the queen of us all. Come with us."

The woman regarded him for a moment. "What's in it for me?"

"Life. If Danae succeeds, you won't have any worshippers left to keep you alive."

"You assume she will succeed." Lasirenn crossed her arms in front of her. "I do not believe she will. What else can you give me?"

"What else do you want?" he asked.

"You," she said.

"I'm not for sale."

"Then, no deal."

As Theo faced off with the water spirit, anger radiated from them both.

"You know we can't do this without you," he said between clenched teeth. "Your price is not reasonable."

"You're asking me to place my very life on the line should we fail. It's completely reasonable to ask for such a reward." She placed her hands on her voluptuous hips.

Theo sighed, his shoulders sagging. He stuck out his hand for her to shake. "Fine. Deal. With one compromise."

Lasirenn's smile deepened as she took his offered hand. "Anything for you, cheri mwen."

He tightened his grip. "You didn't state an amount of time. I'll give you one night."

The smile disappeared from her face, and she narrowed her eyes. Their deal was already sealed, and she knew it. She hissed, pulling her hand out of his. "You're as deceitful as the day you left me."

"Taking advantage of a pretty large loophole isn't deceitful," he said. "And you always knew I would leave. That was no secret."

Lasirenn looked at Sera with disdain. "Just do me a favor and find someone more worthy of you than this one."

Sera's jaw dropped. This woman didn't even know a thing about her or what she had been through losing Hiro. And besides, who said being with Theo was even an option?

Rage flared up inside her, and she snapped her mouth shut. As she took a step forward, she felt a hand on her arm. She glared up at Theo, but he shook his head.

"I'll meet you in the District." Lasirenn untied her robe and let it fall to the ground, standing nude before them.

Despite her anger at the woman's words, Sera couldn't help but gape at the perfect body standing before her. She was exactly what sailors would describe as a Siren calling the ships to shore. She sauntered past Sera and out the door, a salty scent like that of the sea drifting behind her.

"Where is she going?" Sera asked when she recovered enough from the encounter to speak.

His lips pressed tight together, he led her out the door

and pointed toward the naked figure walking into the water of the nearby shore, only visible thanks to the bright light of the moon. Lasirenn's head disappeared under the waves a moment later.

Nothing but the moon's reflection could be seen shimmering on the bay's surface until something disturbed the water. Sera squinted, but it was gone too fast. She was sure she had just seen a large fish's tail.

"One of Lasirenn's other forms is a mermaid," Theo said.

Holy shit! Sera couldn't believe her eyes. Or ears. She had just seen a mermaid. A small shudder shook her shoulders as she imagined Lasirenn meeting an octopus beneath the waves. Leave it to Sera's imagination and her fear of the mollusk to ruin the moment.

"Why does she dislike me so much?" she asked to get her mind off the vile eight-armed creature.

Theo stared out over the water. "A woman scorned and all. That's how she sees herself, anyway."

"But you don't?"

He turned around and started to walk back the way they came. "I loved her, but I was always upfront with her that my time with her was limited. She isn't willing to give up her unique way of gaining worshippers, and that's a deal-breaker for me."

As they walked in silence back to Cassandra's, Sera's only thoughts were about the night he had promised to the goddess, and a knot formed in her throat.

CHAPTER 20

Serafina

"So, what's the actual plan?" Sera asked. Once again, the group gathered in Renee's library, which was now getting a bit too small to house everyone.

Theo had booked flights back to the District the morning after meeting with Lasirenn, although Roseline had clung to Theo's leg, begging him to stay another day. The sight of him kneeling down and comforting the little girl sobbing in his arms had both broken Sera's heart and put it back together again.

Neither of them had talked much on the trip back to the row house, and Sera felt like they had traveled the world in the blink of an eye. Norway, India, and Haiti all within one week, and only a month had passed since the weekend after Thanksgiving, the weekend Hiro had died. It just didn't even seem possible.

Time was moving too quickly to process everything happening, which was probably a good thing in the grand scheme of things. Lack of time meant she couldn't wallow in her guilt over the realization that Hiro hadn't been "The One" or her attraction for Theo. She just hoped getting Bacchus back or stopping Danae would mean the god could halt these feelings before they escalated any further. Hiro still deserved better.

Despite the guilt, Sera couldn't help but wonder if Theo was thinking about his promised night with the sensual water spirit. Lasirenn hadn't arrived at Renee's by the time they had, but Theo didn't show any concern. He leaned against the stones of the library's fireplace with Manny sitting cross-legged at his feet.

"We need to draw Danae out into the open, away from her army, if possible," Theo said. "Then, we summon Hel to release Bacchus and the amulet. The gods will take care of the rest."

"Sounds super simple. What could possibly go wrong?" Nora made a face. She stood with her hands planted on her hips. "How do we get Danae away from the rest of them?"

"That's where Sol comes in. You said you've gotten close to her?" Theo looked to the Bacchae for his nod of confirmation. "Can you think of a way to get her out in the open away from everyone else?"

Sera's nostrils flared. Trusting the Bacchae was not coming quickly to her.

Is it wine time? Or time to whine? Eshu snickered.

The god's tease was both accurate and infuriating. So

what if she wanted to whine a little. Maybe a lot. Bacchus would have understood. She half snorted, half choked, waving away Nora's concerned glance.

Yeah, right, Sera thought. *Bacchus would have agreed with Eshu.*

"She's been staying primarily at the training facility in Virginia, which is on several acres of wooded land, while Lorenzo manages the incoming recruits in the District. It shouldn't be too hard to get her away from most of the Immortals. But her bodyguard, Yumiko, doesn't leave her side. Yumiko is an exceptional fighter."

"What's her story?" Theo asked.

"I don't know. She doesn't have a tongue." Solomon replied. "From what I can tell, it was cut out before she became an Immortal, and Danae was the one to rescue her from whoever cut it out. She'll give her life to her queen without hesitation."

Theo nodded. "Good to know. So we'll have Danae and Yumiko to manage. When is she planning to head back to California?"

"Tomorrow night unless something comes up."

"I see I arrived just in time for the party," a woman's velvety voice came from the library doorway.

Everyone turned to look at the new arrival. Stepping out of the shadows that formed behind her, Lasirenn's dark skin and form-fitting black clothes melted out of the darkness. Her exposed arms glistened as if wet, but no water dripped to the floor, and her eyes fixed on Theo.

Sera glanced at him and saw he returned her gaze, though she couldn't tell if it was with the same desire lurking in his thoughts or not. She swallowed a lump back down.

Nora wants to know what that's about, Freyja's own sultry voice chimed in Sera's head.

Catching Nora's arched brow, she shook her head. *It's too long of a story for right now, but they have a history.*

Obviously. The goddess sniffed.

When Theo introduced Lasirenn to each member of their group, she crouched down to Manny's level and spoke to him in Spanish, or at least some dialect of the language. The boy's face perked up as he listened and talked back.

A sting of jealousy shot through Sera, and she pressed her lips together. Even though she could speak to him through Eshu, he still hadn't opened up the way he did now.

The two gods conversed as well but also in Spanish. Sera could only guess at what Eshu had said when Lasirenn cast a glare in her direction.

"You can speak to the gods?" Lasirenn asked as she stood up.

Sera tried not to get riled up by the other woman's condescending attitude. "Seems like it."

"You make light of a valuable and rare gift?" Her dark eyes narrowed.

Well, Sera had tried. Cheeks burning at the accusation—however accurate it might have been—she opened her mouth to retort.

"Enough." Theo stepped away from the fireplace. "We're not fighting amongst ourselves. Our focus needs to be on stopping Danae."

Putting up her hands in mock surrender, Lasirenn failed to hide a smirk. Ugh, things were not going to go well if the woman continued to bait her.

Theo continued, "We'll use Sera's Gift to coordinate

the ambush." He walked over to his laptop perched on one of the side tables and aimed the attached mini-projector at the blank wall space above the mantle. A press of a button later, a satellite image of Virginia appeared. He narrowed the view down to Lorenzo's training facility.

"This is the best place to confront her." Theo pointed to a specific area on the map. It looked like part of the horse pastures but almost fully enclosed from the view of the compound by the surrounding trees.

This could work, Sera thought, hope lightening her mood.

Tilting his head to the side, Solomon considered the field from his place behind Nora's chair. "I can draw her out with a handful of Immortals for a potential security issue."

"What about a picnic?" Nora suggested.

He looked down at her with wide eyes. "A picnic?"

"You know, a nice, little romantic gesture before she becomes the queen of the world."

Solomon laughed, resting a hand on her shoulder. "I'm not entirely sure romantic gestures interest her, but it's worth a shot."

"Oh please, she was turned as a teenaged girl. She'll swoon as soon as you whip out the basket." Nora reached up to pat his hand.

"I'll trust your instincts."

"Smart man," she replied with a quirk of an eyebrow.

Despite her dislike of the Bacchae, Sera could see how happy Nora appeared in his presence. She practically glowed. That or the goddess Freyja's aura continued to shine around her. But Sera was pretty sure it was just pure happiness. And even though she was more than glad for her best friend, bitter jealousy crept up and made her stomach queasy as she thought about how much she missed Hiro's company and how confusing things were with Theo. For the umpteenth time, Sera wished she had never found the damn amulet and the god within.

Theo's phone rang, and he glanced at it before hitting the end call button. As he took a breath to say something, his phone interrupted again. He let out a sigh. "It's a friend from the station, I'll be right back." He moved into the hallway, leaving the rest of them to talk.

Sera sat in silence, chewing on her lip as she stared at the image of Virginia projected on the wall, and paranoia soon replaced her previous feelings. What if Solomon was playing them all along? He could be leading them straight into a trap. Was she ready to trust her life, *all* their lives to this Bacchae? She plucked at a loose string on her sweater, glancing at Solomon out of the corner of her eye. How trustworthy could he really be if he was willing to rebel against his own queen?

A moment later, Sera jumped from the sudden sound of growling and snarling. She turned toward the door just as Theo came storming back in. His face was a mask of fury, the lines of his jaw moving as he clenched his teeth.

"She's done it. She went on the news." He typed something into his laptop, which was still projecting.

The local news station appeared on the wall, where a reporter announced that the president of the United States had been taken hostage. Sera's blood ran cold as a scrolling banner read, "The undead walk among us. This is NOT a hoax."

The station switched to a full screen of a previously recorded video of Danae, seated on her throne, answering questions asked by someone off-camera. A banner at the bottom continued to scroll with worldly news, announcing government shutdowns across the globe, local leaders withdrawing to their most secure locations.

At least they're taking her seriously, Sera thought, rubbing her arm against the rising goosebumps.

Before ending the interview, Danae addressed the viewers directly, her fangs extended, and her eyes burning red. "I offer everlasting life to any and all who seek it. Come to me, my vampire children. Find one of my Immortal brethren and let them know you wish to become one with the night."

Two of the Bacchae stepped into the camera's view, dragging a bound and hooded figure with them. Dropping the man on his knees by Danae's blood-red heels, one of the Bacchae pulled off the hood, revealing the president. Sera held her breath, tightening her grip on the arms of her chair. The bitch couldn't be crazy enough to kill him. Right?

Before the man could do little more than blink as his eyes adjusted to the light, Danae was at his throat. Her claws dug into the skin of his shoulder and cheek as she held his head sideways. Her extended and very sharp fangs glinted in the light—for dramatic effect, Sera was sure.

And then she struck, blood oozing out from beneath her mouth as she drank. The President squirmed beneath her, his eyes wide with pain and fear.

The screen went black for a moment before switching back to the reporter sitting behind a desk. Sera still had a death grip on her chair, almost afraid to breathe. The scene had been far too familiar.

As his Adam's apple bobbed and sweat dripped down

his face, the reporter pointed to a new clip that showed chaos unfolding in all the major cities. People thought the world was ending.

They were right.

"Well, fuck," Nora said what they were all thinking.

CHAPTER 21

Solomon

Solomon didn't often feel nervous since becoming an Immortal. In fact, he couldn't remember the last time he had. It may have even been when he made his first kill, over two hundred years ago.

But he felt almost jumpy at that moment, and hiding the emotion took significant effort.

From her seat on the throne, Danae looked at him like he had grown two heads. "You want to go on a picnic." She didn't ask it, but the question was there in her raised eyebrows.

"I want to celebrate your success before we return to Paris to check on the Eternals later this evening. You will be too busy for me then." Taking her hand in his, he kissed the back of it. Unlike with Lorenzo's affections, she didn't pull her hand away.

Her face reverted back to a mask he couldn't read. "When?"

"I have it all ready now if you can spare the time," he said, urging his voice and pulse to remain calm and neutral.

She regarded him for another moment before flicking her eyes to Yumiko, who turned and left the hall. Like Lorenzo's mansion, Danae had altered one of the larger rooms of the McLean facility into a throne room, specifically for meetings when she needed to remind Immortals of her place among them as their queen. The vaulted ceiling added to the regal feel of the room, and five stone steps led to the top of the dais where her throne sat.

"All right." Danae rose from her seat and allowed Solomon to lead her down from the dais. Of course Nora had been right about the queen.

"Is Yumiko staying behind?" he asked.

"Why?"

"I packed her a snack as well," Solomon explained. Even though their kind didn't need human food for sustenance, many of them still found the activity itself pleasant. "I figured she would be joining us and didn't want to leave her out."

"Isn't that sweet." Danae's tone didn't convince him of the sentiment. "She will ensure everything continues to run smoothly here for our departure tomorrow."

Relief ran through his mind, allowing him to relax his shoulders. Not having to deal with Yumiko would help significantly.

"You're relieved?" she asked. Her ability to sense mood changes far exceeded the others. He would need to be *very* careful until he had her in place for the ambush.

"Only because we seldom get time alone together. Aside from the bedroom, of course."

Her marble-like face simply regarded him.

Placing the queen's hand on his arm, Solomon led her out the back of the training facility and toward the hidden field. They walked across the grass, which crunched beneath their feet from the frost, and she waved aside any Immortals who sought to accompany them. The field lay on the other side of a grove of pine trees, tall and dense enough to provide sufficient cover for their ambush.

Danae had never been one for conversation, but she listened—or at least didn't interrupt—as Solomon shared some of his thoughts about their newest recruits. The mundane talk kept his thoughts and feelings off the upcoming moment. His voice and the wind rustling the leaves were the only sounds accompanying them.

Although the sun neared the edge of the western horizon, it would still provide enough light for the awaiting group to see without the help of flashlights, and Eshu and Freyja would use their magic to conceal the group from the Immortals' senses. But when they rounded the grove and the blanket and basket came into sight, Solomon's skin prickled. It had been too easy, and yet there was no way she could have known.

Sinking to her knees on the black and white checkered blanket, Danae opened the basket and reviewed the contents. With her head lowered, she wouldn't have seen the others approaching, but he was sure she felt them now. The group formed a circle around her.

Why wasn't she reacting?

"How very quaint," Danae said, her eyes still on the items within the basket.

Serafina stepped closer until the queen raised her head, her eyes fixing on the girl.

"How very quaint indeed," she repeated.

Hatred as thick as congealed honey wafted off Serafina as she narrowed her grey eyes. "Give me the amulet."

"Or else what?" Danae turned to look at each of the members of the group who surrounded her. "Your band of misfits and old gods will take me down?" She started to laugh, still on her knees.

"You will—"

"No, you naive little human. You will obey me, *or else.*" Her eyes flashed red, and a pulse of *influence* washed over Solomon, commanding him to draw near. He lurched forward, resisting, and the talisman provided by Renee that he wore beneath his shirt grew warm against his skin as it counteracted Danae's control. From all sides and angles, the forest bled Immortals until dozens of them surrounded the smaller inner circle.

Danae plucked an apple from the basket and bit into it, crunching as the power shifted.

"How did you know?" Solomon asked, his fangs extending in his anger. He clenched his fists until he felt warm liquid slide down his palm. He had been careful each time he visited.

Had they been betrayed by one of their own?

"Did you honestly think I would trust you? That I wouldn't have your little excursions followed?" Danae asked as she finished her bite of the apple. She gestured toward Nora. "Your infatuation with this pretty human has dulled your senses."

Arriving at her maker's side, Yumiko's eyes showed only white, her pupils covered with a milky film. She raised her arm as a crow cawed in the air above them. The black bird swooped to land on her arm, and Yumiko's pupils returned to their original dark color. Stroking the bird's neck, she smirked at Solomon.

Shock reverberated through to the center of his being. He had heard tales of her kind while growing up, stories of the women and men who could become one with the wild. But he had never thought they were real, even if his mother had sworn they were. He should have known better once he became a descendant of a god.

How had he been so blind?

Yumiko was an animal telepath, able to communicate with animals and see through their eyes. He had never thought to look for anything other than Immortal followers. Now, too many Immortals to count surrounded them. They were grossly outnumbered. He had failed them. He had failed Nora. Defeat swam thick in his mind, knowing he was about to witness the death of his beloved before the queen turned him to dust.

Danae rose to her feet as she finished the apple, tossing the browning core to the blanket at her feet. "Round them up and take them inside. I'm going to enjoy watching them die."

Serafina stood her ground as the queen approached her, a smile pulling at the human girl's lips. "You haven't won yet."

Despite the turned odds, Nora and Renee clasped hands and chanted the summoning spell. Solomon had helped the two women sneak onto the property the night before to prepare the circle. Maybe they could gain the upper hand with this surprise at the very least.

Danae glanced down at the grass, uncertainty crossing her features as she noticed the salt circle just as it burst into flames. Before she could command her army to attack, the ring collapsed into a bubbling tar pit, and Hel's giant horse leaped onto the grass in front of them. The stallion's dreadful whinny threatened to rupture Solomon's eardrums. Most of the Immortals shrank back, some even covering their ears as if that would help.

They had never seen a god in the flesh before.

Hel sat high atop the black horse's back. She pointed at Danae with a skeletal hand, bones showing white in the fading light, and spoke in an ancient form of the Norse language. A leather bag at Danae's waist started to smoke, and the pinecone-shaped amulet fell through a hole that appeared at the bottom. Danae shrieked and bent to pick it up, but the necklace burst into a crimson light. The queen hissed and fell back, Yumiko just barely catching her from falling.

Serafina lunged forward and snatched up the amulet. Holding it to her neck, the ends connected and sealed by themselves. As Bacchus rejoined with the girl, her eyes shone gold as if igniting from an inner sun. An unearthly wind whipped her dark hair around her face and tugged at her clothes. A look of steely determination crossed her features, and she balled her hands into fists at her sides.

Glimmers of hope danced within Solomon.

The Helbeast reared onto its hind-legs and leaped back into the pit, which promptly closed behind the creature.

Deep, booming laughter echoed out of Serafina's mouth. "Oh, you spiteful, insolent children. You have done too much damage this time. Your end is nigh."

Staggering, Solomon struggled to remain in control of himself as Danae used her hive-like *influence* to call the Immortals to her side. The talisman burned into the flesh around his collar as it worked its magic. The Immortals surrounding their group rushed forward to defend and protect their new queen. Shots rang out, and the smell of gunpowder drifted through the crisp evening air.

The sounds of battle raged around Solomon as he sank to his knees, gripping the damp grass between his fingers, the frost melting beneath him. He clenched his teeth, a roar of frustration ripping from his throat as he fought against the urge to protect Danae. He would not fail again. He couldn't.

But he and the talisman weren't strong enough.

The crystal crumbled to dust as the irresistible force of the queen's call pulled him back to his feet and launched him into the fray. The world before him swam in a sea of red, faces undulating in his vision as he knocked bodies to the side. He must protect the queen.

The tiny blonde woman and the grey-haired witch stood back to back, engaged in a magical battle with a handful of Immortals who were trying to break their defensive shield. He grabbed a bottle of wine from the basket as he passed and smashed it against a boy's head, stepping over the shattered glass and limp figure as he stalked toward the witches' threat.

Through the red haze, a dome of wavering static surrounded the two witches, charges of electricity lashing out to obliterate any who approached too close. Glittering dust floated through the air as new Immortals attempted to break through.

Just as he raised the shattered wine bottle above his head, prepared to strike the barrier even if it meant certain death, the bubble popped. It dissolved in front of him, a faint sensation like drops of water hitting his skin.

The queen had won.

A battle cry tore from his throat as he rushed toward the two women, red still muting everything in view. The woman he knew to be Nora looked up at him in fear before the fear faded to something else. Something unbelievable. Something beautiful.

Love.

As he held the jagged edge of the bottle to her throat, a trickle of blood slid down her skin from where the glass broke through. The red haze faded from his eyes as Nora reached up to caress his face, and he slumped forward as her touch broke the queen's hold.

"I knew you were still in there," she said. "But it helps to have a goddess of love on our side, doesn't it?"

As she grinned, Solomon raised his arm to ward off a blow from another Immortal, and his mind refocused on the fight. He directed the slice once intended for Nora at the Immortal's throat instead, and he saw blood spurt from the wound, then he launched a kick at the man's chest. The Immortal went sprawling.

A deep canine growl pulled his attention to the left, where a large, black dog the size of a horse snarled and snapped at the Immortals surrounding it. *Damn.* Serafina hadn't been exaggerating when she described his terror-inducing size.

Lunging forward, the dog clamped its giant jaws on one of the Immortal's necks before ripping the head free from the body. A swipe of one of its paws sent the rest of the Immortal flying before he dissolved into iridescent gold dust.

Impressive work. Solomon had never seen a shifter before, and he was glad to be on the same side as this one.

Serafina wasn't far behind the hairless dog, her eyes still glowing like the midday sun from Bacchus's essence, engaged in hand-to-hand combat with Yumiko. The bodyguard's sword lay a few feet away.

Picking up a knife left behind by one of the slain Immortals, Solomon slid the blade into the back of one of the Immortals facing Nora and pushed up on the hilt to drive it home into his heart. The man dissipated in front of him, Nora's grinning face appearing through the flecks of gold fluttering into the wind.

She began to chant with Renee, the torc blazing with a fuchsia light at her neck. Lightning shot out from the clear sky, striking an Immortal nearby. His body sizzled and popped where the electricity touched him. A moment later, he burst into amber flurries.

Danae stood in the middle of it all, surrounded by a group of Immortals, her face impassive but her eyes calculating. Despite the odds, their group was making quick work of her soldiers. They were facing a group of newer Immortals, who didn't truly understand their skills or how to control them, even after time in the training facilities.

Luck was on the gods' side.

Manny tumbled in front of Solomon before springing

to his feet, a gash on his forehead already congealed and healing. He nodded as he sprinted away after an Immortal running toward the woods. The boy raised his arm and flung a knife at the Immortal, striking her with deadly aim. She fell, and a moment later the boy was on her, finishing the job. He stood and looked for his next mark as the dust settled.

A python the length of a semi-truck was busy swallowing a screaming Immortal whole. The water spirit in another form, he presumed, and not someone he would want to be at odds with.

They might win this thing after all.

A sharp pain shot through Solomon's side, and he stumbled toward the ground. He looked back to see an Immortal holding a spear that had pierced through his skin. Locking eyes on the other Immortal, Solomon pulled the spear toward and through him, grunting as the weapon came out his other side. The Immortal's mouth popped open as he found himself face to face with another, far older Immortal. Solomon thrust his fist through the man's chest and crushed his heart.

As the Immortal crumpled into little more than sparkling ashes, Solomon yanked the spear all the way through, wincing as it continued to do internal damage. He would heal, but it hurt like hell in the meantime.

The last of the Immortals moved closer to their queen or fled toward the training facility.

Danae's eyes narrowed as she saw the tide turn once again. Raising her arms, she chanted her own spell.

Solomon raced toward her, hoping to stop whatever it was she intended to do. Nothing good ever came from that woman. He ducked and swung at an Immortal, his knife connecting with bone in the man's ribs. He ripped it free as the man tackled Solomon. They grappled on the ground, the other Immortal trying to pry the knife from Solomon's hand.

Without warning, the world plunged into a darkness so deep that even his enhanced night vision couldn't pierce the void.

CHAPTER 22

Serafina

I t was eerie standing there in the dark, knowing it had been nearing sunset only a moment before. Sera's ragged breath joined those around her.

This magic fog is too strong to lift without help, Bacchus said. *Find Freyja.*

Freyja! Sera called out in her mind. A bright pink spark flared to life on the right side of her inner eye. She walked toward it, arms out in front of her. A familiar hand reached out in the dark, and a warm tingle spread from the contact. She had found Nora. They clasped their hands together.

Renee's voice joined Nora's as she chanted, and Bacchus lent his energy to the two witches through their joined hands.

Danae's laughter split the darkness, coming from

everywhere at once, even ricocheting within Sera's mind. She winced as the sound threatened to pierce through her skull.

A moment later, the darkness lifted, and everyone looked around in a state of mild confusion as their eyes adjusted to the dusk-filled light. Sera looked toward the group of Bacchae who had surrounded Danae, but the Eternal was nowhere to be seen.

"Where is she?" Sera demanded.

The Bacchae who had protected their queen looked baffled until realization flickered across their faces.

She must have called for the Ordog, Bacchus said, his voice tight with anger.

The bitch had escaped. And so had her silent bodyguard.

The last dozen or so of the Bacchae fled, though Manny continued to chase a few who were close enough. Still in his dog form, Theo padded over to where Sera stood, his tongue hanging out of his mouth as he panted. His head was nearly level with her own.

Chances are she has fled to Paris where the Eternals are held, Xolotl's growling voice said.

We need to go, Bacchus said, a moment before helicopters swarmed over the training facility, spotlights shining down on the compound. The military hadn't taken long to track down Lorenzo's properties. That was a good sign. Hopefully, that meant they had gained control of his home in the District, too.

The group ran from the clearing toward their waiting cars. Theo's canine body shimmered as he transformed back into his human form, accepting the pants Sera offered out the window of the Jeep. He climbed in a moment later and pulled the SUV back onto the dirt road, heading toward the District.

Warmth flooded her body, rolling through like sweet nectar. *I missed you,* Bacchus said.

Danae wasn't good company? She smiled, knowing he could tell how much she had missed him in return.

I had no company. That spell isolated me from the world, and I was so bored. He groaned in emphasis.

Sera laughed, tapping the amulet as an explanation when Theo glanced her way. He nodded and returned his eyes to the road, his face grim. Well, that look sobered her. They still hadn't won. Danae had escaped, and now they needed to track her down in another country as the world fell apart. Great.

We need to destroy the new Council, this "Court of the Everlasting," as she calls it, Bacchus said. His sneer was palpable.

Do you think she went to Paris? she asked.

Yes, he said. *Chances are she has protected her compound in France with the Ordog's dark magic. It will be impenetrable to the mortals who try to attack.*

But not us? Sera asked, hopeful.

We'll see. His response dashed most of her hopes.

"Bacchus agrees with Xolotl that she probably ran back to her place in France," Sera said out loud. "Even worse is it's likely to be protected by the Ordog."

Theo nodded. "That's what I'm afraid of, too. I'm not sure we have the magic to break through, even with all of the gods' power combined. Death magic is intense."

"We've gotta try, right?"

Theo turned his head toward her, the corners of his lips

pulling up. "Right."

Flutters tickled her stomach as she noticed for the first time that he was still shirtless. She could scrub clothes on those abs.

Oh, is that how it is? Bacchus asked with a chuckle.

Her cheeks flushed with heat, but Theo had turned back to the road. *Oh, hush. I'm not at all ready for that, and I blame you for the attraction. You and your love for chaos and sex.*

I do leave quite the impression, don't I? came the snarky reply.

Don't make me regret missing you, she said.

A deep laugh echoed like thunder through her mind.

As they approached the District on a raised section of interstate, Sera's eyes grew wide as she took in the cityscape—burning buildings as far as the eye could see. Smoke drifted high into the night sky, blocking out the stars, and the roads leading out of the city were full of honking cars and more than one fender bender.

The District was starting to crumble.

Sera reached out to Freyja, *Follow us if you can.*

Sure thing, darling, her melodious voice replied.

Avoiding the mess backed up on the interstates, Theo kept to smaller side streets. As they passed various neighborhoods, grim-faced people cast wary glances at the Jeep as they packed up their own vehicles. Clothes, food, and toys littered the sidewalks and streets, abandoned in everyone's haste to evacuate.

To where? Sera gulped, a lump forming in her throat. Where was safe anymore?

After parking on the deserted street in front of Renee's row house, the group filtered into the library. Sera took a look around, checking for injuries.

Manny's shirt was ripped in at least a dozen places, but it didn't look like the skin beneath had been marked. He was too fast. Something had happened to Solomon—his side gaped open, but his blood had congealed and no longer dripped. Theo had donned a new shirt before he entered the row house, but not before Sera had noticed the deep scratches across his chest and back. They didn't seem to bother him now, though.

Hobbling into the room, Lasirenn favored her right leg and lowered herself into a chair with a grimace.

Sera herself had once had scrapes along her arms and bruises that were sure to have formed across her entire body, but Bacchus had healed them in the Jeep. Yes, she had missed his godly powers.

Nora and Renee were in the best shape, protected from any physical attacks by their magical shield. Score one for witches.

"All right, time to plan our next move," Sera said, once everyone was settled.

"We need to be more aware of hive mentality." Solomon winced and touched his side as he shifted his weight.

She blinked at him. "Of what?"

"Because the rest of the Immortals come from the bloodline of an Eternal, Danae can *influence* us all. At once. Like the queen of a beehive," the Bacchae explained. "I found myself wanting to be by her side, fighting for her instead of against her. I couldn't stop it until Nora and Freyja stepped in. These new Immortals will find it even more difficult to resist than I did, especially because they won't want to. This talisman hardly held up, but I'm thankful to have had it." He tilted his head toward Renee, who gave a weary smile in return.

Did you know about this hive mentality thing? Sera asked Bacchus.

Yes, but only Eternals have the ability, and none had used it previously, at least not en masse as she did, he explained.

Can we break it somehow? she asked.

Yes.

How? Although she knew deep down, the answer wouldn't be easy. It never was.

Kill her, he said.

Sera sighed. Why did her gut have to be right? "We need to figure out how to get into her compound in France to free the other Eternals. They might be able to push back on the hive mind and override Danae's control. Anyone have any suggestions?"

Everyone looked around at each other, but exhaustion was quickly settling in for all of them. From his place by the fire, Manny's eyes drooped, and his head nodded. The telltale signs of her impending blackout, a result of the connection with using Bacchus's power, threatened to drop Sera where she stood. Downsides, Theo had said. She would have snorted if she wasn't about to fall over.

"Let's rest for the night and regroup tomorrow with fresh ideas," Theo suggested. He must have seen what she did.

Sera wobbled on her feet, unable to fight it any longer. Steady hands gripped her shoulders, and she looked up into Theo's dark eyes. She hardly noticed who left and who stayed as he guided her up to the guest room. After kicking off her boots, Sera dropped onto her side in the bed, ready to succumb to the overwhelming darkness.

Theo's fingers brushed loose strands of her hair off her face, then his lips gently pressed against her forehead. Not wanting to be alone, she reached up to grab his hand before he could leave.

"Stay," she pleaded.

The mattress sank down where he sat, climbing in next to her. His body felt hot as he curled up behind her and wrapped his arms around hers. Warm breath tickled her ear as he settled in. Feeling comforted in a way she hadn't since before all of this mess started, Sera's eyes drifted closed.

And then she slept.

CHAPTER 23

Serafina

The next morning, Sera found the group back in the library, chatting quietly to each other. Nora looked up from her conversation with Solomon, arching a knowing eyebrow in her direction.

Nora and I both want to know what happened, Freyja's voice chimed in her mind. *In explicit detail, please, darling.*

I don't know what you're talking about. As the memory of the cuddle session flashed through her mind, she avoided looking at Nora. Or Theo. But she could feel both their eyes on her.

Oh, don't play daft, the goddess replied. *Renee said Theo didn't come back downstairs until this morning. He must have cum somewhere.*

If it had been possible for her jaw to unhinge from her

skull, Sera's mouth would have dropped to the floor at the goddess's suggestive comment. Her entire face must have caught on fire.

It wasn't like that, she snapped back.

Freyja sniffed as if offended. *You shouldn't be ashamed of a very natural human instinct. Even the gods have desires.*

Nothing happened, Sera protested. Things were confusing enough with Theo. She didn't need everyone thinking they had slept together, too.

The library had gone quiet, and everyone stared at her.

"Freyja had some commentary about my late arrival," she said. "In my defense, the guest room doesn't have a window, and Bacchus didn't feel like waking me. I didn't know what time it was."

I'm not your father, Bacchus said casually, as if reclining on a chaise without a care in the world.

Thankfully.

Not everyone had gathered together. Lasirenn was noticeably absent. Sera forced herself to look at Theo, who looked back at her with a blank expression. "Where's Lasirenn?"

"She's gone ahead to scout out the area," he said. "We need to know what kind of defenses Danae has set up. We'll meet up with her in Paris."

"What do we do until then?" she asked.

"Prepare."

* * *

A FEW HOURS LATER, SERA found herself alone in the library with Theo, although his eyes never left his laptop screen. Nora and Solomon had left together to run to Nora's place, and Renee had gone out for some last-minute supplies. At some point, the boy had slipped out, but she barely noticed when he came and went anyway. He was sneakier than a fox stalking a chicken coop.

Glancing up at Theo a few times, Sera tried to work up the courage to say something. Only what she wanted to say, she had no clue.

Shall we pour a glass of liquid courage? Bacchus suggested.

No, we're not getting drunk, she said and glanced at Theo again.

After the fifth time, he sighed and looked at her. "Let me guess, you want to talk."

"I just want to say thank you." She closed the book she was pretending to read. "And I'm sorry. I didn't mean to make things more confusing by asking you to stay."

"We're good. Let's focus on the plan. I've booked flights for everyone for tonight," he said, returning his gaze to the laptop.

Give him time, Serafina, Bacchus said, sending calming waves into her shoulders. She hadn't realized how tense she had become until her shoulders pulled away from her ears.

Time isn't something we have a whole lot of at the moment, she thought.

Sera held back her sigh of frustration as she gave in to the god's request. "Even Manny?"

"No, he has his own way of getting onto the plane that doesn't involve going through security. He'll join up with us when we get there," Theo said.

"Don't tell me he's going to be in the cargo area. It's freezing!" she protested.

Before he could respond, the sound of the front door

opening followed by a howling wind echoed down the hallway. A moment later, Nora and Solomon entered the library, their faces red from the chill.

"Everything is shutting down—the Metro, buses, stores," Nora said, holding her hands in front of the fire. "The airports, too."

Colei! There goes our plan. A sea of gold undulated in Sera's vision as Bacchus barely restrained his anger. *She must be moving faster than we thought.*

Cursing under his breath, Theo pulled out his cell phone. "I may be able to get us a plane and a pilot, but if they've grounded all flights, we're going to have a hell of a time getting out of here. I'll be right back." He stood and left the room, holding the phone to his ear.

"How is it out there?" Sera asked as Nora settled into a chair, Solomon taking the one next to her.

"Crazy. People legitimately think it's the end of the world. We saw so many houses with boarded-up windows and doors, and the roads are a mess. I think this place is going to be a ghost town in another day. Of humans anyway."

"As opposed to animals?"

"No, we saw, what? Five?" Nora turned to Solomon for confirmation. He nodded. "Five different patrols of Bacchae. They've basically seized the city."

"What about the military? Has martial law been declared?" Sera asked, her palms starting to sweat. This didn't sound good at all.

Nora and Solomon exchanged a look.

"The Bacchae swarmed the bases in the area," Nora said. "They've been taken over."

Despite a stream of Latin expletives pouring into her mind, only some of which she knew from her studies, Sera sat speechlessly. She obviously knew Danae had planned to control the world—hell, the bitch had outed the entire supernatural community and fed on the president—but it still hadn't felt completely real until that moment.

Theo walked back in, his expression grave. "We've got a plane, but my guy isn't so sure we'll get off the ground. We've got to meet him at the Leesburg airport in three hours. Let's get moving." He looked around the room. "Where's Manny?"

Call to Eshu. We must go, Bacchus said, his voice still tight with fury.

Eshu! We've got to get out of here. Where are you? Sera pushed the thought as far as it would go.

A sensation of pain mingled with fear flashed through her mind, but the accompanying words were too distant to hear. Her mouth went dry as she imagined what trouble the boy could be in.

"I think something bad happened," she said. "But I can't hear him. Just emotions."

"Can you track which direction it's coming from?" Theo asked.

I can help, Bacchus said, a tingling feeling crawling through her skull as he lent her his power.

She closed her eyes and focused on the feelings coming from Eshu. "Yes. He's not too far away yet."

Theo nodded. "Okay, let's go."

As the four of them bundled up and left the house, Nora sent Renee a message to meet them back there as soon as she could. Their plan was to find Manny and Eshu, grab

Renee, and head out to the Leesburg airport before dark. Hopefully, it would all be that simple.

Unlikely, though.

Cracking the window as he drove, Theo sniffed the air while Sera directed him toward the sounds from Eshu. She couldn't believe how drastically different the city looked after just one night—a night of terror and panic. She knew it had been bad, both from their drive back from Virginia and Nora's description, but seeing it unfold before her was unreal. Just how many Bacchae had Lorenzo created?

Sera pulled her phone from her pocket and clicked on her father's contact image. She had never been more relieved he lived in suburban Virginia, but she needed to warn him about what may be coming.

After several attempts to get the line to connect, the lack of signal at the top of the screen caught her eye.

"Crap, I don't have any signal," she said.

"Me neither," Nora said from her seat in the back.

"The number of people trying to make calls must have crashed the networks," Solomon said.

Biting her lip against the rising panic, she reminded herself that her father was a survivor and well-equipped to keep himself safe. Chances were he would be keeping his neighbors alive, too.

Eshu's words became clearer despite the incessant honking of cars and distracted her from her thoughts as they neared Interstate 395, which ran along the District's eastern edge.

What about the... Can you see...

Eshu! She shouted with her mind.

Sera? What're you doing here? Genuine surprise in his tone.

We came to help. I could feel something wrong.

Eh, nothing a little trickery won't handle, he said. *But I guess if you're already here…*

She rolled her eyes. "He's pretending like they don't actually need help."

"Did he tell you what's happening?" Theo asked.

What's the situation? she asked Eshu.

A group of these dolts thought it would be fun to tie us up and throw us in the back of their armored vehicle. The trickster god snickered.

How many are in the group?

Well, I only counted three other vehicles before they shut the back of the truck, he said.

Sera groaned. "He's in the back of an armored truck, with at least three other trucks of Bacchae nearby. There could be more, though. He couldn't see once they closed the doors."

Theo grunted and sniffed the air again.

"We're close." He parked the Jeep at the base of the entrance ramp, cars with panic-stricken people blocking the street as the interstate itself was at a complete standstill. Their group exited the Jeep as horns honking and crunching metal filled the air, along with muffled screaming.

"What the hell is that noise?" Nora covered her ears with her gloved hands. They ran up the on-ramp toward the sound.

The scene before them was chaos.

Cars and trucks faced in all directions as four heavy armored vehicles plowed through them, smashing and crushing the other cars in their wake.

Theo glanced at Solomon. "We doing this?"

The Bacchae grinned, a wicked gleam in his eyes. "It's too late for secrecy."

Deep growling filled Sera's mind and ears as Theo's body dissolved and reshaped into the giant, black hairless dog that was his other form, his clothes shredding behind him. He snapped his powerful jaws, droplets of foamy drool spattering the ground beneath him.

Leaning down, Solomon planted a kiss on Nora's lips before he faced the trucks. With his fangs extended and eyes blazing red, the Bacchae's face morphed into a snarling mask.

The dog jumped onto the hood of a car and bounded after the trucks, which were moving slowly due to the pileup of cars. Solomon followed, agile as he executed parkour-style moves to keep up.

Bacchus's laughter filled her mind. He, of course, loved the chaos. *Let's go!*

Freyja's eagerness radiated beside her, tangible as a pink aura shimmering around Nora. The two women ran after the dog and the Bacchae, dodging cars as best they could with the help of the gods.

Metal groaned in front of them. Solomon stood on the step leading up to the driver's side door of one of the trucks, wrenching the door free of the moving vehicle with one hand. He reached in and pulled the surprised driver out, throwing him to the ground.

The giant dog grabbed the Bacchae's leg in his jaws and crushed it, the Bacchae screaming in agony as blood sprayed from his limb like a fountain. Theo let go to close his teeth around the Bacchae's middle, then swung him toward the next truck. The body crashed onto the front windshield with a sickening wet sound, surprising the two Bacchae inside.

People screamed around them, exiting their cars to run away or watch in horror. The smell of burning tires filled the air as some tried unsuccessfully to get past the congestion with sheer horsepower, but there were just too many cars. Sera tried not to focus on them as she ran past. Guilt at inciting such terror could come later.

Which one is he in? Bacchus asked as they closed in.

Reaching out with her Gift, she found Eshu's essence coming from a truck on their right. She pointed Nora in that direction.

All four trucks came to a halt as Solomon and Theo destroyed the leading two, which allowed Sera and Nora time to reach the truck holding Manny. The two Bacchae in the front cab jumped out to face the women.

Bacchus's energy flowed through her limbs like warm nectar, and she released herself to his control. Fighting it had consequences, she had learned. Her hands reached down to the bumper of a nearby car and pulled, ripping the metal free of the frame as if it were nothing more than a weed. She might have won prizes at the Bacchanalia with that move.

Rolling thunder rumbled overhead as she faced one of the Bacchae with the bumper. She wielded it as both a shield and staff, catching the bullets shot her way, then knocking the emptied gun from the woman's hands. Just as she ducked one of Sera's swings, the Bacchae was swept up into the air by a surge of wind, swirling with magic, and landed on the sharp point of a light post a hundred feet away. The body dissolved into glittering dust. Blinking in surprise, Sera turned to look at her friend, who winked and grinned.

Bacchus and Freyja's laughter rang in Sera's mind—

both gods relished the frenzy.

As they turned to face the next Bacchae together, the back of the truck opened, and three more Bacchae jumped out. They lifted their guns just as Sera caught a glimpse of Manny's face inside, tied up but grinning behind the gag. The kid actually looked like he was enjoying himself.

She launched herself at the Bacchae before they could shoot, using a flurry of kicks and jabs with the bumper to whack guns from outstretched hands.

Ah! The cavalry has arrived, Eshu's voice snickered.

You're welcome. Sera smiled despite her sarcasm. She ducked under a Bacchae's fist, feeling the air whoosh by her head.

And so humble, too, he bantered.

The black dog leaped into the fray, pinning a Bacchae to the ground before ripping the man's arm free from his body. The screams of pain were brief as Theo raked his massive paw over the Bacchae's chest, tearing through skin and bone before chomping down on the heart. The body shook once then dissolved.

As Solomon hurdled his way over cars, he and Theo made quick work of the few remaining Bacchae. When the last of them exploded into dust, Solomon found Nora and checked her over, smoothing back her hair and kissing her forehead.

Nora laughed and punched him playfully. "I'm fine!"

Although she tried valiantly not to, Sera grinned at the sight of her friend in love. Even if it was with a stupid Bacchae she had vowed to hate for all eternity.

Jumping inside the truck, Solomon wrenched the chains free from the metal wall. Manny hobbled toward the front, where Sera broke the manacles binding the boy's wrists before pulling him in for a tight hug. After a brief moment, his arms wrapped around her waist. Tears pricked the corners of her eyes. He may not have said much in their time together, but he had already found a place in her heart.

Clapping and cheering sounded all around them. The people who had stuck around to watch the fight were out of their cars, phone cameras held up to record video as the group rescued the teenage boy.

Well, I guess Bacchae may not be the only supernatural beings "out" now, she thought to Bacchus, tucking stray hairs behind her ears.

He chuckled. *The world is about to get a whole lot more interesting.*

CHAPTER 24

Solomon

Within a half-hour of getting back to the witch's row house, they were back on the road again in two vehicles as the sun edged toward the horizon. The world was deteriorating fast, and they had no time to waste. Solomon wasn't normally a praying man—his god lived in a necklace around the neck of an annoying human girl—but he sent thoughts out into the universe that they arrive safely and without incident.

Just in case.

Theo led the way in his Jeep, knowing back roads to get them out of the District without too much of a holdup, while the witch drove Solomon and Nora. Having a few more decades of driving experience than she did and no real need to rest anytime soon, Solomon had offered to drive, but

Renee had declined. She and the "rusty wagon," as she called it, had a history, and no one knew it as well as she did. To her credit, she had no problem keeping up with Theo.

On a good day, it would take at least an hour to get to the rural Leesburg airport, and they had already used an hour getting the boy back. They needed to make up as much time as possible so they wouldn't miss the detective's pilot friend. Theo had made it clear the pilot wouldn't wait long after dark.

Even though they avoided the interstates and major bridges as they drove, Solomon could still see them piled up in the distance and hear horns blaring into the darkening sky. They drove through red lights and stop signs, not bothering to comply when the world was in such shambles. Helicopters buzzed overhead, their spotlights pointed at various areas of the ground below. He couldn't tell if the pilots were human or Immortal.

Either a god answered his prayer, or they got lucky. Kind of lucky, anyway.

No roadblocks barred their way to the airport, but once they arrived, a small mob surrounded the entrance building, clamoring to be let in. A bright spotlight at the corner of a building revealed armed guards and thick chains barricading most of the doors, allowing limited entry through just one. No one had broken through or started to climb the fences yet, but the rising tension and fear building in the air told him it wouldn't be long.

Renee parked next to Theo's Jeep on the dirt shoulder, a hundred feet or so away from the edge of the crowd.

"I didn't expect so many people here," the witch said, removing her glasses and tucking them into her satchel.

"My guess would be local charter pilots and their families." Solomon rubbed his chin as he surveyed the crowd. "But I don't know why there are guards. The airport doesn't typically have them on staff."

"Theo is letting the pilot know we're here," Nora said out loud, her eyes glazed over as she communicated within her mind with the goddess and Serafina, presumably. "As soon as the plane is ready for take-off, we'll head in."

"No offense intended, Solomon, but I'd like to avoid any bloodshed if at all possible," Renee said, catching his eye in the rearview mirror.

"None taken, but I'll do whatever's necessary to keep Nora and the group safe. I can smell the panic from here." He couldn't fault her for her apprehension. Eyeing the crowd, he tried to determine if the smell was concentrated in one area they could avoid. Unfortunately, it seemed to permeate the entire mob.

Nora reached out to intertwine her fingers with his. Lifting her hand to his lips, he kissed the back of her soft skin.

"He's ready," Nora said, squeezing his hand one more time before opening her door and stepping out. Solomon and the witch followed.

The detective waved them over to join Serafina and Manny, both of whom were blowing warm air into their hands.

"The gods are getting antsy," Theo said. "We're all surprised the airport hasn't been taken over by the Bacchae yet, which means they're most likely on their way."

A shot rang out in the air, followed immediately by screams and angry shouts.

"I said stay back, or the next bullet aims for you," a voice bellowed from somewhere in the crowd.

"Freyja and I will do our best to calm these poor people down," Nora said.

Solomon couldn't see any changes, but he could *feel* a wave of soothing energy flow from Nora and settle like a blanket over the crush of bodies.

As they approached the only building allowing entry, panic-stricken faces turned their way. Some glared, and one bold fellow wearing a baseball cap reached out to stop Nora, who led the way.

Solomon gripped the man's wrist, using some of his Immortal strength to make a point. The man's face changed to a grimace of pain, and he pulled his injured arm back, rubbing the red marks with his other hand. After that, no one attempted to stop them, but the crowd jostled and pushed at each other with muttered curses.

Two men at the door stood with guns drawn, aiming at the mob. At close range, their uniforms made it clear they were Capitol Police Officers, not hired guards. They glanced warily at the approaching group, but their fingers moved back from the triggers as Freyja's magic washed over them.

"No entry until the senator's plane takes off," one of the men said.

That explained the security and possibly even the amount of people trying to get into the airport. Did they really think a senator would let them on board his aircraft?

"We have diplomatic clearance to enter," Theo said as he raised his police badge. "Our pilot should be here at any moment with the paperwork."

As if on cue, the door opened behind the guards, and a

uniformed pilot stepped out.

"Just in time, kids. Let's get this bird in the air," he said, waving the paperwork in one of the guard's faces. He didn't wait for a response as he directed their group inside.

Shouts of protest came from the crowd behind them, and it surged toward the door.

A deep rumble sounded down the darkened road, but it took a few moments for the humans to hear it above the din. All heads turned to look as five armored trucks formed out of the shadows. Screams split the air, and the crowd rushed the door or turned to run.

Solomon and Theo pushed their group inside the building then turned to face the crowd. Letting his fangs extend, Solomon bared his teeth, his eyes shifting into the red, vertically-constricted pupils of the Immortals. Beside him, a growl erupted from the detective, his fingernails extending like claws under the glow of his golden eyes.

Uncertainty turned to terror as the people closest to them realized the new threat they faced. But the people behind them either didn't see their otherworldly display or decided the trucks coming closer were the more significant threat. Humans fell to the ground and were trampled as others pushed from behind.

"We need to go," Solomon said, knowing it would turn into a slaughter if they stayed any longer. The smell of fear was intoxicating to his predator side. His fangs longed to sink into that flesh, releasing the liquid life within. He shook his head to clear his thoughts and ducked inside.

Theo let loose an earth-shaking roar before following him in. Solomon locked the doors, and together they hauled over one of the enormous couches, standing it on its side to bar the entry. It would not last long.

Running outside to rejoin the group already on the aircraft, the two men raced toward the awaiting plane, which was taxiing toward the runway and retracting the attached airstair used to board the craft. Solomon leaped inside the opening with ease and turned to give the detective a helping hand.

A roaring truck engine pierced the air before one of the armored vehicles burst through the chain-link fencing surrounding the airport. Headlights landed on their plane, illuminating Theo.

"Get in! Now!" Solomon yelled, holding out a hand.

Without hesitation, Theo jumped, reaching out his arms to catch the side of the doorframe and Solomon's hand before the airstair closed. Solomon dragged him the rest of the way in, pulling the airstair completely shut and locking it. His heart thudded against the inside of his chest.

"Everyone buckle up! It's gonna get bumpy!" the pilot shouted from the cockpit.

Solomon took the seat across the aisle from Nora, relieved she had made it on board with no issues. She held hands with the boy and chanted a spell. Although she flinched as gunfire erupted outside the plane, she didn't break her hold.

That's my girl, he thought with a smile.

As the nose of the plane tipped up, the gunfire ceased. A quick glance out the window showed the Immortals on the ground lowering their guns, squinting against the sudden wind and confusion on their faces.

"There. That should do it," Nora said, with a release of her breath. She fell back against the leather seat. "We expanded Eshu's concealment magic to cover the entire plane. We should be invisible."

"Let's just hope none of the bullets hit the plane," Renee said, facing Solomon from her seat. She closed her fist over the handful of crystals in her palm. "I can't be sure how powerful my wind enchantment was from inside."

"From what I could tell, both spells worked," Solomon reassured her.

Grinning at the boy, Nora held out her hand for a high-five. He glanced at her hand then curled up on the chair, pulling his hoodie over his head.

CHAPTER 25

Serafina

Sera wished she could have enjoyed the luxury of the private charter plane, from the comfortable leather seats to the champagne-stocked wet bar. There was even a bedroom in the back, which Renee and Nora claimed. Magic consumed a lot of energy, and both women drooped with exhaustion.

But even with Bacchus's help, Sera hadn't slept well on the reclining chair. The nightmares of Danae winning and turning everyone she loved into caged livestock had invaded her mind once again.

Several hours later, the small plane landed with a jolt and stirred them all from a light, restless slumber. It was still dark out, but they had made it to Paris. Well, Sera assumed they were in Paris.

"Y'all were sleeping," said the pilot, "but half the city's on fire, and the other half's in complete darkness. Radio's sayin' the power grid's failed. I had to land on the Beauvais–Tillé airstrip. We're 'bout 50 miles out from the city. Charles de Gaulle looked like it'd been blown up."

A murmur of frustration rumbled through Sera's mind as each of the gods reacted to the news.

The pilot looked grim as he gestured toward the open airstair. "I hope y'all know what you're doing."

Chills ran up Sera's back as the group exchanged glances. Did they know what they were doing? She wasn't sure.

We may not know what we're doing exactly, but we're a hell of a lot smarter than a teen witch, Eshu remarked, along with a brief image of a man in a top hat placing a monocle over one eye and winking. *Not to mention the bag of tricks I've got up my sleeve.*

He's right, darling, Freyja's voice chimed in. *We gods have survived this long, and we're not about to let Bacchus's mistake be the end of us.*

Xolotl growled his agreement.

Reclining on a Roman chaise, Bacchus chose to focus on finishing his glass of wine instead of defending himself. Probably for the best. Sera allowed herself a small smile at the gods' confidence.

Theo thanked the pilot as they disembarked the plane, then led them toward the terminals using the few flashlights they had brought.

With all the electricity off, the entire area was blanketed in deep darkness and silent in a way she wasn't used to, in city, or even suburban, life. Her skin prickled, imagining what monsters might lurk in the depths of the shadows.

"Bienvenue à Paris," a woman's rich voice drifted to them from out of the dark.

Whirling around, Sera prepared for a fight.

Easy killer. It's not a monster, Bacchus said, as a soothing sensation rolled through her body, reassuring her.

With her dark skin and clothes still blending with the shadows and her footsteps silent, Lasirenn practically slithered into view. Her eyes locked on Theo.

Are you sure about that? Sera asked.

The god chuckled.

"Or at least welcome to what's left of the city," the water spirit said.

"How bad is it?" Theo asked.

"Bad."

He nodded, his lips pressed into a thin line. Apparently, that lack of information was enough for him. Sera rolled her eyes, only kind of hoping she couldn't be seen in the dark.

"And Danae?" he asked.

"Well protected, but there are cracks. We should wait for daylight before we launch our assault. Come, I have a vehicle." Lasirenn sauntered away, hips swaying.

Sera caught Nora's elbow dig into Solomon's side and almost snickered. She knew that feeling.

Oh, honey, he only has eyes for you, Sera heard Freyja reassure Nora. *But if you'd like me to remove his eyes to be sure, just say the word.*

Nora laughed and winked at Solomon when he looked her way. Reaching out to catch her hand, he intertwined his fingers with hers before kissing the back of her hand.

While Sera appreciated the goddess's confidence in the Bacchae and the man's display of affection, she also wanted to stake him right through the heart. Apparently, it was going to take a lot more time for her to be okay with him dating her best friend.

Wine always helps, Bacchus quipped, raising his refilled glass.

The vehicle the water spirit mentioned turned out to be a blue and red tour bus, complete with sight-seeing ads plastered along the sides. Piling in, the rest of the group dozed as much as they could as Lasirenn drove toward wherever it was they'd be staying until the sun came up.

Everyone except Sera. Her thoughts ran in dozens of directions as she thought about the potential battle on their horizon and the night Theo had promised to Lasirenn—should they survive that long. Oh, and they needed to come up with a solid plan for everything, too.

She held in a snort. Bacchus probably loved the chaos.

Well, when you put it that way.... His voice dripped with sarcasm. *But yes, yes, I do.*

They drove on the outskirts of Paris, but the devastation that Danae's army had caused to the ancient city made itself known. Fires burned across the horizon and whole buildings had collapsed in on themselves, their skeletal remains crumbling to ash. For the most part, the dark streets remained devoid of moving cars and humans, but reflected in the glow of the fires, glass and assorted supplies littered the sidewalks in front of storefronts, indicating the mass hysteria and rioting that must have occurred.

Sera hoped that the city's treasures had been removed or protected from the flames, but chances were that much of their history would be lost. What a damn shame.

As the sky began to lighten with the new day, Lasirenn parked the bus in front of a two-story stone cottage, surrounded by overrun vegetation and thick woods.

"We're far enough away from her compound that they shouldn't notice our presence, but close enough that we'll be able to move in quickly. Come, I have fresh food waiting for you all." Lasirenn led them inside.

Coziness radiated through the main living area, with two large couches and a giant shag rug placed in front of the fire. The fireplace itself was massive, the kind Sera could walk straight into if she wanted to. The warmth from the flames seeped into her weary bones, reminding her just how exhausted she really was.

"Took you guys long enough," a familiar playful voice said from behind her.

Turning around, Sera found Hareni leaning against a doorframe, one ankle crossed over the other, and her hands cupped around a steaming mug. The young woman had pulled her black braid over her shoulder again, and a blue tunic length sweater draped over her slight frame. Leggings covered in a colorful flower pattern disappeared into thick fuzzy socks that came up to her calves. An incredibly comfortable and casual look, as if the world wasn't ending.

Sera's mouth dropped open. "I thought Durga said she wouldn't be joining the fight."

"Hashtag truth. But that doesn't mean *I* can't," Hareni said.

Theo dropped his bag on the ground by the door before stepping forward to shake her hand. "We appreciate your willingness to fight, but with all due respect, this will be too dangerous for a human."

Hareni held his hand a moment longer than necessary. "I see you took my advice about keeping the beard. And yes, I know it's going to be dangerous, but it's going to be worse for me if Danae wins. I'm kind of hoping Durga will change her mind."

She took a sip from her cup. "Besides, I brought back up."

* * *

JUST TWO HOURS LATER, they knelt in the bushes on the outskirts of Danae's property. While the rest of the group had been in the air, Lasirenn had become familiar with the compound's security patrols.

If the water spirit was correct, they had a perfect window of time in just under two minutes to make it onto the property before the next patrol. It would take all of their combined god powers and magic—and possibly a miracle— to break the Ordog's defensive shield protecting the building holding the Eternals.

Once the shield was down, they would free the Eternals before Danae launched her counterattack. If they failed... well, Sera didn't want to think about that. It might be a long shot, but it was their only shot.

Hareni's backup turned out to be a reasonably sized French militia. Because the focus in the cottage had been solely on getting into Danae's compound, Sera hadn't found out how the young woman had found them or convinced them to join her. But she was sure the girl's charismatic personality played a role.

The militia and Hareni hung back, waiting for their signal that the defensive shield was down.

Theo checked his watch. "It's almost time. We'll move in as soon as the patrol passes."

Taking a deep breath, Sera tried to settle her quivering, adrenaline-fueled muscles. A moment later, a blanket of calm settled around her.

Thanks. She breathed a sigh of relief. *I hope this plan works.*

You need to believe it, Bacchus cautioned. *With every fiber of your being.*

Closing her eyes, Sera focused her thoughts on her loved ones. Images and memories of her mother, father, Hiro, Nora—everyone she had ever cared about—flashed through her mind. In one, her mother grabbed her hand, pulling her out into the rain to dance in the puddles. Her beautiful auburn hair stuck to her rain-kissed face as she laughed.

Oh, if only Sera had known back then that her mom was a witch. It made perfect sense now why she had loved the rain and being outside so much.

And then Hiro. The doctor who treated cancer patients as if they were his own family, who cared so deeply for anyone and everyone who entered his life, who somehow loved *her* despite her flaws, despite her obsession with her career. She hadn't made him enough of a priority while he was alive, even though she now knew why; she would do better with honoring his memory.

She had lost too much already; she wouldn't let that monster take anything more from her. Her heart ached, but determination steeled the last of her frayed nerves.

A rough hand slipped into hers, giving it a gentle squeeze. She opened her eyes to see Theo and his damn adorable dimples smiling at her. Yes, they would be successful. They *had* to be successful. She had too much to lose, including this unknown, very tempting opportunity.

A movement in her periphery pulled her gaze back toward the compound. A patrol of four Bacchae walked past, chatting amongst themselves and oblivious to the threat lying just a few feet away. With Freyja's help, Eshu had once again surrounded their group with concealment magic, keeping them invisible to the Bacchae's heightened senses.

Even though she trusted the magic, Sera let out her held breath after they passed. The nearness was unnerving.

"Let's go," Theo said as he stood.

Biting her lip, she crept forward with the others onto the grass surrounding the stone building, forming a line and connecting hands. Solomon stayed back, ready to protect the group from any unexpected and unwelcome visitors.

Her skin tingled as Bacchus joined his essence with the other gods. The two witches began to chant, Freyja's musical voice ringing out from Nora's mouth as she and Renee raised their linked hands toward the sky. Pink, gold, blue, and black auras shimmered across the line of joined hands, swirling around the two women like cotton candy as each of the gods lent their power to the spell.

A tornado-like wind rushed around them, tugging at Sera's clothes and whipping her hair around her face. She clenched her teeth as she stood her ground, squinting against the dirt that spattered against her face. Grips tightened as the group held on to each other.

Dark clouds rolled in and hid the sun, thunder crashing within the murky depths. The volume of chanting increased as the two witches willed their magic to break the shield. The sky lit up as three bolts of lightning shot down like a trident, sizzling as they connected with the now visible barrier, a wavering dome encompassing the compound.

When the lightning dissipated, the smell of burning plastic lingered in the air, and the shield remained. Low snarls from the Aztec god filled her mind, along with angry curses from Bacchus.

"It's too strong!" Nora's voice called out, frustration evident in her tone.

Sera's hopes plummeted faster than Icarus plunging to his death. This had been their only chance, their only plan to stop the girl queen. Failing now meant she would win, and the world would be doomed. Tears pricked the corners of her eyes. She needed to get back to her father before the Bacchae did.

The next patrol of four Bacchae appeared around the side of the building, their eyes glued to the darkened sky in confusion. Sera gripped Theo and Renee's hands tighter, wanting to scream in frustration and rage.

Their time was up.

Without hesitation, Solomon moved in front of Nora and raised his gun, loaded with silver bullets, toward the Bacchae. He pulled the trigger three times in quick succession. One of the Bacchae stumbled back as the bullets found their marks, and he exploded into a cloud of golden dust. His comrades shouted as they recognized the attack and ran toward them.

A terrifying roar exploded through the area, vibrating within Sera's bones and shaking her to the core. It took all of her willpower not to break the line to cover her ears. Had

Danae come so soon?

Bushes in the woods rustled before a familiar orange and black striped tiger leaped onto the grassy area.

Durga!

Hareni had been right. The giant cat bounded across the field, jumping onto the back of one of the Bacchae. Her massive claws sank into the man's back, mauling his skin into shreds. She closed her jaw around his head until amber flurries disappeared into the air.

Holding her breath as the tiger quickly dispatched the remaining two Bacchae, Sera couldn't believe their luck. But would the goddess's added energy be enough? Manny let out a whoop at the end of their line. Apparently, she wasn't the only one getting her hopes up.

Hot damn, Durga. Talk about making an entrance. Eshu whistled his approval.

The goddess's feline form softened and shifted into the many-armed woman as she ran, wielding a weapon in each hand. A new arm grew and stretched out from her side, allowing her to join hands with Manny, whose excited grin was contagious. Her orange aura swirled down the line of connected limbs, burning like an icy fire as it passed through Sera's arms, and into the mix of colors around Nora and Renee.

A moment later, the barrier around the buildings popped, the magical remnants melting into thin air.

Renee lit a match, sending up a signal flare with the help of a spell, alerting the militia to move in. Men and women in dark uniforms surged out of the forest, holding guns loaded with silver bullets, and took up defensive positions as they surrounded the entire compound.

As her hopes lifted, Sera wanted to give in to her excitement like Manny had, to jump with joy or grin like an idiot. But she bit it all back. Even with their reinforcements, their group would be outnumbered. She hoped the militia would be strong enough to slow the Bacchae army down until the gods could free the Eternals. And convince them to do the right thing by standing down and surrendering, of course. Their entire plan relied upon that one small detail, and then Sera would kill Danae. Justice would be served.

It *had* to work.

The group of gods ran to the smaller building housing the enslaved Eternals and streamed inside the entryway. Surprised Bacchae guards looked up from their places around the room. Durga and Solomon made quick work of the guards, and they all moved farther into the building.

What she saw inside made Sera sick, bile burning its way up her esophagus. Four Bacchae—the Eternals, she assumed—hung as if dead from chains attached to a stone wall. Their forearms and hands were a mess of burnt skin, most down to the bone. The skin that remained on their emaciated bodies prominently displayed their skeletons beneath. She wasn't even sure they were aware of the group's presence.

Bacchus's anger sparked like lit gunpowder within Sera, his magic surging through her and out her arms like a cannonball. The magic flowed toward the prisoners like a stream of water and crashed against their chains. A moment later, the metal clattered to the floor, as did the occupants.

The Eternals looked up in surprise at their rescuers.

"Is Danae gone?" one of the women asked. Despite holding her destroyed arm to her chest, she glared at the door, her sunken eyes filled with fierce hatred.

"Not yet," Theo said as he helped her to her feet.

As if on cue, an unearthly scream split the air, coming from every direction, including within Sera's mind. She covered her ears, grimacing as she staggered to stay upright.

She's coming, Bacchus said, although he sounded more amused than anything.

Gunfire erupted outside.

"Listen," Sera said to the Eternals, "Danae will be here soon. We will help you in exchange for a peace treaty. Once she's gone, you need to use the hive mind on the rest of the Bacchae across the world, making them stand down and surrender to local governments. Deal?"

Without hesitation, three of the Eternals agreed.

One of the men looked at the others with disdain, shaking his head. "Absolutely not. We will be destroyed without question."

"Well, you kind of deserve it right about now," Sera snapped at the Eternal. "Your kind feeds on humans for fuck's sake, and not always from willing volunteers. But we're going to insist on immunity as long as you agree to these terms. Capisce?"

As he opened his mouth to retort, one of the women placed her skeletal hand on his arm. "Eratosthenes, enough. It's over."

Eratosthenes glared at each one of them in turn before reluctantly agreeing. They would need to watch that one after this was finished.

The doors burst open, and a team of Bacchae poured in to face the intruders, clearly oblivious to the threat of the gods. Giving herself over to Bacchus, Sera launched into the fray, using whatever she could get her hands on as a weapon. Growling, hissing, and maniacal laughter filled her mind as the gods used their human hosts to decimate the Bacchae.

After a burst of glittering dust settled around her, Sera caught sight of a familiar salt-and-pepper head of hair on a Bacchae. She ground her teeth together, her jaw clenching in revulsion.

Chad, she and Bacchus thought at the same moment.

A guttural roar of fury tore its way up from her core as she screamed at the man who—for months—had made her feel so small, so insignificant. The man who tried to force himself on her as he had with other young women, or worse. Of course the arrogant son of a bitch would become a Bacchae.

Cringing from the sound of her roar, he looked her way, surprise spreading across his face as he recognized her. Then he grinned, his new fangs flashing in the light.

Oh, that will be your last mistake, she thought.

She strode toward him, knocking aside Bacchae like flies. Just before she reached him, she ripped an arm free from the closest Bacchae and brandished the limb like a sword, blood and gore splattering around her. She would use their claws against them as they had done to her.

Chad raised his gun and pointed it at her. Although he had new Bacchae strength and power on his side, he was no match for a god, nor Sera's rage. She dodged the bullets with ease and used the limb she held to rake him across the face. For a brief moment, blood spilled down his cheeks from his scored skin before the wounds healed again.

"If you can't play nicely with your toys, then they get taken away from you," she said. Before he could react, she grabbed him between the legs and crushed the flesh there, ignoring his howls of pain.

As much as Sera wanted to extend his torture for all eternity, she had a battle to win, and Chad needed to become an afterthought. She pulled her other arm back, fist clenched, and punched it into his chest. Bone and tendon gave way beneath her hand until it came out his other side, holding his still pumping heart.

Wiping the golden flurries and the memory of the man from her hands, Sera turned to face the next Bacchae. As she raised her arm to block his attack, he stopped, his eyes glazing over and his mouth dropping open. In fact, all of the Bacchae stopped and stepped back.

Confused at the behavior, Sera turned to look behind her. The Eternals stood together, holding hands.

They're using the hive mind to control the others nearby. She comes, Bacchus explained, his voice quivering with glee.

The girl who called herself queen stalked through the open doorway in dangerously high stilettos. Pulsing red arteries snaked out from her eyes, her irises blazing a fiery crimson. Her bodyguard Yumiko was right on her heels. Danae snarled, baring her fangs as she caught sight of the group and the Eternals set free.

She hasn't noticed yet. Eshu's giggle rippled through her mind. *Where's the popcorn?*

Sera's own lip curled up as the Bacchae witch confronted them. Here was the woman—the little *girl*—responsible for ruining her life. Here was the destroyer of the world, the queen of the doomed. But damn, Sera had to admire the blood-red stilettos. Maybe she would take them as a memento.

Nah.

"It wasn't enough for me to take your dreams, now you want to die, too?" Danae hissed. She snapped her fingers as if ordering a silent command. "So be it."

Yumiko unsheathed two of her daggers and stepped forward, grinning at Sera.

Wait for it... Bacchus urged, childlike delight barely hidden in his tone, as the bodyguard prepared for the fight.

A look of uncertainty crossed Yumiko's face as she glanced around. She must have just realized she was the only Bacchae heeding whatever command Danae had given. Oh, this was going to be good.

Waiting for the girl to figure it out, Sera crossed her arms in front of her, smirking. Although she really did try not to gloat, her body just wouldn't obey. Maybe Bacchus was gloating. Yeah, that must be it.

Her face betrayed no sudden realization, but Danae's pupils faded to their regular blue, tinged with a stormy grey, and the snake-like arteries faded back into her olive-toned skin. She placed her hand on Yumiko's arm, lowering it.

"You think you've won." A lazy smile tugged at Danae's lips.

Oh, that bitch is going down, Eshu said with a sassy snap of his fingers.

"Pretty sure I don't just think it," Sera said, grim excitement spreading through her limbs.

The Eternal who had been holding her destroyed arm earlier stepped forward, no marks to be seen on her flawless skin. "It is over, Danae. You've caused enough damage to this world. We will pick up the pieces."

Danae's eyes flicked to the other Eternal. "You always

did want to rule the world, Liviana. I just made it easy for you."

Doing a double-take as she looked at the Eternal, Sera couldn't believe she hadn't recognized her. The dirt, grime, and sunken skin didn't help, of course, but the face from her dreams was unmistakable.

Liviana shook her head. "We will return the world to its rightful rulers. With a little hope, luck, and possibly some help from our new divine friends, we may not be destroyed outright."

"Except you," Sera said as she bent to pick up one of the broken silver chains that had held the Eternals, her eyes locked on Danae's.

Liviana bowed her head, silently assenting to Sera's judgment.

"Oh, Serafina. You're not going to kill me." Danae's lips quirked up.

Freyja's tinkling laughter rang through Sera's mind. *She's a peach, isn't she?*

Sera almost laughed, too. "You think I wouldn't kill the creature responsible for ruining my life? You're sorely mistaken, lady."

"Don't you want to know what happened to your mother?" Danae's blue-grey eyes bored into hers.

Sera bit down on her tongue hard, blood seeping into her mouth. "No. I don't want to know how you killed her." She gripped the chains in each fist and stepped toward her, ready to end Danae's life. "Goodbye."

"I didn't kill your mother." Danae tilted her head to the side and smiled with a bone-chilling calmness. "Your mother is alive."

Time stood still as Sera's world came to a pinpoint of vision, Danae's words echoing in her ears and mind: *Your mother is alive.*

"How?" Sera asked, her voice sounding foreign and far away.

"The witches were my first offering to the Ordog. He holds them in his realm, alive but almost certainly not well." She smirked. "Only I can bring them back, and if you kill me, they die."

I cannot detect any falsehoods in her words, Bacchus said quietly.

Her mind reeled. Her mother. Alive! Could it even be possible? Did that mean Sera could bring her back?

CHAPTER 26

Serafina

Sounds, shapes, and colors faded into the background as Sera tried to make sense of what had just happened, what she had just heard. All her life, she had believed her mother died while caving, even though her body had never been found. Just over a month ago, she learned her mother had been a witch and killed at the hands of a monster—this *same* monster—while trying to escape.

But the truth?

If Danae wasn't lying, then the reality was far worse than any of that. Sera's breath caught in her throat, her pulse pounding in her ears. Her mom, and the other witches who were with her, lived as prisoners of the Ordog, a treacherous god of the underworld. Horrors beyond imagining swirled through her mind as she considered what that actually meant—a prisoner of the devil.

But that was only *if* Danae told the truth.

Sinking to her knees, Sera's arms went limp, the chain dangling from her hands. "I can't do it."

All feeling except pure defeat fled from within until she was nothing but a hollow husk of a body. Danae had won. She had been holding the ultimate card to play, and it worked.

The immortal girl had to be telling the truth. It was too farfetched a lie to be one. But even if it ended up not being true, Sera had to know for sure. She had to be certain before she doomed her mom to hell for all eternity.

Danae would live.

But only for now. Hiro still deserved justice in the form of Danae's golden ashes. Sera had promised his mother that she would avenge him, and she wouldn't let the woman down. Never again.

Dark brown eyes appeared in the haze of her vision, and rough, yet gentle hands cupped her cheeks. "Sera."

She blinked, allowing her gaze to focus on Theo's concerned face.

"We're going to figure it out. I promise," he said.

As she nodded, still numb inside, a figure attempting to back away unseen caught her eye. When she recognized the bodyguard's boots, Sera leaped to her feet, pushing past Theo and tightening her grip on the chains once again. Before anyone could react and stop her, she wrapped the silver links around Yumiko's neck and pulled in opposite directions as hard as she could.

Yumiko's hands reached up, trying desperately to pull

the chain away from her throat, her eyes bulging from her head as her skin started to smoke. With a sickening sizzling sound, the silver seared through the Bacchae's skin and bones like she was made of butter.

The head slid from her neck and fell to the dusty floor, rolling to a stop in front of Danae's stilettos. Rotting before their eyes, the body slumped sideways before exploding into a cloud of amber sparks, which faded into daylight.

A look of horror, and possibly even grief, flashed across Danae's face before she caught herself. It was short-lived but satisfying. Sera locked eyes with her with cold ferocity. That would be the last time the bitch underestimated Sera.

* * *

TWO DAYS LATER, SERA woke from another nightmare, only instead of Danae, this time the Ordog showed her the torture he inflicted upon her mother every day for the past twenty years. She really had no idea what kind of life her mother had lived over the past two decades, or even *if* she truly lived, but Sera hoped beyond all else that it was better than what she saw when she slept.

Bacchus had offered his help to suppress the dreams, but she had turned him down, wanting—maybe even needing—to use her grief and fear to keep her going, to fuel her journey to find her mom. No one seemed to know whether it was possible to bring her and the others back from the underworld, the realm of the dead.

No one alive had done it.

Shuddering, she swung her legs out of the cottage bed. She looked back to the other half of the full-sized mattress, empty though Theo had laid down next to her the night before, providing nothing but unassuming comfort once again. She was sure he had left France without saying goodbye.

Wincing as her bare feet touched the cold stone floor, Sera scrambled to throw on some warm socks and the rest of her clothes. Theo and Lasirenn would take Manny back to Haiti to live with Cassandra, and Eshu would be back among the Yoruba people who worshipped him still.

Sera did her best to ignore the feeling of dread growing in her stomach and made her way to the bathroom to splash water on her face and brush her hair. She did her best to not think about the night Theo had promised to Lasirenn, whether it would happen while the two were away, and if it would reignite the spark between them. She swallowed all the feelings of guilt that accompanied those other thoughts, guilt about Hiro and not loving him the way he deserved, and about her mom and the horrors she must be living.

Sera had bigger things to worry about than one night to fulfill a necessary promise. One night that didn't mean anything more.

That's what she kept telling herself, anyway.

Over the last two days, the mortal world struggled to find its way out of the darkness Danae had plunged them into. The Bacchae army had only managed to take over the American and French governments but knocking out the North American and European power grids had devastating consequences for millions. There had even been fear that North Korea or China would take advantage of the situation to assert their own world dominance.

Thankfully, nothing of the sort had happened, and most countries had been sending aid to all the areas in need. Sera was fairly sure the threat of unleashing the Eternals and all the Bacchae they controlled held any attacks at bay.

The four remaining members of the High Council had followed through with their agreement to turn themselves over to world leaders and use hive mentality to control any Bacchae uprisings. Even Eratosthenes, though his complaints never ceased.

The secret was out; the Bacchae could no longer live in the mythos of vampire lore, but they could figure out a way to live side by side with mortals. What that meant exactly, no one was sure.

Liviana had quickly taken charge of Danae's capture, requiring a cell constructed solely of silver to house the Bacchae witch as part of their submission to France's government. For now, she lived as she had done to the others: in silver chains and manacles burning away the continuously healing flesh beneath, receiving only enough animal blood to keep her from crumbling into ash.

It seemed fitting.

The president of the United States had been found alive within Danae's French compound, though his mental state was still a bit shaky at best. Had he been drained—or worse—the mortal population may have demanded justice. The monster was caged, and that seemed to be enough for the time being.

Despite all that had happened, Sera almost enjoyed getting to know Liviana, the girl who had quite literally haunted Sera's dreams for several months until she learned the truth about the Bacchae. Unlike the other Bacchae she had met so far, Liviana and her progeny had worked in the background for over two millennia to help the mortal community flourish. She had been a natural choice to join the High Council when it was created over a millennium ago.

Through their discussions, and Bacchus's random quips, Sera learned that the Council had been formed after the Bacchae population rose to unprecedented levels and threatened the secrecy of their existence. The Council's primary function had been to control the creation of new Bacchae, requiring all nominations to be approved through them. Monitoring Bacchae activities and blocking any attempted uprisings such as Danae's had been a close second.

Unfortunately, they had grown lax in their duties after they were stripped of most of their abilities.

She still hadn't found out why Danae and the rest of the Council were at such odds, and Bacchus remained tight-lipped, saying it wasn't his tale to tell. Reminding him of the dreams he had sent her way, sharing Liviana's story, did nothing to change his mind. The hypocrite.

In her own words, Liviana was glad her sister Octavia hadn't lived to this day, or else she and Danae would have become quite the devious duo. Sera shuddered to even imagine what the outcome would have been.

The earthy aroma of already-made coffee met her nose just before she reached the downstairs kitchen. The owners of the cottage had renovated the space over the last decade to bring in more rental revenue but left many of the old-world touches like the brick hearth and oven, still used for baking.

Most of the cabinetry had been replaced with a newer cream color, which really brought out the mint green accents of the wooden ceiling beams and window frames. A myriad of baskets graced the tops of the cabinets and dangled from hooks in the rafters, and copper pots and pans hung from a suspended cookware rack above the island.

But the real centerpiece of the room was the oblong table. It filled the space between the end of the cabinets and the hearth and could comfortably seat eight adults. Scratches and dings marred the dense wood, adding charm and character to the dark walnut color.

The cottage's kitchen had become her home away from home, and she loved it.

Renee was already awake, of course, seated at the table even though the sun wouldn't fully rise for at least another hour. She looked up from her newspaper with a smile as Sera approached.

"I got the sense you'd be up soon," the other woman said, tilting her head toward the freshly brewed pot. Coffee really wasn't Renee's thing. She preferred a steaming mug of tea, as did Nora. Maybe tea was a witchy thing.

"A little psychic humor?" Sera smiled at their joke as she poured herself a cup.

Renee chuckled. "Still having nightmares?"

"Yes. As crazy as it sounds, they help keep me going," she said.

Renee nodded.

You know, I could just keep you going, Bacchus chimed in.

As tempting as his offer was, she felt like it was cheating. The nightmares terrified her, threatened to overwhelm her, but it could only be worse for her mom. She would honor her the only way she knew how right now, by sharing in her torture.

"So, what's going on in the world today?" Sera asked,

leaning forward to grab one of the pages Renee had set to the side. Journalism was alive and well even if most of the airports were still shut down. At least they weren't in a rush to return home. Not until they had more answers anyway.

"Nothing that interesting." Renee winked.

The two women sat in silence, reading the newspaper as if the world hadn't just fallen apart. As if they could finally go back to a normal life, whatever normal meant now. As if they were simply on vacation in the elegant Parisian countryside reading the paper together.

The sun peeked above the horizon, spraying its golden light through the kitchen windows.

EPILOGUE

Solomon

New Year's Eve. The last time Solomon had truly enjoyed the day before a new year, he had been nine years old. His mother had given him the very last gift he'd ever receive from her—a doll made of straw. Although he had loved it, uncertainty and embarrassment crept in over the next few days. None of his friends played with dolls, only the girls did. His mother had been crushed when she found the doll burning in the fire.

He would give just about anything to go back in time, to give his mother proper thanks for all the things she did to try to shield him from the horrors of their lives. Slavery had not been kind to her—to anyone—but she always had a smile for him, even when they took him away. He knew now she only smiled so he wouldn't be as scared.

As he stared at the wood crackling and shifting in the fireplace of Nora's apartment, Solomon wrapped his arms tighter around the tiny blonde woman who had stolen his heart, pulling her in close on her cream-colored couch. Her oatmeal scent was stronger in the warmth of the room.

He would do better with her. He would make sure she always knew how much he loved and appreciated her. Nothing would stand in his way.

She tilted her head up, green eyes twinkling as she smiled at him. "What are you thinking about?"

"Just that I never thought I'd have this opportunity. To love someone as amazing as you." He kissed the top of her curly hair as she snuggled into him again, her head against his chest.

"Let's just hope the world gets its shit together so we can actually enjoy it," she said.

He grunted in agreement.

Two weeks had passed since they stopped Danae. The United States was still a shambles, people only traveled in groups they trusted, and military patrols scoured the streets. But the American and French governments had mostly been restored. There was a tentative peace agreement—although very precarious—between the humans and the Bacchae while Liviana and the other Eternals met with each of the world's rulers to establish rules for their cohabitation.

Video footage of the fight on the District Interstate where they rescued Manny and Eshu had leaked, but authorities had quickly covered up any talk of other supernatural creatures. All parties had agreed that the world only needed to know about the Bacchae. Adding in the reality of the divine would only create more chaos.

The group of gods disbanded, going back to their homes with renewed promises to keep a more watchful eye on the Bacchae should they try anything of the like again. Theo had returned from Haiti, sans water spirit, and he and Serafina were spending their time researching options for entering the underworld in the hopes of finding Serafina's mother, Rachel Finch.

The trick was getting back out again—alive.

Solomon was sure they were also spending their days and nights getting to know each other... intimately. Their attraction to one another had been undeniable. If only the girl could get over whatever guilt she felt for Hiro, they might have a real future together.

Speaking of which, he and Nora had quite a bit to discuss themselves.

"Do you have any resolutions for the new year?" he asked, stroking her hair.

A ripple of mirth shook her shoulders. "Does not getting kidnapped or killed count?"

He smiled, though she couldn't see it. "Has Freyja convinced you to merge with her yet? You two make quite the formidable team."

Nora stiffened beneath his touch before sitting up to face him, her fingers brushing the golden torc. "I've been thinking a lot about that, and I think I've made up my mind. No, I've definitely made up my mind."

He waited for her to continue, holding his breath.

"I'm not interested in immortality. Freyja's explained that immortals can't procreate, and I want a family. Probably more than anything else in the world. I mean, not yet. But someday. I've still got to kick ass at my exams and become

Dr. Eleanor Eisler, first of her name." Her mouth quirked to the side.

He wasn't surprised. Not really. Despite her flirtatious nature and proclivity for partying, Nora had expressed her desire several times to settle down and make offspring. Just like she said, not yet. But what did that mean for their relationship? Would he have to watch her grow old and die in the arms of another man, a human man?

His nostrils flared as he struggled to control his jealousy. The thought of giving her up to someone else just about drove him mad.

"I understand. I'm just not sure what that means for us," he said, keeping his voice calm. "I have no intention of losing you."

Biting her lip, she took his hand in hers. "What if... what if you could become human again?"

His lungs constricted, forcing the air from his body. Hope could not even come close to how he felt at those words. "Is that even possible?"

"Freyja says it is, but it's risky."

"I'd risk everything for a mortal life beside you," he said.

Her eyes lit up, sparkling as they filled with tears. "You're sure?"

Pulling her to him, he let his lips respond as he pressed them to hers. She returned his kiss, their tongues dancing a familiar dance, before she pulled back.

"Would it be okay if we just... *existed* for a bit before we go on any more adventures, though? Maybe let the world settle down a bit?" she asked.

He laughed. "That sounds good to me."

As they settled back down into the couch, Nora's head resting against his chest, they watched out the windows as light snow began to fall.

Thanks for reading!

Please consider adding a short review on Amazon and Goodreads to let other readers know what you thought.

I love to get to know my readers. You can reach me on Facebook, Instagram, or Twitter **@stephaniemirro**. Sign up for my mailing list to get new release information, special deals, giveaways, become a part of my ARC team, and more. I look forward to hearing from you!

www.stephaniemirro.com

GLOSSARY

Gods, Mortals, & Others

Alexander – Bacchae; created by Lorenzo Vicari; *deceased*

Bacchae (Bock-eye) – the vampire-like creations of Bacchus

Bacchus (Bock-uhs) – Roman god of wine, chaos, festivities, and frenzies

Berenice (Bare-a-nees)– Bacchae; one of the Eternals on the High Council

Cassandra – friend of Theo's living in Haiti; has the Gift of Sight like Renee

Charles "Chad" Lambert – professor and world-renowned archaeologist

Cheryl – server at The Morning Grind

Danae (Duh-nigh) – Bacchae; one of the Eternals on the High Council; possibly the oldest Bacchae among those still living

Durga (doo-r-gah)– Hindu warrior and protective mother goddess

Eleanor "Nora" Eisler – Serafina's best friend

Eratosthenes (Air-uh-toss-the-nees)– Bacchae; one of the Eternals on the High Council

Eshu (Eh-shoo) – Yoruba messenger and trickster god

Eternal – an original Bacchae, one created directly from Bacchus's blood before they could create new Bacchae from their own blood

Freyja (Fray-uh) – Norse goddess associated with war, death, love, sex, beauty, fertility, and gold

Hareni (Har-en-ee) – Durga's human apprentice

Hiro Saito (Hee-ro Sigh-tow) – Serafina's boyfriend; *deceased*

Imhotep (Im-hoe-tep)– Bacchae; one of the Eternals on the High Council

Immortal – a name the Bacchae have given themselves

Joseph – Haitian gang leader

Julia Dixon – DCPD detective; Theodore's partner; *deceased*

Lasirenn (La-seer-en) – African water spirit; also known as Mami Wata

Leif Karlsson – witch; previously a member of Renee's coven

Liviana – Bacchae; one of the Eternals on the High Council

Lorenzo Vicari – Bacchae; created by Danae; Solomon's maker

Manny – human teenager chosen by Eshu

Ms. Patton – Sera's elderly next door neighbor

Nestor – Bacchae; one of the Eternals on the High Council

Nidheesh "Nidhi" (Nid-heesh) – taxi driver in Kolkata; one of the Others

Octavia – Bacchae; sister to Liviana; *deceased*

Others – generic term given to witches, Bacchae, gods, etc.

Rachel Finch – Serafina's mother; presumed dead

Renee Colette – witch; Serafina's mentor

Robert "Bob" Bernard – DCPD detective

Roseline (Rose-a-leen) – Cassandra's daughter

Serafina "Sera" Finch – archaeology student chosen by Bacchus

Solomon Jones – Bacchae; created by Lorenzo

Susan – Serafina's father's new girlfriend

Theodore "Theo" Pratt – DCPD detective; merged with the god Xolotl

Tiana Williams – DCPD detective

Xolotl (Sho-low-till)– Aztec god of lightning and death

Yumiko (You-mi-co) – Bacchae; created by Danae; closest bodyguard to the queen

Sera's story continues in…

REVENGE

OF THE

WITCH

IMMORTAL RELICS BOOK THREE

ACKNOWLEDGEMENTS

Publishing this series has been a dream come true, and the outpouring of support from my family, friend, and fans has kept me going on the hardest of days.

To my parents, who always supported me and believed in my ability to live my dream, *thank you*. To my husband, who has shown me unconditional love and support while I wrote, edited, and marketed, *thank you*. To my kids, who continued to take great naps (up until the last month) so that mommy could work, *thank you*.

To my editor, Donna Royston; my critique partners, authors Savannah J. Goins and V.M. Darkangelo; to my beta readers: Linda Mirro, Thomas Mirro, Martin Wilsey, C.J. Ellisson, Leilani Lopez, James Siedenburg, Renee Siedenburg, Erica Rue, Don Anderson, Roseann Hanson, Devon Lawson, Lauren Harr, Shannon Edwards, Leah Edwards, Lindsay San Giacomo, Kimmie Stack, Lauren Dunn, Taylor Shelby, and Christie Klump; and the members of my local writing group, the Hourlings, who provided invaluable guidance, support, and critique, *thank you*.

To Christian Bentulan, who created the stunning cover that caught your eye, *thank you*.

To all my family and friends, who showed their support in so many ways—asking how writing was going, becoming Patrons on Patreon, and following me on all things social media—*thank you*.

To you, my dear reader, for picking up this book and making it through to the end, *thank you*.

We made this magic happen. Together!

ABOUT THE AUTHOR

Stephanie Mirro's lifetime love of ancient mythology led to her majoring in the Classics in college, which wasn't quite as much fun as writing her own mythology stories as she did growing up. But that education, combined with an overactive imagination, being an active fantasy reader, and having a vampire obsession, resulted in the *Immortal Relics* series.

Born and raised in Southern Arizona, Stephanie now resides in Northern Virginia with her husband, two kids, and two furbabies. This thing called "seasons" is still magical.